FALLEN

Toggling for an unscrambled channel, Shakov called out to the local militia that was scattering before him, "Surrender!" He never saw the enemy *Falconer* open up with its gauss rifle, caving in his BattleMech's left knee joint.

The raw kinetic force of the hypersonic mass shattered what was left of the armor, snapping the *Exterminator*'s leg straight out and wrenching it back. Warning lights flared as the huge machine spun lazily to the right. Shakov fought the gravity of the *Exterminator*, his muscles straining against the control sticks, but he knew it was a losing battle. Arcing his body in a last ditch to salvage the situation, he heard the shriek of stressed metal as the 'Mech toppled over, slamming down onto its right side with a bone-jarring impact and the sickening crunch of crushed armor.

As if that wasn't bad enough, a loud, determined voice yelled over the comm system.

"To blazes with you and your traitor-prince," the militia commander screamed. "This ends now!"

BATTLETECH®

STORMS OF FATE

Loren L. Coleman

A ROC BOOK

ROC
Published by New American Library, a division of
Penguin Putnam Inc., 375 Hudson Street,
New York, New York 10014, U.S.A.
Penguin Books Ltd, 80 Strand,
London WC2R 0RL, England
Penguin Books Australia Ltd, Ringwood,
Victoria, Australia
Penguin Books Canada Ltd, 10 Alcorn Avenue,
Toronto, Ontario, Canada M4V 3B2
Penguin Books (N.Z.) Ltd, 182–190 Wairau Road,
Auckland 10, New Zealand

Penguin Books Ltd, Registered Offices:
Harmondsworth, Middlesex, England

First published by Roc, an imprint of New American Library,
a division of Penguin Putnam Inc.

First Printing, April 2002
10 9 8 7 6 5 4 3 2 1

Series Editor: Donna Ippolito
Designer: Ray Lundgren
Cover art by Fred Gambino

 REGISTERED TRADEMARK—MARCA REGISTRADA

PUBLISHER'S NOTE
This is a work of fiction. Names, characters, places, and incidents either are
the product of the author's imagination or are used fictitiously, and any
resemblance to actual persons, living or dead, business establishments, events,
or locales is entirely coincidental.

For Mort and Judy Weisman.
It has been an honor and a privilege.

ACKNOWLEDGMENTS

It is amazing what changes can come about in such a short time. As this book was being outlined and written, FASA decided to close its doors, the BattleTech® property was sold to WizKids Games, and what seemed like The End of this story line (but not BattleTech®) approached. In one way or another, that transition was eased by the following great people.

I would like to express my appreciation to Jordan and Dawne Weisman, Ross Babcock, Mort Weisman, Donna Ippolito, and Maya Smith for their support and friendship. Also to anyone and everyone who helped make FASA what it was: Randall, Bryan, Mike, Sharon, Chris, Annalise, Rett, Jill, Sam, Dan, Diane, Jim, Fred, and all the rest of you whom I never got to know as well as I'd have liked.

Special thanks to the rest of the "Final Five," who all signed on to bring the Civil War to its end. Randall Bills, Blaine Pardoe, Thom Gressman, and Chris Hartford. And Mike Stackpole, a continued friend of the court.

A special acknowledgment to my agent, Don Maass, who always makes things easier. And congratulations on the new book!

Love to my family, Heather, Talon, Conner and Alexia.

Special mention for the cats—Rumor, Ranger, and Chaos—who are all sleeping in a sunbeam at the moment of this writing. Sometimes I wonder if you guys aren't terribly overrated. (I'm going to pay for that.)

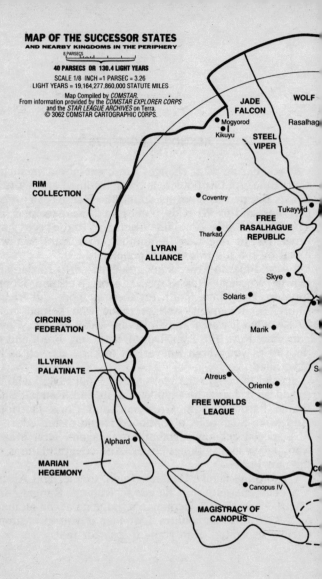

MAP OF THE SUCCESSOR STATES
AND NEARBY KINGDOMS IN THE PERIPHERY

8 PARSECS

40 PARSECS OR 130.4 LIGHT YEARS

SCALE 1/8 INCH =1 PARSEC = 3.26
LIGHT YEARS = 19,164,277,860,000 STATUTE MILES

Map Compiled by *COMSTAR.*
From information provided by the *COMSTAR EXPLORER CORPS*
and the *STAR LEAGUE ARCHIVES* on Terra.
© 3062 COMSTAR CARTOGRAPHIC CORPS.

JADE
FALCON

WOLF

Mogyorod
Rasalhag

Kikuyu
STEEL
VIPER

RIM
COLLECTION

Coventry

Tukayyid

FREE
RASALHAGUE
REPUBLIC

Tharkad

LYRAN
ALLIANCE

Skye

Solaris

CIRCINUS
FEDERATION

Marik

ILLYRIAN
PALATINATE

Atreus
S

Oriente

FREE WORLDS
LEAGUE

Alphard

MARIAN
HEGEMONY

CO

Canopus IV

MAGISTRACY OF
CANOPUS

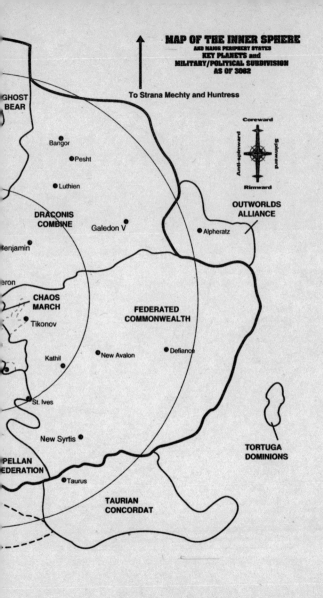

MAP OF THE INNER SPHERE
AND MAJOR PERIPHERY STATES
KEY PLANETS and
MILITARY/POLITICAL SUBDIVISION
AS OF 3062

To Strana Mechty and Huntress

Coreward

Anti-spinward · Spinward

Rimward

GHOST BEAR

Bangor

Pesht

Luthien

DRACONIS COMBINE

Galedon V

Benjamin

OUTWORLDS ALLIANCE

Alpheratz

eron

CHAOS MARCH

Tikonov

Kathil

New Avalon

FEDERATED COMMONWEALTH

Defiance

St. Ives

New Syrtis

TORTUGA DOMINIONS

PELLAN FEDERATION

Taurus

TAURIAN CONCORDAT

The Ides
of March

1

The Press Center was a collection of rooms tucked into the furthest reach of one wing of the Davion Palace. It smelled of stale cigarette smoke and cheap coffee, odors Archon Princess Katrina Steiner-Davion always associated with the nervous intensity of political reporters. She imagined the stench trailing them through backroom meetings with anonymous sources, onto the sweatshop floors of publishing giants, and into the cramped offices of their hypertensive editors. But it also found its way here, rubbing off on the wood-paneled walls and spilling over the expensive carpeting of Davion Palace. *Her* palace.

Like dogs continuously marking their territory, Katrina thought. Half-wild dogs, always sniffing around, baring their teeth, ready to lunge at the first scent of weakness.

Except that today there would be no snapping or barking. No wounded howls. Two hundred empty chairs greeted her as she swept into the Media Room with a confident air, leaving her aides at the door, out of sight. A two-man holocam crew stood a lonely vigil in the center of the room, already recording. Katrina had chosen a dark navy suit to warm up her cool blue eyes, and her golden hair was braided tightly along either side of her head for a professional appearance.

She nodded perfunctorily to the men on her way to the stage. "Good morning," she said, making it sound as if she addressed a large crowd instead of just two crewmen.

Not that the press frightened her. She kept the pack leashed, making friends with the safer mutts and turning the best scrappers against each other in dominance games. It had worked for her whole life, with the media in harness as she rose to power. They'd received her favorably after she *borrowed* her grandmother's powerful celebrity, making the shift from Katherine—such a mild and flavorless name—to the stronger, respected Katrina. The media stayed with her as she seceded with the Lyran Alliance and accepted—reluctantly, of course—the mantle of the Archonship. She was the resurrection of a true House Steiner, and never mind her Davion heritage.

At least, not until she'd needed it, setting her sights on the other half of the Federated Commonwealth. While Victor was away chasing glory with the Star League army, the media had helped convince Yvonne to step down as their brother's regent and to hand over to Katrina the reins of the Federated Suns.

And Victor came home to glory all right, but he also found himself a ruler without a throne. It had surprised Katrina that her warrior-prince brother had so peacefully accepted the situation. That lasted a year, until the mysterious assassination of Arthur, the youngest Davion brother. Victor had seized unfairly on his death, daring to publicly accuse Katrina of involvement in it. Then he'd rallied the Davion "old guard" and built a grassroots campaign in the Lyran Alliance, launching a civil war for the return of his thrones.

If Katrina had made any mistake, it was in underestimating the amount of damage her brother could do to her in the Lyran Alliance. It was her stronger base of power, after all. For the longest time, she'd refused to even acknowledge the fighting as a civil war, treating Victor's supporters as rebels and traitors. That strategy had died when he captured Coventry in the second wave of his advance down through the Lyran Commonwealth. Coventry was the second-strongest industrial world in the entire Alliance, and winning it was both a political and military coup for Victor. It underscored his history as a war hero, and by bringing Duke Harrison Bradford to his banner, he regained some of the political weight that Katrina had worked so hard to deprive him of.

Victor also began to gain ground in the propaganda battle. The longer he opposed her and the more victories he won, the harder she had to fight to hold on to public support. Which was the reason behind today's broadcast and her decision to exclude the media. This speech was intended to assure the common man and woman that Katrina continued to hold a firm—but fair—grip on both interstellar nations. It didn't matter that she had no recent military gains to parade; if reports were to be believed, those would be coming soon enough.

In the meantime, putting her face in front of the people was just as important. Perhaps more so.

Katrina took her place behind a low podium emblazoned with the gauntlet-and-sunburst crest of the forever-sundered Federated Commonwealth. She gave the hem of her suit jacket a quick tug, having selected this particular outfit for the same reason. Blue would appeal to her Lyran citizens, yet each gold button on the jacket was etched with a Davion-style sunburst. It was a studied presentation of neutrality and fairness.

She was ready.

Katrina rested her folded hands on the podium's slanted top and smiled as if recognizing a friend among the imaginary correspondents. The wood felt cold against her skin.

"Thank you all for being here," she said. "I know that many questions have come up regarding the recent setbacks we have experienced in my brother's bid for power. Despite the media's supposed fascination with violence, I know how much you—how much we all—wish the situation could be otherwise.

"Perhaps today, I can offer everyone some hope." She paused for emphasis, knowing that the camera would take her carefully constructed image and send it almost instantaneously to the worlds of both empires under her rule.

The command circuit of HPG stations was one of her proudest accomplishments, and she had invested heavily to create it. The holovid feed would travel from this room to the various media interests on New Avalon, with only a ten-second time delay engineered for intelligence concerns. Just in case. The signal also sped along the communications spine of hyperpulse generators that connected the hundreds of worlds of her two nations, jumping instantly between star systems as the address made its way toward Tharkad—capital of the Lyran Alliance and traditional seat of power for House Steiner. Within moments of speaking, her words commanded the attention of billions of lives. It was a public relations coup her brother could never duplicate.

"It has been better than a year now since my brother encouraged and sponsored rebellions on several worlds within the Federated Suns and Lyran Alliance, plunging us into this dark and bitter civil war. To be precise, it has been one year, two months, and twenty-nine days. I know. I have felt each one crawl by with painful clarity."

True, and despite her best efforts to silence Victor once and for all.

"In this time, we have all seen the horror my brother has loosed. Media coverage," she said, playing to the nonexistent press corps, "has been exemplary. It has certainly helped control panic by keeping the public informed of all necessary steps we are taking to end this threat to their safety and security."

And of that, Katrina promised them silently, she would continue to be certain.

In another wing and several sublevels beneath the palace proper, Lieutenant Jorge Gavrial, a junior analyst officer, oversaw current activity in the small, private war room once known as the Fox's Den. A bank of monitors covered the west wall, each one tuned to the Archon Princess's public address, which was preempting the civilian news stations that usually cycled through on computer-timed intervals.

Gavrial reached past one of the on-duty technicians to adjust the input controls, and suddenly the nine-by-nine array of monitors formed one large composite picture. Katrina's image looked out over her military administrators, blue eyes alert, always watching.

Most of the room's NCOs were hard at work, laboring over computer workstations, sifting through incredible amounts of data for facts that, when verified, would be translated onto strategic maps. Covering the northern wall, a floor-to-ceiling projection displayed the whole of the Inner Sphere.

Gavrial spared it a quick glance. The realms of House Kurita, Marik, and Liao, as well as the occupied territories held by the Clans, were blanked out in solid, primary colors. What remained was an outline of the old Commonwealth, the super-state conceived with the marriage of Hanse Davion to Melissa Steiner, and into which Gavrial had been born. Like an hourglass cocked far to one side, the Lyran Alliance formed the upper bulb and the Federated Suns the lower. Connecting the two was a small stretch of unaffiliated systems known as the Terran Corridor. Stars filled both halves like grains of sparkling sand.

"Also in this time," the Archon Princess continued, "our loyal forces within both realms have performed the difficult but admirable job of containing Victor's excesses. For every world where Victor *claims* to hold an advantage, I have seen reports of our continued, defiant resistance. Coventry and Alarion will not be his for much longer. Kathil and Wernke are all but ours again. I could not be prouder of our serving militaries."

Gavrial shook his head, trying to coordinate what he was hearing with what he could see for himself. On the star map, he could read at a glance the status of the civil war. Systems supporting Victor burned with a golden hue, those in favor of Katrina a calm blue. Red indicated fighting, or at least severe political unrest, and there were more red-burning stars than either gold *or* blue. Even as he watched, the important Federated Suns world of Kathil began to flash between red and gold, showing that the advantage had turned seriously in favor of Victor. Tikonov didn't look good either, and Axton was all but lost if reinforcements couldn't be found.

Katrina knew about the rebel gains. She had to. Gavrial decided that she simply didn't want to alarm the average citizen. As if reading his mind, her image on the monitor was saying, "The fires of treason may burn hot where they rage unchecked, but the gains claimed by the rebels are not so complete as they would like us to believe. They are mostly inconsequential, and those flames will soon be quenched."

Up in the Alliance, where Victor had built a strong grassroots movement, Gavrial traced out the Prince's path. He had traveled down from distant Mogyorod to Inarcs in the first wave. In the second wave, Victor had continued on to Coventry, another critical manufacturing world. Then, most recently, he had taken Alarion—truly a prize for his third wave. Men and materiel, those were the keys. Inarcs, Coventry, and Alarion all held out in a steady, damning gold on the star map.

Those worlds were hardly inconsequential, Gavrial thought. With the strength of just those three alone, you could invade the whole Capellan Confederation.

Elsewhere in the Crucis March, Roxanne Blake drifted slowly through one of the most extensive art collections on the planet Marlette, or anywhere in the Federated Suns, for that matter. Jericho City's Sheffield Gallery specialized in contrasts, and her weekly visits always turned up something surprising. Colossal statues dwarfed patrons who crouched over microscopes to review rare pieces of micron sculpturing. Painted, two-dimensional portraits stared out into abstract holographic scenery.

Rough-welded constructs smelling of oil and scorched metal crowded next to organic, living exhibits.

As she strolled through the rooms, entranced by some of the newer pieces, a voice intruded on her reverie. "You must always remember that it is the methodology of rebels to undermine and divide," the voice said, ringing through the gallery. "It is just as true that faith and perseverance can armor any nation against such subversive efforts."

Startled, Roxanne almost lost her footing. She glanced about sharply, wondering if it was part of some new exhibit. Then she recognized the voice, and wondered how it was possible that Katrina Steiner-Davion was on Marlette without anyone hearing about it.

"The people are the underlying strength of a ruler, and in you I have found a wellspring of spirit and courage that has helped me face the trials of this last year. Just as I know you have all faced your own difficulties," the Archon was saying.

Looking around, Roxanne saw where the voice was coming from as a crowd began to gather around a large piece of neo-performance art. With a start, she realized that the piece was actually broadcasting. A pair of holovision projectors were mounted inside a hologram-augmented diorama that constantly monitored the local networks, displaying two competing channels onto a simulated battlefield. Of course, both stations were given over to the Archon Princess, and the podium had been morphed by clever programs to sprout weapons. While twelve-centimeter-high BattleMechs lumbered along a clay-streaked ridge or walked callously over the scurrying-ant formations of unarmored infantry, one projection of the Archon Princess fired on the other with everything from ruby-tinted lasers to the lightning-whip of a particle projection cannon.

Roxanne watched as the dueling Katrinas led first one side and then the other to victory. Suddenly, the wave of the crowd pulled her away, toward the adjoining exhibit, where she suddenly found herself caught in a calm eye developing between two competing storms.

Mounted on a post and surrounded by a large expanse of walled-off empty space was an unframed original painting by one of the Lyran Alliance's most controversial talents. People crowded the glass walls, but Roxanne's better-than-average height let her view the piece from a few steps back. As always, Reginald Starling's work pulled her into his savage world, and she felt a chill up her spine as she grasped the image. She glanced nervously back at the diorama.

Around her, others were doing the same, glancing back and forth and comparing the two works. Scattered whispers welled up into an excited buzz, with finger-pointing and loud comparisons regarding the distorted subject of the painting and the battling holograms. The face appeared twisted, as if seen through a heat-induced shimmer, but the ice-blue eyes stood out with perfection, as did the subject's long, golden hair. Which, apparently, was enough realism for the artist, who had knifed in the rest of the body with broad strokes of red and black. In some areas, the red clung to the canvas so thick that it looked like clotted blood.

That seemed equally appropriate to the title of the piece. "Bloody Princess VI," read the placard.

"It takes a certain strength of character to stand up for your ideals," the image of Katrina said as she chewed her second avatar to shreds with a firestorm of autocannon fire. "To espouse the truth, tear down the falsehoods, and expose that which is not wholesome."

Even more light years away, in the distant Capellan March of the Federated Suns, Sergeant Preston Davis of the Fifteenth Deneb Gravediggers Company paused in the shadow of a grounded VTOL, the chill shade of the helo-transport offering some relief from Tikonov's afternoon sun.

The battle had passed through the Retsin River Valley hours earlier, but there were still "military concerns" that required attending. Rubbing at his nose through the surgical mask he wore, he stared out over the ruined wilderness and listened to the end of Katrina Steiner-Davion's address, which was coming to him live.

"So my challenge to you all," she said, "is to remain steadfast in these trying times. To place your faith in me, and in each other. And above all to stand behind the loyal militaries of the Lyran Alliance and Federated Suns so that both realms may endure. They deserve your support. They deserve so much more than what has been thrust upon them in this last year. Don't we all?"

Davis settled one end of the burden he carried onto a growing pallet of similar black nylon bags, then nodded for the corporal to go help with another. Listening to Katrina, he grunted in response, his eyes traveling over the ruined countryside.

Where the river had once wound calmly around a bend, the waters now ran up against a mass of twisted metal that channeled the river back down into a narrow torrent. Lying face-down in the riverbed, the body of a fallen *Atlas* formed an impromptu dam, with only its right shoulder and the stub of one arm resting on dry bank. A stone's throw downstream lay an overturned *Pegasus* hovercraft, still smoking where hot metal poked above the muddied water.

Like every other battlefield Davis had ever seen, this one was strewn with the corpses of several dozen 'Mechs and fire-gutted vehicles. Armor fragments had plowed into the chewed earth, and trees had been knocked over or simply crushed under the weight of the awesome military machines. He was glad to see that more of the metal corpses belonged to Victor Steiner-Davion's allied force than to Katherine's loyalists, but it was close. The ground was stained with coolant, fuel, and blood. Heading northwest were the deep depressions of BattleMech footsteps as the few survivors returned to their staging area.

The Fifteenth Deneb Gravediggers Company were the only live bodies left on the battlefield. The wounded and the dispossessed had been evac'd out hours before, and no general planned to tour this site. Davis and the others wore surgical-style masks, partly to block the acrid stench of propellant and scorched earth but more to keep out the slaughterhouse smell of blood that always accompanied their work.

His men worked busily, prying the remains of warriors free of 'Mech cockpits and ruptured tanks, then carrying them into the shadow of an old "eggbeater" VTOL, where others worked two-to-a-team to identify and toe-tag each body. From the helicopter's cockpit, the Archon Princess's address blared out over the Armed Forces Radio Network. Most of the gravediggers tried not to hear, just as they tried not to see.

It was often better to forget, Davis knew. Sleep came easier that way.

But Katrina's voice continued to ring out loud and clear. "And my promise to you, the brave men and women who defend us that we may continue to live free from harm, is that you will not be forgotten. You will never be abandoned. And we *will* bring you home," she promised, "safe, whole, and welcomed.

"So help me God."

2

Salisbury Plains, York
Alarion Province
Lyran Alliance
13 March 3064

The retreat of Victor Steiner-Davion's allied forces from York was deep into its twenty-fifth hour, holding only through sheer determination. Strapped into his *Daishi*'s sweltering cockpit, he blinked away the sweat burning at the corners of his eyes. Perspiration soaked his light clothing, and one annoying lock of blond hair had become matted over the ridge of his left ear, right where the bulky neurohelmet prevented him from scratching. Condensation from evaporated sweat fogged the ferroglass shield of his cockpit, but he could see enough to know that his people had about reached their limit.

Before being pressed into this final, pitched battle, he had admired York's straw-colored sky and the way it seemed to reflect the golden clay and tall, feather-topped yellow grasses of Salisbury Plains, stretching for a hundred kilometers in every direction. Now, aerospace fighters tore that sky apart with vapor trails and the greasy, black smoke dragging behind burning craft. Occasionally, one two-fighter element dipped down long enough to make a support run, intruding on the slower but no less savage ground war where the Eleventh Arcturan Guards continued to press forward against the shortened lines of ComStar's 244th Division, the Prince's Men.

Victor's final stand.

BattleMechs anchored each side into place, walking titans more deadly than any weapon known to mankind's long history of warfare. Between and around their positions, packs of armored vehicles wheeled about in an uncertain dance, like wild herds spooked by competing predators. Long, thick lances of laserfire and the arcing, white-hot lightning of particle projection cannon signaled brief but violent clashes between the allies and their enemy. Missiles swarmed in on gray contrails, pock-marking armor, the ground, infantry formations. Tongues of flame licked out from smoking barrels, the rattling reports of so many autocannon rolling over the plains in constant thunder.

The sound roared past Victor's position, then scattered into hundreds of echoing, hammer-like blows as uranium-tipped slugs pounded at his OmniMech's legs and lower chest. The *Daishi* trembled as some of its armor dropped to the ground in a rain of sharp-edged splinters. He gripped the 'Mech's control sticks tightly, fighting to keep his cross hairs in the general vicinity of the *King Crab* piloted by enemy commander Linda McDonald. The targeting reticle jumped around his tactical screen in fits, flashing only partial sensor lock.

Victor knew it would have to do.

Pulling into his primary triggers, he unleashed the *Daishi*'s full ire. His twelve-centimeter autocannon missed wide to the right, but his laserfire aimed true. One ruby lance slashed an angry wound across the *King Crab*'s left flank while a second stabbed deep into the arm on the same side. His trio of pulse lasers spat out a flurry of emerald bursts, tracking in on the assault 'Mech's left leg. McDonald's armor all but evaporated, spraying off in a molten mist. More ran in a fiery stream down her 'Mech's leg, leaking past the armored skirting that protected the knee joint to foul the leg actuator. Following them, a six-pack of short-range missiles corkscrewed in to gouge a few more craters into the *King Crab*'s armor.

McDonald staggered, keeping her hundred-ton behemoth upright as much by luck as by skill. She had been about to take a step, with most of her 'Mech's weight already on its right leg. Victor could imagine her twisting in her seat, ducking her head to the right so that her neurohelmet could translate her sense of balance into a signal that would be fed into the assault machine's gyroscope.

Alarms rang in his ears, including the harsh blare that warned of reactor shutdown. The extreme power spike created by the demand of his weapons had pushed the *Daishi*'s fusion chamber past the capacity of its improved heat-sink technology. Victor toggled an override, pre-empting the safety feature.

But nothing could prevent the waste heat of such a power draw from bleeding past the reactor's physical shielding and up through the cockpit decking. The slow wave of heat seemed to broil him alive, scalding the bare skin on his legs and arms and making his vision waver from hyperthermia. He gasped for breath. The ozone scent of heat-stressed electronics burned his sinuses. His life-support vest, lined with thin tubes that circulated coolant through the sleeveless jacket, labored to keep his body's core temperature within safe limits. Just.

"General, your 'Mech's thermal image shows a very unhealthy glow," he heard Demi-Precentor Rudolf Shakov say in his headset, the transmission crystal-clear.

Peering through his ferroglass shield, Victor could see the oily smoke of scorched myomer musculature bleeding up past the *Daishi*'s forward-thrust head. He had already reversed his throttles, but the OmniMech's heat-addled myomer responded sluggishly. With slow, halting footsteps, it shuffled backward at a pace any determined infantryman could match.

He used the spare seconds—an eternity in a hot firefight—to survey the scene. The Prince's Men still held a tight line, retreating slowly to the south, where a battalion of his Outland Legion waited impatiently in reserve.

A fighting retreat was one of the most difficult strategies to pull off, and Victor's forces on York were currently engaged in two such actions. Far to the southwest, the Sixth Crucis Lancers were falling back in a similar line against the combined weight of the Alarion and Carlisle Provincial Militias.

Had the odds been equal, the Prince's Men and the Lancers—singly or together—could probably outfight their attackers. Even two to one would have been enough, considering that the Eleventh Guard and the Alarion militia were ill-trained to fight at regimental strength.

At some point, the enemy's greater numbers simply won out as they hit York with more than enough troops to make up for their lack of ability. The irony was that Victor had never intended to fight here. York should have been only an advance base for the final drive of his third wave. The struggle was supposed to occur on Alarion, a district capital and site of the Alliance space docks. In a surprise move, the loyalists had let Alarion fall without a fight, and had thrown themselves at Victor on York instead, where he least expected it. He'd been forced from his strongholds and out onto the plains.

The loyalist assault had also eaten up the last of his grace. A mistake out here by either allied regiment would be devastating. Hard, flat, and open, the Salisbury Plains were unforgiving. You couldn't even start a good grass fire to hide in the smoke. The wet grass smoldered but refused to burn.

The only advantages were in the shallow depressions or the occasional low rise where squads of battle-suited infantry could hide. And what Victor had, he used. Already a pair of Sloth suits had sneaked under a *Caesar*'s sensor net, planting their anti-Mech mines in its crotch as it strode over them. Tiaret, his security chief and bodyguard, was also out there somewhere, encased in her Elemental suit and tormenting the Arcturan Guards with her repeated hit-and-fade tactics. It was enough to slow the enemy advance. That, and a determined resistance, might let them all escape.

He turned his *Daishi* to keep an aggressive angle on Patricia McDonald, who was limping back for the safety of her own lines. Her *King Crab* was a formidable machine, but with a gimped leg, it could fall prey to a lighter, faster design. Such as Shakov's *Exterminator,* which had begun to run toward her across the open ground, weapons blazing. His quartet of medium lasers had no real chance to hit, not at that speed and distance and coming in at a cross-body angle, but his long-range missiles did manage to chip away at the 'Mech.

"Get out of there, Rudolf," Victor struggled to say, his throat raw and bloodied from breathing the scorched air. "Don't play games with that *Crab*."

Fusion ports lit off along the *Exterminator*'s back as Shakov engaged his jump jets. The sixty-five-ton 'Mech took to the air on columns of superheated plasma, rocketing up and sideways in a short arc that landed him in a crouch just to the left of Victor's Clan-designed 'Mech.

"You're one to talk, sire," Shakov said. "You promised Tiaret you'd watch out for yourself. She and Precentor Irelon both ordered me to make sure you do. You're trying to get me in trouble."

Victor couldn't help a smile. Rudolf Shakov was one of the few ComStar people he'd ever met who could boast a sense of humor. "We'll see how much trouble you get into when Irelon reviews my battleroms and sees you grandstanding with an assault 'Mech," he threatened. "Stay in line."

As his heat sinks finally began to shunt away the excess heat, Victor carefully probed with his lasers at the ever-encroaching Arcturan Guards. Return fire had fallen off with McDonald's temporary retreat, though an occasional low-caliber autocannon continued to worry his armor. He ordered his line back another five hundred meters. When his rear monitor showed some laser-equipped jump infantry climbing into a transport hovercraft to join the retreat, he throttled down to a slower walk. He didn't give a damn for any promise he'd made to take care of himself. He wouldn't leave men behind. Not when escape was within reach.

He dialed up the magnification on his rear monitor. South, far behind the Prince's Men, a line of dark, rounded shadows on the horizon created the illusion of mountains. Even as Victor watched, the bright glow of a drive flare cut one of the shadows free. It rose slowly into the pale sky on a pillar of fusion-born fire. Two more, and then a third, joined it. The four leviathan DropShips were the second group to slip free of the noose being drawn around his forces. They were on their way to rendezvous with his waiting JumpShips.

"Luck," Victor said softly, knowing they still had to brave a cordon of enemy fightercraft and assault-class DropShips. His troops were good men and women who deserved better than to pay such a high price for his strategy gone wrong. Besides, he couldn't afford to lose them if he was ever going to end Katherine's tyrannical rule. Although he might not get the chance to do that if he, too, didn't break free of the trap.

His comm system crackled to life again. "Godspeed, and protect the Prince," he heard someone say. The words were faint, washed with the static of a long-distance transmission. Victor checked the chronometer, thinking that the first flight of DropShips to flee York might be reaching its rendezvous point right about now.

"Shakov, was that—" His sound-activated mic opened a channel while ComStar's voice-recognition software dialed for his private frequency with Shakov.

There was only the briefest pause as Shakov's *Exterminator* stabbed out with a quartet of medium-class lasers, deviling a Plainsman hovertank that had cut in too close.

"Right," Shakov said. "That was the captain of the *Pharos,* one of the Lancer JumpShips. I have corroborating reports on three other channels. They're clear!"

Which meant that two *Hercules* DropShips had beat the aerospace cordon. Eight hundred men and women belonging to the Sixth Crucis Lancers, clear! Victor manually toggled for his all-hands frequency.

"The first transport is away," he called out, and was rewarded with a brief backwash of cheers that filled the airwaves for several long seconds. He was also rewarded by the sight of intensified fire against the Arcturan Guard line, as his men threw them back. Victor added a pair of extended-range lasers to the brief offensive, stabbing at the *King Crab* limping after him just at the edge of weapons range. The flush of heat was hardly noticeable this time.

"This is going to work," he said, his spirits lifting for the first time since York fell under the loyalist assault.

"Hold that thought," Shakov warned, knowing enough not to respond on a common channel. "New message coming through, from Cranston, and the news isn't good."

Jerrard Cranston was one of Victor's oldest friends as well as his chief intelligence officer. Just now, he commanded the Outland Legions' second battalion, patrolling for flanking attempts by Katherine's forces. They had received reports earlier of a possible new unit making planetfall on York. If Jerry had found them, and they were loyalists, then the news was actually very bad.

Victor wanted to demand more information, but controlled the impulse. It often surprised him how Demi Shakov knew of incoming transmissions before Victor heard anything on his command channels. Maybe it was because of Shakov's long-time service in ComStar, one of the two organizations that maintained and operated the Inner Sphere's interstellar HPG communications network. The man was a MechWarrior first, but his ability with battlefield communications sometimes bordered on the miraculous.

"Cranston's being jammed," Shakov said, "but I have enough to give you his situation. The Outland Legion just made contact with another regiment, repeat *regiment*. The First Alarion Jaegers."

"Another regiment. How the hell did we miss that?" Victor grumbled as the Arcturan Guard pressed forward with renewed vigor. Had they just received news of this support regiment too?

"They couldn't have arrived at the nadir point with

the others," Shakov said, "or we wouldn't have missed it. They burned in from a pirate point on the backside of the planet. Victor, they've got WarShips with them."

"WarShips?" Victor echoed. "As in plural? More than one?"

"Affirmative. Two *Fox*-class corvettes. Enough to hold off the *Melissa Davion*," Shakov said, naming Victor's one WarShip on location. "Sire, it's time for you to leave."

Victor ignored that. His crosshairs burned the dark gold of target lock, and he fired, carving two angry wounds into a Fulcrum hovertank. The Eleventh was probing forward again.

"Forget it," he said, rubbing uselessly at the collar of his neurohelmet. His neck was stiff from holding up the helmet's weight for so many hours. There were still two retreats to bring off. People to rescue. "We're not finished here."

"*You* are," said a new voice.

Victor had no problem recognizing the gravelly tones of Precentor Raymond Irelon, currently healing a broken leg and holding down Victor's command post from the hangar bay of one of the DropShips on the horizon. "You left me in strategic command, and now I'm exercising the right to *order* you from the battlefield. If it means anything to you, Jerrard Cranston and Colonel Vineman concur. You are to report to the *True Spirit* for immediate lift."

"Then we all go," Victor replied even as he dropped his targeting crosshairs over the blocky outline of an old JM6 *JagerMech*. Both ruby laser beams caught it square in the chest, cutting through the last of the *Jager*'s ruined armor and flooding the torso cavity with destructive energy. A blossom of heat on his thermal scanner showed engine damage, but not enough to bring down the machine. The *JagerMech* fell back. "We turn and make a run for the cover of the DropShips."

"Once you're away from the line, I will consider it," Irelon said. "Demi Shakov, your people will form an escort for the prince."

Waiting for his lasers to cycle, Victor took a second

to check the Eleventh's relative strength. "No good, Raymond. If you pull away a third of our strength, the Guard will envelop the rest and cut them to pieces."

"They will be otherwise engaged. On my command, Demi-Precentor Hullinger will launch a preemptive strike aimed at Colonel McDonald. If you're gone, Victor, I can concentrate on bringing home as many as possible."

Victor slammed one fist against his control console, gashing himself on a metal burr. In his anger, he barely felt the pain. "Damn it, Irelon. If you think I'm going to walk away from these people—"

"You'll do it," Irelon broke in, "because it's the right thing to do. You'll do it to prevent the useless sacrifice of good men and women. And you'll do it because there's no one else we would follow to oppose your sister."

Irelon's final comment got through to Victor, where no other words would have. It was so easy to lose himself in the heat of battle, to dedicate his loyalty to the men and women fighting at his side. But Victor also had responsibilities to the citizens of the Lyran Alliance and the Federated Suns, to the worlds in open rebellion against Katherine, and to the soldiers facing Katherine's wrath if he should fail to bring her down once and for all.

Irelon was right. "Damn," he whispered, his voice choked with anger.

Slamming the throttle forward and grinding on the foot pedals, he turned his *Daishi* into a tight pivot that pointed him away from the battle, away from the fate of his warriors, before he could change his mind. He raced for the distant haven of the DropShips at more than fifty kilometers per hour, every pounding step echoing the sound of defeat in his ears.

York was lost. The lives spent defending it, spent bringing off this forced retreat, spent in exchange for his safety—they were lost to him as well. It tore at him. Worse, it begged a question that tormented him constantly.

How much more would he have to lose before this war was finally over?

3

Omi Kurita walked the flagstone path of her palace gardens with measured steps, the picture of dignity and studied calm despite her troubled heart. Today, she wore a kimono of jade green silk loosely gathered at the waist by a golden obi, and the fragrance of the gardens teased her onward as her underskirts brushed the top of her sandaled feet.

Distraction. That was what she sought. Something to occupy her mind, to compartmentalize her inner turmoil over Victor's latest message. It was more than the longing and the pain that always came with reminders of how much separated them. It was more than the gulf between their cultures or the feuding legacies into which they'd been born. It was the frustration that she was too far away to share his burden. The onus of civil war weighed so heavily on Victor's *seishin*—his spirit—that she could almost hear it straining in every word he recorded for her.

"How much more will we lose, Omi?" he'd asked. *"How much has been lost already?"*

Omi couldn't forget the haunted look in his blue-gray eyes. Though her brother Hohiro insisted that the defeat at York was not strategically critical, Victor had taken it hard. Her brother couldn't understand that, of course. In the Draconis Combine, a samurai's duty was to serve and, if necessary, to die for the state—for House Kurita. Victor took his losses far more personally, and Omi knew that fighting a civil war against his own people only made it worse.

But it was more than that. She understood that his real question was how many more times would they be forced to subordinate their private relationship to the demands and obligations of their birthrights? He missed her terribly, she knew. On Mogyorod, they'd wanted only to remain together, but the war called him away. Now, Victor was afraid that their love was not to be. Omi was one of the few people in whom he could confide. And even when he tried to hide his pain or his fear, he couldn't. Not from her. Never from her.

Her own sorrows she had hidden, for the sake of everyone but herself. Victor's message had stirred up the pain, and she could not think clearly. If she was ever to find a way to answer him, she needed to occupy herself with some mindless diversion.

Her Palace of Serene Sanctuary offered little in that regard. She had never bothered with the dojo, leaving it to the agents assigned to her by the Internal Security Force and the Order of the Five Pillars. Besides, intruding on the O5P business offices would cause too much disruption to allow for such selfishness. She might have sought out Isis Marik, who was inhabiting a suite of apartments in the Palace of Serene Sanctuary, but that too would be selfish. Isis was still grieving the end of her relationship with Sun-Tzu Liao and the loss of her place in the Free Worlds League. Omi didn't want to burden Isis even more. The poor girl deserved some peace to rediscover herself after so many years of forced up-rooting.

And so Omi had come to wander in the garden. Spring roses climbed the palace walls, splashing the polished ivory stone with their blood-red color, though the early-blooming nasturtiums almost obliterated their scent. She welcomed the warm touch of the afternoon sun, its fingers working out the tensions in her neck and shoulders. She smiled as the sunlight gleamed along one sleeve of her jade kimono, the richness of the silk at odds with her simple surroundings.

Ahead, an elderly palace worker was polishing the flagstones, hunched over a straw broom likely made by his own hand. The dry whisk of his short, determined strokes reminded her of the sounds made when palace gardeners raked the beds of colored gravel into wonderful designs.

The Zen garden had always been among her favorite retreats, and she had spent more time here than anywhere else since her return to the Draconis Combine and Luthien. More time even than at Unity Palace, the seat of power for House Kurita, despite the great suffering of her father. She and Hohiro longed to comfort him, but they knew that the great Theodore Kurita must not be seen as dependent on anyone, so they stayed away. Even some time playing with his grandson had not helped comfort the coordinator's grief, a child in the palace reminding him of his lost wife. And so Minorn had taken the child away.

So many losses, even within her own family. Was that the answer to Victor's questions? For Omi to explain how hard hit her father was by the loss of his wife? Kurita honor remained intact and the family persevered, but to know that the *Dragon*—the Coordinator of the Draconis Combine and elected First Lord of the Star League—had been humbled by events outside his control, even if for only a moment . . .

But she wouldn't have to explain any of that to Victor. He understood without having to be told. Had it been beyond his ken, the two of them could never have loved each other. And they did. Past prejudices and reason, they did.

Omi walked up to the sweeper. The old man stepped aside and knelt, his arthritic knees cracking loudly. He laid his rough-fashioned straw broom on the ground in front of him and bowed until his head touched the ground. Omi considered stopping to speak a few kind words, but knew it would only frighten such a simple man to be recognized. So, she simply bowed in honor of his service. He never saw it, but would accept that she had done so.

Acceptance. As deeply ingrained in the Combine's samurai culture as honor and duty. So many tragedies, Omi thought, thinking of both her and Victor's families. So few rewards. That was what it meant to be born into one of the Inner Sphere's ruling houses. She accepted that. Victor did, too, despite his occasional, wishful forays into the workings of a "perfect" universe. She couldn't resist a sad smile. In the Combine, it was believed that imperfections were what truly defined life.

It was also what drew Omi's attention to the disturbance of her gardens.

Along the northeastern wall, where afternoon sunlight reached year round, were the garden beds Victor had planted and personally tended during the first months of his exile. Omi remembered that time well, for she had shared with him the pain of losing his realm to his sister. Without a nation—without any true political standing in the Inner Sphere—he had retired for a time to her palace garden, to work with his hands in the soil and to reflect on his life and his future. Such periods of reflection were nearly sacred in Combine culture. Omi had once vowed to never regret sharing with Victor her spirit or her body, and he had justified her faith in those days, honoring her with his decision to remain close.

The nasturtiums, in fact, were his. Planted in the partial shade of the spring roses, surrounded by a bed of crushed white marble, their bright colors drew the eye whenever direct sunlight found them. Their strong perfume could be overpowering, even dizzying. They were *direct,* which was how Victor preferred to be whenever possible. They were also strong and forgiving. That was Victor as well.

"Take this," he had said when they separated on Mogyorod, still shaken by the failed attempt on her life. Victor had handed over the *natami* stone she'd given him at Christmas the year before. The one he'd named Warrior's Path.

Omi tried to refuse it. "It should stay with you."

Victor smiled and shook his head. "It deserves a home. A place to feel comfortable. For me, that will always be with you. Plant it in the garden on Tukayyid, where you first gave it to me. And if you return to Luthien, set it among the nasturtiums at your palace, back in a shady corner."

He'd chosen an excellent spot from memory. The stone was shot through with veins of reddish-blue quartz that sparkled when they caught the occasional sunbeam. There was also a staggered line of crystalline flakes across one barren stretch, which Victor had named "the trail of tears." Omi often retrieved the stone from its spot, holding it up so that the crystals caught the bright sun. They twinkled like tiny stars, reminding her of Victor's progress since Mogyorod. From Newtown Square to Hood and Winter. Then, on to New Capetown and Coventry. Followed by Alarion and York—which had almost been the end of him—and, now, soon to Halfway.

Omi knew the stone as well as any piece of her palace. And it had been moved.

The disturbance was subtle, as if someone had picked it up and then carefully replaced it, readjusting the stone's position on the ground. It bothered her. The gardeners knew to leave these flowerbeds alone, that the stone was Named. They were all aware that she made a habit of visiting it. *Natami* stones were a very personal matter.

Still, Omi could think of a half-dozen reasons why someone might have stepped into the flower beds and disturbed the stone. A gardener might have thought to wipe it clean of dirt or perhaps had moved it in the work of spiking the soil with additives. It was also possible that one of the master gardeners might have decided that the stone needed to be turned for a "new look."

Omi didn't desire a new look for Warrior's Path. If she sought distraction, she'd found it. Careful of the nasturtiums, she stepped off the flagstone path and onto the hard-packed, crushed marble. Leaning in carefully, one arm extended for balance, she reached to pluck the stone from its nest. Her fingers brushed against it, found purchase, and pried the fist-sized rock partly from its resting place.

A sharp whisper of sound startled her with the accompanying pain. She'd been stung. Twice, in fact—two separate pinches at her underarm. A third pulled at the sleeve of her kimono, and some activity among the roses above the stone made Omi think of darting insects. Still bent over the flowerbed, she pulled her hand away slowly, frowned at its heavy weight and how she had to twist the entire arm to see her wrist. Two needles were stuck into her arm, one of them through the jade-green sleeve of her kimono. No larger than a sewing needle, each one was tipped with a small plastic plug.

Omi felt the blank look weighing on her face. She closed her eyes, tried to rock herself back onto the flagstone path. "Oh, Victor," she murmured.

His name was the last thing Omi Kurita would say.

"Omi-*sama*? *Tasukete*! *Ima, ima*!"

She heard the alarm given by the old sweeper, felt the numb pressure of hands at her shoulders and massaging her cheeks. Fighting the weariness, Omi managed to force her eyes open. She couldn't focus on any of the faces hovering over her, the ones blocking out her view of the never-ending blue sky. The pungent aroma of the nasturtiums faded as her breathing slowed. Omi tried to talk, but the paralytic had already silenced her voice.

Her mind registered when they began the assisted breathing of CPR. Then came the pain of arrythmia as her heart raced in a frantic effort to provide oxygen to her brain. The world shrank down, dimmed, until only a single memory dominated her mind. A face. *His* face.

Peering at her from a great distance as he bent down to
set something on the ground. She wanted to speak so
badly . . . just one last whisper . . . to tell him . . .

 Victor . . .

Shouting at the Rains

4

Bune, Halfway
Bolan Province
Lyran Alliance
14 May 3064

As his *Exterminator*'s high-pitched alarms warned of missile lock, Demi-Precentor Rudolf Shakov held his ground under the first pounding wave of missiles. More followed, a barrage of LRMs that speared through the windbreak of tall, gray-barked alders, all that separated his position in a railroad trestle bed from the city of Bune's waterfront industrial area. The industrial park consisted of a flat, paved area, broken only by some warehouses and huge stacks of timber that eventually gave way to docks and the wide Graham River.

Fiery explosions lopped off a half dozen trees with brutal efficiency, shattering boles into burning splinters. Bursting easily through the thin branches, the warheads rained scorched leaves onto the gravel-covered ground, trailed sooty paths over a double set of train tracks, and fell into the advancing Com Guard line.

A double-handful of warheads escaped Shakov's missile-defense system, leaving his *Exterminator*'s armor pockmarked over both shoulders. Next to him, a newer *Excalibur* staggered forward onto one knee under the pounding. Then, still crouched, it raised its right arm and hammered back with its gauss rifle. The rail gun's nickel-ferrous slug blurred through the thin line of alder, and Shakov hoped it would make life miserable for one of Halfway's valiant—if obtuse—militia.

The *Excalibur* could stand off at range from the militia's position. He could not. Not as effectively, at any rate. Rocking the throttle lever forward, Shakov ran his *Exterminator* toward the treeline, speeding out from under the umbrella of incoming missiles. Checking his tactical screen with a practiced eye, he saw that most of his unit had already done the same. They had easily dodged the concentrated missile barrages, once more profiting from the inexperience of Halfway's small militia. Not that Victor's allied forces were rushing to show leniency in favor of ending prolonged fighting. The defeat at York was too fresh.

The bulk of Prince Victor's escort regiments had escaped York to rendezvous here. Though Halfway was their second choice, Shakov thought it was, in some ways, the better site for a base. A predominantly agricultural world, Halfway was defended by a single rump battalion with only limited armor support. The planet had also felt Katherine's spiteful hand early on. In the face of civil unrest, she had authorized martial law and restricted shipping, such that many export crops rotted in the warehouses and the world's largest timber concerns were nearly forced into bankruptcy. The public outcry had died down quickly, but resentment continued to simmer. Now, with liberation at hand, the general populace was vocal in support of Victor's opposition to his sister's rule.

In other ways, though, Halfway was the worse of the two. The planet had less in the way of military support infrastructure, and Katherine's minions had viciously purged the local militia of any potential Victor supporters. That strategic maneuver placed a fanatical force with no avenue of retreat in the allies' path of advance. The militia fought as if demon-possessed, despite nonexistent support by the locals and odds of five to one. Their combined fear and love for Katherine was, apparently, stronger than any thought of self-preservation.

Shakov shook his head over the unnecessary losses. Soldiers should know when they were defeated.

A new wave of missiles passed overhead, falling into the near-deserted rear of the Prince's Men. A few Battle-Mechs, such as the *Excalibur,* and one small formation of slower armored tanks were all that remained in the killing zone. The tactical icon for one of the armored vehicles, a venerable but well-respected Burke design, flashed the signal for incapacitation. Shakov figured it was probably a blown tread or maybe engine trouble. With logistical support at an all-time low, the loss of any 'Mech or armored vehicle was painfully felt. He wished the crew safe, but could do nothing more than try to take the pressure off them.

"Staggered advance," he ordered. "Jumpers first, and quiet those missile boats."

Shakov fired off his own jump jets even as he gave the order, his sixty-five-ton *Exterminator* lifting into the air on twin columns of plasma. He controlled the flight with his foot pedals, feathering one set of lifters or the other, rising over the alders in a graceful leap

Two militia companies of mixed BattleMechs and heavy armor held defensive positions close at hand. They were old machines mostly, with a light sprinkling of updated designs, though none newer than the militia commander's *Falconer.* Under normal circumstances, the mechanized core of Shakov's new command, the Loyal Subjects, would have matched them quite evenly. In this case, Precentor Irelon had also augmented his force with extra machines from the division's Broken Chains battalion and battle-suit infantry borrowed from what was left of Demi Hullinger's Strongmen.

All told, Shakov had six BattleMechs and a quartet of the rare, jump-capable Kanga hovertanks distracting the militia, drawing their fire as three battle-suit squads raced for the cover of timber stacks or to leap for purchase on the enemy 'Mechs themselves. Behind him, another half-dozen 'Mechs shouldered their way through the wind-break, creating passages for the two score armored vehicles following.

The *Falconer*'s particle projection cannon drew a steady beam across the ridged chest of Shakov's 'Mech even as it hung in the air. The manmade lightning gouged deep into protective armor but failed to find any previous wounds. A steady hand on the controls evened out any tremors, but Shakov noticed the silver blur that passed a few meters to the left of his ferroglass shield, between the *Exterminator*'s head and shoulder. He swallowed hard and counted himself fortunate, knowing how close the *Falconer*'s gauss rifle had come to smashing through his cockpit.

Tightening down on his jets, he dropped faster for the ground, absorbing the shock of landing with a slight crouch, then immediately stepped out into a lateral maneuver that made him a harder target. His targeting cross hairs fell over the *Falconer*'s hunched outline, but Shakov pulled away from the shot to target a nearby LRM carrier instead. His orders had been to silence the missile barrages, and a good commander followed his own orders.

Whenever possible, at least.

The crosshairs flashed from red to gold, and he reached out to the limit of his range with medium lasers. The scarlet beams stabbed into the right side of the armored vehicle, sloughing away armor and opening up large wounds into which a pair of Kanga hovercraft poured two streams of autocannon fire. At least one salvo of the uranium-tipped slugs managed to rupture an ammunition magazine. A gout of flame erupted from the LRM carrier's wounded side, the explosive force tearing away the entire right side of the vehicle and propelling it up into the air in a lazy, side-for-side spin. Follow-up detonations rocked the vehicle's corpse while still in the air, and what finally hit the ground again was totally unrecognizable as a war machine.

Heat pulsed up through the cockpit decking as the

Exterminator's fusion reactor spiked to meet the power demand of its lasers, but the hike in temperature was only a degree or so, and would dissipate quickly. The *Exterminator* was a very heat-efficient killer, an old, treasured design, incorporating improved technology that ComStar—in its former capacity as the caretakers of knowledge—had jealously guarded for centuries. Except for the most hard-fought battles like the one on York, Shakov usually fought with the chill touch of his coolant suit aching in his muscles. This shooting-gallery battle for Halfway had him shivering with cold.

Two other carriers had gone the way of the first. A fourth retreated under heavy fire from a pair of *Wyverns*. With this immediate relief, the bulk of Shakov's forces cleared the treeline and spread into the waterfront area. He toggled for an unscrambled channel, one he knew was monitored by the Halfway militia.

"Surrender!" he called out to his opposite number just as the *Falconer*'s gauss rifle caved in his BattleMech's left knee joint.

The raw kinetic force of the hypersonic mass shattered what was left of the armor, snapping the *Exterminator*'s leg out straight and wrenching it back. Warning lights for his 'Mech's upper leg actuator and hip joint flared red, and the machine spun lazily to the right.

Shakov fought gravity for control of the *Exterminator*, his muscles straining against the control sticks. His neurohelmet helped out, taking a reading on his own equilibrium and feeding it as a regenerative signal into the sixty-five-ton machine's massive gyroscope, but it wasn't quite enough. Arcing his body left in a last-ditch effort to salvage the situation, he heard the whining shriek of stressed, high-speed metal as his gyroscopic stabilizers complained. The *Exterminator* toppled over, slamming down onto its right side with a bone-jarring impact and the sickening crunch of crushed armor.

A shaken Rudolf Shakov stared up through his forward shield at an overcast sky. Exploring with his tongue, he felt the chips grinding between his molars. "I'm giving you this last chance, Major Dobson," he said through clenched teeth, though he was sure the offer would have sounded better with his 'Mech on its feet.

The *Falconer*'s PPC washed argent fire over the back side of Shakov's downed 'Mech. Energy bled through into the chest cavity, and a new failure light winked on to warn him that his anti-missile system had been destroyed.

As if that wasn't answer enough, a loud, determined voice yelled back over the comm system, "To blazes with you and your traitor-prince, *ComStar*," Dobson screamed. "This ends now!"

Shakov crabbed his *Exterminator* around, such that the *Falconer* could find no good angle on his back. Working his damaged leg under him, he managed to stand back up in place just as a trio of militia BattleMech made their last charge.

It was the best assault Dobson could manage. Most of the Halfway militia was presently tied up swatting away battle-suited infantry or being hounded by Com Guard assault vehicles at four-to-one. Into that chaos walked the BattleMechs of the Prince's Men, pressing back and putting down the defenders with bright laserfire, hard-pounding gauss rifles, and the furious storms of heavy autocannon.

Shakov watched as a ninety-ton *Highlander* decapitated one of the militia *Enforcer*s with a well-placed gauss slug. A lance of Lightning hovercraft made swift runs past a damaged *Wolfhound*, their pulse lasers spitting a flurry of emerald darts into the BattleMech's flank and finally severing one leg at mid-femur.

A pair of hunchbacked *Raijin*s stalked up on either side of Shakov's *Exterminator*, squatting on their backward-canted legs as they joined him in facing the abbreviated militia charge. Alternating their PPCs and their SRM systems with their pulse lasers, they kept up a blistering storm of destructive power that felled first a militia *Nightsky* and then the deadly *Hatchetman*.

Shakov kept his fingers tight on the *Exterminator*'s triggers, firing lasers and missiles as fast as they cycled. The scarlet energy scythed through armor, worrying the

Falconer's right side and exploiting earlier damage. The right-arm gauss rifle burst apart as ruined capacitors discharged through half-melted accelerator coils, dancing arcs of electricity up the arm and shoulder of the militia BattleMech.

Still, the *Falconer* rushed forward, slipping under the effective range of Shakov's long-range missile launcher. Not only did the 'Mech outgun Shakov, but with the *Exterminator's* ruined left leg, the other machine outperformed him. He kept his 'Mech on its feet under the furious energy barrage, returning what damage he could with his quartet of lasers. He tensed when it seemed clear that Major Dobson intended to charge directly into him, slamming his seventy-five tons of animated metal into the crippled *Exterminator*. The crashing blow would certainly finish him off.

Except that it never came. Several dozen meters short of Shakov's position, the *Falconer* shuddered in midstep. It staggered through two more awkward steps before one leg twisted beneath it. The diamond-cut tread finally lost purchase on the paved surface, and the 'Mech fell shoulder-first to the ground. Sparks danced off the abused metal, which in turn dug gravel out of the dark ferrocrete as the machine skidded along in an ungainly pile. For a few moments, Shakov thought he had somehow struck a mortal blow to the *Falconer's* gyroscopic stabilizers.

He was half-right.

A battle-suited infantryman clung to the *Falconer's* back, having burrowed into the lower gyro housing and then ridden out the worst of the fall. It was an Elemental suit, specifically designed for the Clans' genetically bred infantry troopers. Victor had brought a few bondsmen back with him from the Star League assault that destroyed Clan Smoke Jaguar, but only Tiaret had accompanied Shakov today. She was Victor's bodyguard and one of the most coldly efficient warriors he had ever met.

"I suppose I should thank you," he said over the division's common frequency, knowing she would never accept the praise, "but didn't that fall into the category of interfering with a personal match?"

His gentle humor wasn't meant to poke fun at the Clan concept of single combat so much as to acknowledge Tiaret's sacrifice—accepting a mark against her honor to help save an ally and friend. She quickly disabused him of that idea, however.

"I had prior claim," she informed him over her private channel with Shakov. Which was likely true, since the battle-suit infantry had rushed forward while he dealt with the missile carrier. "He foolishly chose to ignore me, and in firing on you, he released any claim to single combat. His skill could not match his bid." She let that piece of Clan wisdom hang unanswered for a moment. "He was correct about one thing," she added. "It ended now."

Shakov surveyed the battleground, running his gaze over the thinning ranks of the Prince's Men as he tallied the holes in his unit. Each loss haunted him. Every fallen man and woman meant one less warrior for the next battle. One less shield for Prince Victor. No one had forced them to leave ComStar to take Victor's side in this civil war, but that didn't mean Shakov accepted the sacrifices without misgiving.

And he didn't want to correct Tiaret here, even on a private channel, but they were both wrong, she and Dobson. It didn't end now at all. It couldn't end. Not for him, at least.

Not until he saw Victor Steiner-Davion safely through to New Avalon.

5

As he entered the large dining room of the brothel known as the Happy Harlot, Victor was struck by the intimate atmosphere the dark mahogany wainscoting and garish red wallpaper seemed to lend to the place. And made all the more so by the thick, maroon velvet curtains someone had drawn over the large windows that overlooked the rear courtyard and gardens.

The place was like something straight out of an old holovid. Twin crystal chandeliers hung over the long, cherrywood table, and gold leaf decorated the lintels and the arched supports of the vaulted ceiling. Five large hutches displayed china and other delicate items collected from the treasures hauled between worlds by servicemen and business travelers. A faded outline on the wall showed where a sixth hutch had been replaced by a large computer station and a portable holographic projector.

Colonel Patricia Vineman and four of the men waiting for him stood when Victor entered the room, their heavy chairs scraping against the hardwood floors buffed to a golden sheen. Even Precentor Raymond Irelon rose, despite the pneumatic cast that still imprisoned his right leg. Tiaret was already on her feet, dwarfing a nearby hutch as she stood guard at the room's set of wide doors. Morgan Kell, Grand Duke of the Arc Royal Defense Cordon, stepped over to give Victor a brief, one-armed embrace. The sleeve of his right arm was pinned up to the shoulder, the limb lost in the same blast that had taken the lives of Victor's mother and Morgan's wife.

Only Phelan Kell, Morgan's son and khan of the exiled Wolf Clan, remained seated. He leaned back in his chair, stretching out in his comfortable Clan leathers and looking far too at ease in the garish surroundings. His green eyes lit with amusement, he tossed Victor a casual wave. Phelan delighted in thumbing his nose at formality.

Victor shook his head in mock reproof. "My faith in the universe has been restored. Phelan, you never change."

Phelan rocked forward and came partway to his feet in one fluid motion. He extended one hand to give Victor's a warm clasp. "But you do," he said, then glanced around pointedly. "I can appreciate the unspoken military value of such establishments, Victor. But I never thought to find you in a bordello."

Victor nodded toward Jerrard Cranston, whose face was the picture of innocence. "Jerry's idea. After what happened on York, he and Tiaret thought we needed something unconventional to prevent an easy strike at our command center. Who would think to look for me and my top generals here?"

Phelan nodded. "You do realize, I hope, that after this war, the guests are going to find a large plaque in the front hallway that says 'Victor Davion slept here.'" He smiled wickedly. "You've turned this place into a landmark. What will Omi say?"

Victor's frown didn't last long against the poorly hidden grins of Morgan Kell and General Caradoc Trevana. "I'll worry about that later," he said, suddenly bothered by the room's faint hint of flowery perfume. Not that he truly worried about explaining himself to Omi, but it was painful being reminded of her after so long without a single word. He took a seat between Morgan and Doc Trevana. The eight men present occupied only the forward third of the long table, and Victor had expected ten.

"Christifori?" he asked, wanting to get down to business.

"Running late," Cranston said from where he was working at the computer station. "He wanted to see about his crew and command company."

"I sent Demi Shakov for him, Highness," Precentor Irelon said. "Rudolf will move things along."

Victor nodded curtly. "Then let us do the same. York was to be our advance base for the balance of the third wave. I want to know what went wrong, and how much it hurt us."

"What wasn't wrong?" Cranston asked, tapping a few keys on the work station. He stepped back as a basic, two-dimensional stellar map of the Lyran Alliance was projected into the air over the holographic display. "Incomplete intelligence, rushed implementation, and too heavy reliance on tactical advantages versus strategic planning. The same problems we've faced from the beginning."

True enough, Victor knew. From Mogyorod, a Lyran world at the far edge of the Inner Sphere, he had been in probably the worst position possible to organize a civil war. In fact, he'd been overwhelmed and almost killed in his first battle. Only the defection of the Prince's Men from ComStar and their timely arrival had saved Victor and the war effort. It had allowed him time to gather further support, rally troops and establish a base of power. Hard-pressed fights won on Newtown Square and Coventry marked those early waves of the civil war.

Then came Alarion, a district capital and important manufacturing world, home to the Lyran Alliance's main shipyards. It had fallen without a struggle—not a single shot fired. Victor's forces landed uncontested, finding only vacant military bases and rumors of a single infantry regiment in hiding. There was not a trace of the provincial militia or the Alarion Jaegers.

"As near as I can piece it together," Cranston said,

"someone ordered Alarion vacated, reserving the local forces for a proactive assault rather than the usual defensive stand. They pulled back, probably to Carlisle, where they rendezvoused with the Carlisle militia and the Eleventh Arcturan Guards. From there, they hit us on York.

"It really has the markings of a genius," he continued, stroking his blond beard. "Giving us Alarion forced us to pare down your escort, Victor. We have to garrison the world now. All for little gain."

"What about the shipyards?" Patricia Vineman asked. "Certainly those are worth something." She had joined Victor's force at York, replacing the Thirty-ninth Avalon Hussars left at Alarion. Just in time for Victor's first major defeat of the civil war.

Cranston grimaced. "The *Robert Kelswa* was the only WarShip close to completion, and it was removed prior to our arrival. There are two *Fox* corvettes and one *Mjolnir*-class battle cruiser still in space dock, but we don't have either the financial resources or the necessary time to complete them. At best, we might press a few DropShips into service."

He shook his head wearily. "We're denying the shipyards to Katherine. That's about all at this point."

"If that's the case," Doc Trevana put in, "why did you worry about York at all?" He rubbed the bridge of his large nose, his gaze riveted on the stellar map. "Why not simply bypass it altogether?"

Victor poured himself a glass of ice water from the sweating pitcher on the table and took a drink. "Like Jerry said, hasty implementation. We moved on York and Alarion at the same time, in case we might have to bypass Alarion. We'd been in contact with Patricia's Sixth Lancers as well as the Seventeenth Skye Rangers, both of which had moved in from Periphery guard. They were to secure York, giving us a fallback position."

Morgan Kell's weathered face creased into a deep frown. "And instead, you were stalked there and trapped." Though Morgan no longer commanded the legendary Kell Hounds, his mind was still razor sharp when it came to tearing apart military operations. "A bit of martial judo, turning your own plans against you. Any idea who you have to thank for that?"

"I don't think it's Nondi," Victor said, naming his aunt, Katherine's marshal of the Lyran armies and her regent on Tharkad. "She's old-school Steiner, and this was far too subtle. Jerry and I are putting money on Maria Esteban, commanding general of the Eleventh Arcturan Guards."

Cranston nodded. "She even had us chasing ghosts with false intel that placed her at Triesting, supposedly preparing to move on Loxley and then strike at Coventry."

Phelan smiled with dark humor. "See what happens when you open your military academies to an old enemy?"

"Esteban may be a graduate of the New Avalon Institute of Military Sciences," Cranston said, "but she's Lyran to the core and something of a dictator. She'll allow little dissention, and she'll keep coming after us."

Patricia Vineman's voice was tight with anger. "If the Skye Rangers had actually shown up, Esteban wouldn't be a problem anymore. We'd have hammered her force into scrap." She also poured herself a glass of water, then set it down without taking a drink.

"We're still trying to locate them," Cranston said. "They may have been delayed. They may be destroyed."

A knock at the door interrupted any further comment. Tiaret cracked the door open, blocking the view with her large, muscular frame. Apparently satisfied, she then swung the door back enough to show the ComStar acolyte waiting in the hall. He shifted nervously from one foot to the other, and gripped a noteputer in one hand. Precentor Irelon excused himself from the table and hobbled out on his crutch to deal with the matter. He would judge if the news was worth interrupting the meeting.

Silence followed Irelon's departure. A few of the others also poured themselves glasses of water and sat sipping quietly. Victor stared at the table, tracing the pattern of the dark wood grain with his thumb. The smooth, lacquered surface belied the rough textures trapped underneath. It reminded him of his motley collection of forces.

"So," he finally said, "we're left with the Sixth Crucis Lancers, the 244th Division, and the Outland Legion, which is currently hovering at around two battalions of disjointed units."

Despite the Legion's disparate nature, Victor couldn't help feeling a touch of pride for them. It had been formed piecemeal from soldiers who had fought with him in the Clan homeworlds, its members staggering in by ones and twos and the occasional lance when Victor had first issued his call to arms. They had come from the Combine and the League, from the Capellan Confederation and even one of the smaller Periphery realms, rallying to his cause even though they owed allegiance to rival nations.

"Morgan, did you release the Twenty-third Arcturan Guard from the ARDC?" Victor asked.

Morgan nodded. "They're en route. General Killson's aide, Colonel Hebl, accompanied me here. He'll liaison with your people until they arrive."

Patricia Vineman leaned forward. "The Twenty-third are good troops, but we need something with more teeth. Where are the Davion Guards?"

"Sidelined," Cranston said. "Katherine decimated the First RCT and stranded the Heavy Guards on Galax without transport. The Light Guards and the Third RCT are too far out of position to rendezvous. The others are up to their cockpits in hard fighting on four different worlds."

Victor brushed a hand over the table's surface. "I take what I can get, Patricia. I'd like to bring over my Revenants, but the Tenth Lyran is still stuck on Robinson."

She folded her arms across her chest. "Stuck?" she asked, obviously not buying it.

"All right, not stuck," Victor said coolly. "If I ordered them to seize transport and join me, they would, and James Sandoval couldn't do much about it. For now, they stay on Robinson until I see how Tancred manages. If necessary, the Revenants can back Tancred in ousting his father."

"You just might need that, no matter what Tancred

decides," Morgan said. "But don't forget your big problem, Victor. There's only five months until the next meeting of the Star League. You *have* to get this civil war back on track, or Katherine will bury you politically."

Doc Trevana nodded. "So far, First Lord Kurita has backed your position that this war is an internal matter, which leaves us staging a justified resistance to Katherine's rule. But your sister will be a front runner in the election of the new First Lord. If she brings the Star League Defense Force in on her side, or convinces Thomas Marik to support her side if he's elected, we're lost."

Victor nodded. Then, it wouldn't be about tactics *or* strategy. It would be all politics. If Katherine's forces began to fly the flag of the Star League, Victor *had* to lose. "So we need a big victory, or some kind of symbolic gesture. The question remains, what else can we try?"

"Donegal or Hesperus would both make excellent choices," Doc Trevana suggested, "though we'll need more support out of the ARDC. Both those worlds have good manufacturing capabilities, which we can use, and enough political weight to give you a boost going into the Star League conference." He paused, considered. "Skye would be another good choice, and it's right in line with your path into the Federated Suns . . ."

"But Robert Kelswa would use that to force a new bid for Skye independence," Victor finished, thinking of his cousin and the myriad troubles that branch of the family had brought on him in the past. "It's a problem I've been putting off, though I'm sure that sooner or later I'll have to deal with Skye." He looked around. "Other ideas?"

"Bolan," Patricia Vineman offered. "It's a district capital, and close."

Phelan looked up, eyes practically glowing. "Tharkad," he said simply.

Leave it to the Wolf, Victor thought. Go straight for the throat and damn the political considerations.

Raymond Irelon chose that moment to rejoin the meeting, slipping through the door under Tiaret's always-watchful gaze. He carried a noteputer over to Victor while Morgan Kell was explaining the potential consequences of an attack on Tharkad to his son. While listening to Morgan, Victor noticed that Irelon's face was ashen and that the look in his eyes was worried.

"Tharkad is an armed camp waiting for Victor to make a stab there," Morgan said. "If we attack under Victor's personal standard and lose, it's over."

"That's an unlikely if," Phelan said. "We won't lose."

Morgan shook his head. "You know better. Too many things can go wrong. It's the difference between a risk and a gamble, Phelan. If we risk something and fail, we can recover. If we gamble and fail, we're through."

"We can do it," Phelan insisted. "We'll mobilize the entire ARDC, plus my Wolves, the Kell Hounds, and whatever elite forces we can strip off the Jade Falcon border—"

"Impossible," Victor cut in. He stood up, holding the noteputer in one hand and bracing himself on the table with the other.

"The regiments in the ARDC aren't going anywhere," he said as he passed the noteputer to Morgan.

"We've just been trumped."

Pulling up at the far west end of the Torrence Spaceport, Rudolf Shakov parked the jeep just inside the open doors of the 'Mech hangar. Unfolding himself from the driver's seat, he noticed that the first drops of rain began to patter against the ferrocrete outside. Soon the thin coating of dust that lay over the 'crete, milled by the grinding steps of BattleMechs on the move, would turn into a sticky gray muck. The technicians and port laborers caught in the downpour would spend some time chipping the plaster-like mud out of their boot treads tonight. The roads would be running slick with grime and oils leached up from the surface. He made a mental note to give the rains at least an hour to wash the pavement clean before driving back to Atholl.

It was an hour he wouldn't have.

He dismounted from the jeep, clipping a small, black

ComStar personal comm unit to his belt. Threading his way past running technicians and stacks of crated ammunition, he headed toward the back of the hangar, where a dozen 'Mechs stood racked in their maintenance alcoves. From the thirty-ton *Battle Hawk* to the older but still-impressive *Banshee* that topped out at twelve meters and ninety-five tons, each of the machines was of Lyran manufacture. Each was also painted in the Steiner-blue and emerald trim of the Freedom March Militia. And each showed considerable battle damage.

Shakov had little difficulty finding his quarry, even though Archer Christifori still wore his utility jumpsuit. Except for the red stripe sewn down the side of each pants leg and a MechWarrior's service pin, his clothing was identical to the garb worn by many of the technicians. Shakov noticed that Christifori had already found a new rank device to go along with his promotion to leftenant-general. By the sound of things, however, his rank carried little weight with the local master sergeant.

"I *need* those parts, Sergeant. It's not a matter of stockpiling. Look at my machines." Christifori stabbed a finger at the combat-weary 'Mechs, the gesture that had first caught Shakov's attention. "Don't tell me I hauled twelve 'Mechs all the way here from Odessa just to be stonewalled. If I'd left them behind, they'd at least be serviceable. I take them outside now, and I'd be lucky if my MechWarriors even stayed dry."

"I understand that, sir." The sergeant hefted his note-puter in one hand. "But we're on a strict priority list until logistics reopens our supply lines back to Alarion."

Shakov slowed his approach, wanting to further observe how *General* Christifori handled the problem. The man's recent rise in rank was impressive—from major to colonel and now general, all inside four years. His list of achievements in that time was equally impressive, but it didn't reveal anything about *the man*. Even within ComStar, the Lyran officer corps was often the butt of any joke that had to do with cocktail-party commanders and social generals.

"I appreciate your position, Sergeant," Christifori said

evenly. He seemed to value and respect the enlisted man's duty. "But we're in a war zone, and my command company's 'Mechs couldn't fight their way through a pack of space scouts. Certainly that bumps us up a few notches on the list."

The master sergeant frowned. "I've heard no reports of Lyran activity." Like most soldiers in Victor's force, the man wore the uniform of the Federated Suns. Although mostly a public relations move to give Victor a stronger appearance of legitimacy, quite a few warriors had come to accept this as the natural order. The sergeant likely didn't realize he'd just insulted the senior officer.

Nor did Christifori use it to take the man's legs off at the knees. "Sergeant, *I* am a Lyran. And about as active as I can be, in Prince Victor's name. But I take your meaning. Now try to understand mine. I consider anything within fifty light years of Victor Steiner-Davion a war zone. I want my 'Mechs both ready *and* able, and I'm not leaving until we at least find a compromise."

Shakov stepped forward and smiled. "Even though you have orders to report to the Prince at once, General?"

Christifori glanced quickly over one shoulder. "It's also my duty to remain ready for battle. Preparation supercedes planning. The Prince will understand." Nothing in his voice suggested that he saw anything in Shakov that might help him. That was no surprise, considering Shakov was also dressed in utilities and a simple leather jacket. At a glance, he would easily look civilian.

"Well, let's not test that further than we have to," he said, holding out one hand for the sergeant's computer. "Maybe I can help."

He used the small function pad to scroll out of the Depleted Stores records and into Transfer Requisitions. He used a stylus to scribble his signature into the noteputer's memory, and added an authorization code that the supply master for the 244th Division would recognize. "Sergeant, this will allow you to draw anything the general needs from our supplies. Please see to it."

Thunder from the growing rainstorm echoed through

the hangar as the master sergeant nodded and quickly called together a team for their supply run. The dampness of the storm mixed with the dry gunpowder scent that always accompanied crated munitions. Shakov thought it a wonderful contradiction. Kind of like a Com Guard officer who would trade his Primus for an exiled prince.

"You're a demi-precentor?" Christifori asked, finally noticing the small, silver star emblem on Shakov's jacket collar. "You don't look ComStar."

"The 244th Division severed its ties to the Com Guard when we went to Prince Victor's aid on Newtown Square, so technically, I'm not. Officially, I suppose we're listed as deserters. Oh, and heretics." He extended his hand. "Demi Rudolf Shakov."

Christifori shook his hand and smiled warmly. "Archer Christifori. And we have something in common. I imagine my listing with the Lyran Armed Forces currently reads about the same. Scratch heretic, but insert any other vulgar insult, and you'll be close enough." He glanced at the retreating sergeant's back. "I'm not costing you any needed supplies, am I? We'll make do with whatever you can spare."

"From each according to his abilities, to each according to his needs," Shakov said.

Christifori's grin wilted. "Is that some wisdom of Jerome Blake? I thought ComStar got rid of their mysticism when Word of Blake decided to go their own way."

Shakov shook his head. "Not Blake, General. It's an old slogan of another famous Terran. But it fits the military mind well enough, don't you think?" He was glad to see Christifori's smile return, but any further banter was interrupted by the vibration and the low-frequency buzz of the comm unit attached to his belt.

He reached for the communicator. "Information waits for no man," he said. "Now, *that* is Jerome Blake." He disconnected the remote earpiece from its cradle and settled it into his ear with the thin wire extended out along his jaw. "Don't let the messenger ruin the message, General."

"Call me Archer," Christifori said, then waited quietly as Shakov thumbed the activation button on his belt-clipped base and answered the page.

The conversation was very one-sided, with Shakov nodding and humming quick affirmatives. He was aware of the concern in Archer Christifori's eyes, and thought it was probably a reflection of his own.

Then he disconnected the call, pulled the earpiece away from his face, and shoved it into a pocket. "Time to get you to Prince Victor, Archer," he said, taking Christifori's arm and steering him back toward the waiting jeep. "Apparently, wars wait for no man either.

"The Jade Falcons have just attacked across the border."

6

The Davion Palace on New Avalon had several military planning rooms, staffed with specialists who worked over the newest equipment. The Office of the First Prince—now that of the First Princess—had never been meant to serve that purpose, however. It was cozy and comfortable and seemed to Katrina more like a small den.

Wood paneling and built-in bookshelves covered the walls. A large desk of blond ash occupied one side of the room and an antique collection of a sofa and three chairs the other. The sitting area was arranged around a small fireplace, only recently added, which burned ceramic logs on a gas-fed flame. The sofa and one matching chair were upholstered in a pattern of ivory and gold leaves. An uncomfortable-looking ebony chair was tucked into a nook next to the hearth. The remaining chair—her chair—was dark leather wrapped around rich wood.

Katrina paid little attention to the men gathered together in the room—her most senior officers and aides. She sat facing the eye of a wall-mounted camera, posing in studied calm. Above the camera, a newly installed holovid screen displayed the head and shoulders of the man attending this meeting through a virtual interface that had cost Katrina—or more specifically, the Davion state—billions in contributions and ComStar maintenance agreements.

On the screen, Gavin Dow pulled his mouth into a thin line as he finished his courtesy update on the Jade Falcon attacks and waited for her response. The collar of his powder blue smock was trimmed in gold, a slight variation on the regular Com Guard uniform. The pure gold clasp that held his cape over his left breast proclaimed his rank as Precentor Martial, *pro tem*, of course. Dow was Precentor Tharkad, the man responsible for ComStar operations in the Lyran Alliance, but was also Victor's temporary replacement as head of ComStar's military arm.

"And the names again of the worlds under attack?" Katrina asked, reaching up to casually push some strands of golden hair away from her face.

The delay between her question and Dow's answer was measured in microseconds, and she couldn't help marveling at the powerful system she'd help develop. Hyperpulse generators provided instantaneous communication between worlds within fifty light years of each other. Normally, however, an HPG station received incoming transmissions, then had to swing its massive dish around to tight-beam the batched comms to the next world. The relay could take days to travel from one side of the Inner Sphere to the other, and that was with priority routing. By funding ComStar to build an extra station on a number of worlds between Tharkad and New Avalon, her two seats of power, she had formed a command circuit of stations that could line up for a real-time network.

ComStar's spur tapped into that system, joining their current seat of power on Tukayyid to the network. Katrina had thought that opportunistic when she'd first learned of it. Now, it was proving itself invaluable as ComStar—or Dow, at least—shared information about the recent attacks by Clan Jade Falcon into Lyran space.

"Blue Hole is lost," Dow confirmed. "The Falcons

have also struck Kikuyu, Kooken's Pleasure Pit, Ballynure, and Newtown Square. Only on Newtown Square were they thrown back." The recital came quick and certain. Dow didn't bother to check notes or ask an aide. Katrina had heard rumors that he possessed a near-perfect memory, and she believed it. He never forgot *anything*. Unless he wanted to.

"And our request for a coordinated strike into the Clan occupation zone?" She was careful not to glance sidelong at her officers, which would tell Dow he was being observed. "I'm told that from Tukayyid you could launch an assault that would clip the end off the Falcon invasion corridor. That would relieve pressure on the Lyran military." And allow her more freedom to continue opposing her brother's damnable revolts.

Dow's yellow-green eyes darkened, as if he'd drawn a mask over his face. Which, in a way, he probably had. "That will not be possible at this time," he said slowly, carefully. "You have to understand, there are two other Clans hovering over Tukayyid, waiting for the chance to strike at Terra and claim the title of ilClan. The Com Guard and SLDF must act in a manner that protects *all* of the Inner Sphere. Your Federated Suns as well as your Lyran Alliance."

An excuse Katrina and her advisors had anticipated and one not without merit. Since being displaced from Terra by the Word of Blake, the Com Guard had fallen into a very reactive posture. The undevoured portion of the Free Rasalhague Republic was little more than a Com Guard armed camp now, waiting for a Clan—any Clan—to strike forward. Clans Jade Falcon, Wolf, and Ghost Bear already occupied a large wedge of the Inner Sphere's coreward space. They could not be allowed to advance any deeper.

But predicting Gavin Dow's refusal on this matter was only one step toward Katrina's true goal—convincing him that ComStar's military should begin supporting her efforts to put down Victor's rebellion. Dow was a politician as well as a soldier. He knew Katrina's expectations and the political process of give and take.

Obviously foreseeing her next maneuver, he moved quickly to counter. "I have also had little success with our Primus and the First Circuit concerning your earlier request to place Com Guard divisions under local command. Primus Sharilar Mori, I'm afraid, takes too much direction from First Lord Kurita, and we know the First Lord will remain adamant about nonintervention."

Katrina narrowed her eyes, letting a hint of her displeasure show through. "There must be some room for negotiation, Gavin Dow. Your Sixty-sixth Division on Tharkad has openly declared that they will defend my Lyran capital from any outside aggressor. Neither you nor your Primus has censored Precentor Kesselring for that declaration."

"Dag Kesselring was the son of a Lyran noble before joining ComStar, and that buys him some leeway. Given his insight into Lyran matters, I have prevailed upon the Primus to allow him such discretion."

"That does not seem much," she said coldly.

"As you would have it, Highness. It is the best I can accomplish at this time." Gavin Dow nodded once, his silver hair gleaming under the bright lights. "I remain your faithful ally, Archon Steiner. You will come to realize that soon enough."

The screen went dark, and Katrina glanced at the two officers sitting at military attention on the sofa to see how they had taken Dow's final words. By dropping all reference to her as First Princess or as a Steiner-*Davion*, he drew a closer relationship with himself as Precentor Tharkad. A not-too-subtle method of confirming where priorities—for him, at least—lay.

One of the two officers was Simon Gallagher, field marshal of the Crucis March and the "Prince's Champion." He chewed on one arm of his square-lensed glasses and brushed the top of his balding head with the other, smoothing down what was left of his stringy gray hair. Gallagher had been born to the Lyran state, and he regarded Katrina first as Archon, then as Princess.

The other officer was Jackson Davion, her cousin and Marshal of the Armies for the Federated Suns. In a separate reality, he might have been the man Hanse Davion might have wished as his son and heir. Tall and strong, with the chiseled features and reddish-blonde hair of the Davion men, he was an officer's officer. Fortunately, he was also a true patriot, and accepted Katrina as the Federated Suns' legal ruler. His fealty, once sworn, would never be compromised. Still, his blue eyes clouded with anger at Gavin Dow's snub of his nation and Katrina's Davion heritage.

"I don't trust him," Gallagher said. "He's out for his own ends, Highness. You can be certain about that. The Precentor Martial of ComStar cannot command his own troops into battle? Even a small force, hitting the Falcons from behind, would undercut their strikes into Lyran space."

Katrina leaned back against her high-backed chair. She drew her feet closer and smoothed the emerald-colored skirt over her legs. The mellow scent of the chair's smooth leather was comforting, a reminder of the days this office had belonged to her father and she had visited it as a child. She remembered pretending to run the magnificent ship of state that was the Federated Commonwealth. Now, that childhood fantasy was finally a reality, though she'd had to split the two realms apart to make it so. A threat to either realm was a threat to her rule.

"What if we found another ally against the Falcons?" she asked innocently, waiting to see if either officer took the idea to the next level. In the corner seat, Richard Dehaver, her chief of intelligence, straightened perceptibly.

Jackson Davion frowned. "The Draconis Combine? They would have to skirt both the Ghost Bears and Clan Wolf to strike at the Falcon OZ. Help from them is not too likely, especially with Duke Sandoval's unsanctioned attacks against them last year. And I'd say their recent news blackout suggest that they have other concerns."

"Such as?" Dehaver asked, joining the conversation. "Do you think they're preparing to attack us in retaliation?"

"Could be." Jackson tugged his sleeves straight. "When

the Dragon goes silent, something is going on. Last time, it had to do with the purges of their Internal Security Force. And now . . ." He paused in thought. "JumpShip traffic has crawled almost to a standstill. Communication across the border has stopped, and I mean completely. They're keeping something from us. Count on it."

"We'll find out what it is," Katrina promised. She couldn't keep from glancing over at the empty chair, where her advisor from Lyran intelligence should have been seated. "In the meantime, I want other options. Dow said the Falcons were thrown back from Newtown Square. That's Adam's world. We'll send him to coordinate with Marshal Bryan."

"And the ARDC?" Dehaver asked tonelessly.

Thinking of Morgan Kell and his Arc Royal Defense Cordon, Katrina's hands clenched angrily. She forced them to relax, wanting to act in cold confidence rather than anger. "Morgan wanted authority over a portion of the border, so let him deal with it."

Katrina would profit no matter who won that battle. In a perfect universe, the Falcons would confront the Kell Hounds and Phelan's exiled Wolves, and they would finish each other off.

"That is all for now, gentlemen." She nodded a dismissal to her two senior officers, who stood up instantly as if the semblance of sociability had been overly taxing. Katrina was in her element when it came to informal meetings, and if that gave her more power over men such as Jackson Davion and Simon Gallagher, so much the better.

Davion paused to wait for Gallagher to leave. "If the Combine military is gearing up to strike at us, Highness, we are in poor shape to meet them."

Katrina met his gaze evenly, held it. She nodded once. "Take appropriate steps as you need to, Jackson. You have my complete trust."

He stiffened, bowed at the waist, and withdrew from the office.

"Make certain Gallagher is kept abreast of his actions," she told Dehaver. "If I need to get around Jackson Davion for any reason, my 'champion' is still the best way."

"Of course, Highness." Dehaver stood, walked over to the empty chair, and sat down comfortably against the ivory and gold upholstery. If not for the man's soulless eyes, his red hair and boyish freckles might have made him look completely harmless. "You know he's right. The Draconis March is not ready for an assault."

Of course Katrina knew that. Among all the flare-ups and rebellions, the Draconis March held by Duke James Sandoval was in the worst shape. All because Tancred Sandoval, the duke's son, was Victor's supporter and had turned the entire March upside down in opposing his father. The duke had to divide his time and his forces between a lifelong hatred for the Draconis Combine, careful and limited support for Katrina, and the new threat raised by his own flesh and blood. "You still caution against the use of force to remove Tancred Sandoval, I assume?"

"Despite the current *political* animosity between father and son, the Sandoval family remains a cornerstone of the Federated Suns. The duke's profile suggests that he would turn on you in an instant if he believed you had directly harmed his family or his people. As it is, while dealing with Tancred, he will still deny Victor any easy avenue through the Draconis March."

Gathering up her long hair in both hands, Katrina tied it into a makeshift knot that lifted it off her shoulders. Dehaver was one of the few men *not* affected by her beauty or presence. With him, she could be comfortable.

"Perhaps the Clan assaults will distract my brother as well. He never could pass up a chance to go at them."

Dehaver let the comment hang unanswered for a moment. Then, "Your suggestion about finding another cat's paw who might distract the Falcons, Highness. Did you have anyone in mind?"

Katrina collected herself, guarding against any nervous gesture or flash of emotion. "What do you think, Richard?"

He shrugged, rubbed his hands together. "Looking at

the situation objectively, the most obvious threat to the Jade Falcons is actually Clan Wolf."

"So it would seem," Katrina agreed cautiously, waiting for more. She stroked the smooth, carved arm of her chair with one hand, feigning a casual attitude she did not feel. She wasn't about to mention her unofficial relationship with Vladimir Ward, Khan of the "other" Wolf Clan.

The temptation was there, certainly. If Vlad struck at the Falcon rear while she carried out a counterstrike from Lyran space, they could divide the Falcon occupation zone and rid the Inner Sphere of yet another invader. And if not for her troublesome brother, who seemed to go on living despite her best efforts, Katrina might have personally invested the time and effort to arrange such a venture.

It always seemed to come down to that. *If not for Victor* . . . After a year of his resistance, she was beginning to regret not turning the assassin against him rather than his precious Omi. The attack on Omi—intended to crush Victor's spirit, to punish him for opposing her rise to First Lord of the Star League—had failed on Mogyorod. Worse, it had cost her twenty-five million kroner, half the blood price paid in advance, with nothing to show for it.

Feeling the onslaught of a dark mood, she tightened her mask and waved a dismissal at Dehaver. What she wanted now was to enjoy a glass of wine and her warm fire while planning for the Star League conference to take place in November. This time, nothing could stop her rise to First Lord.

Always dream large, her father had once told her. That had been before the War of 3039, likely while he was still planning his triumph over the Draconis Combine. He had failed in that, and Katrina never forgot. Dreaming wasn't enough. Planning. Manipulation. Action! She fully intended to succeed where her father left off, attaining the station of which he had only dreamed. First Lord of the Star League.

And once she had it, she would never let it go.

"There is one other thing," Dehaver said, interrupting her reverie. He was on his feet now. "A man named Reg Starling."

Katrina felt her composure slip for the briefest of milli-seconds, but she knew that Dehaver had seen the brief lapse. He'd been watching for it, springing the words on her like a trap. Reg Starling was a name she knew well enough. It was the adopted identity of Sven Newmark, a man who had previously helped her with some "busi-ness" dealings.

"Reg Starling is dead," she said. Suicide, according to the official report, which she studied closely when the Lyran Intelligence Corps finally brought it to her.

"The fact that you even know that, Highness, attaches greater importance to him than I would have thought. May I recommend that you never acknowledge his name outside this room?"

She cocked her head to one side, at once curious and cautious. "Why would I?"

"When someone brings up his latest series of paintings, it would be best to dismiss it as a novelty *far* beneath your station."

"New series?" Katrina hated Dehaver's way of side-stepping into a conversation. "Speak plainly, Richard."

"It's called the 'Bloody Princess' series, and I'm afraid you are the subject of his study in what I believe he calls 'politics by the knife.' Each original is signed, dated, and verified *after* the date of his *supposed* suicide. We're looking into this now, but my question to you is, how important is it that this man *remain* dead?"

Katrina caught the emphasis Dehaver placed on the dates and the now-questionable fact of Starling's death. "Why didn't Matthew bring this to me?" she asked, nod-ding at the chair Dehaver had just vacated, the one her LIC advisor would have occupied during the earlier meeting.

"I intercepted him and reassigned Matthew to head up an immediate investigation," Dehaver said. "I don't think he wanted to be the one to tell you, regardless. So, unless you object, I will coordinate LIC efforts with the local ministry of intelligence."

A second level of buffering between Katrina and the investigation. But also a step up the ladder of power for Richard Dehaver. Katrina did not miss *that* implication. Not in the slightest.

"You are quickly becoming an indispensable advisor, Richard. Or an incredibly dangerous liability." She let that sit with him a moment. "Handle this as you see fit," she ordered. Then she nodded a final dismissal, which he was smart enough to take.

"As you say, it is beneath my notice."

7

Phoenix Studios
Bremmerton, Upano
Coventry Province, Lyran Alliance
24 May 3064

The burned-out office building had been an eyesore to the city of Bremmerton on Upano for nearly three years now. Squat and wide, the two-story, red brick building was boarded up and dark on the lower level, with a padlocked chain-link fence securing the front entrance. Scorch marks licked up the brick facing and around the partially caved-in roof. The second-floor windows, left open to the elements, stared down on the street with blackened eyes, and the scent of ash and charcoal from the fire still wafted from them after a heavy rain.

Keeping the building untouched and preferably ignored by the city had been no easy feat, even though the place stood on Bremmerton's less-than-fashionable east side. It had required promises of refurbishment and gratuities disguised as political contributions and charity donations. It had required constant recycling of work permits and new plans for the building, including a nine-month diversion as all avenues to declare the building a historic landmark were exhausted.

It had turned out to be one of Francesca Jenkins' more difficult missions.

Now, it was time to close up shop, though not by their choice. Francesca checked the padlock for signs of tampering and then signaled Curaitis before moving inside. He caught up with her in the debris-choked stairwell, where separately they checked each telltale as they proceeded up the stairs, careful to pass over the steps that they had either rigged with pressure trips or undercut to give way under weight. Only one other person knew all the traps, and if he had slipped up on *this,* it was all over.

By the time they reached the second floor, both former agents of the Intelligence Secretariat were convinced that no one had beat them here. Francesca nodded in satisfaction at Curaitis, who stared straight through her, his ice-chip eyes unreadable. She didn't mind. She was used to it.

The studio apartment was hidden at the end of a short hall closed off by two well-sealed doors. There were no windows to betray movement. No way for someone outside to glimpse any light.

Stepping through the second door was like entering another reality. Charred plaster and collapsed beams gave way to hardwood floors and paneled walls, with new drywall tacked up on the ceiling. The great-room design had plenty of space for an open kitchen, a living area, and sleeping quarters separated off by a shoji-panel screen. Fully half the room, though, was taken up by Phoenix Studios, the name Francesca had privately given Reg Starling's new home. A stack of blank canvases leaned against one wall, and three easels draped with bilious green cloths stood in the middle of the area. Paint was spattered over the floor, some of the dried splotches so thick someone could have tripped on them.

The great Valerius still slept, though it was almost noon and the lights had come on with a preset timer. The paneled screen was arranged so that it threw a shadow over his bed, a problem Curaitis solved by knocking the screen over so that it hit the floor with a loud wooden slap. The mountain on the bed jumped and rumbled like a plaid island caught in an earthquake. A thick arm swept away half the covers, and Valerie Symons' heavy face stared up at them.

"You don't even want to know how ticked I am," Francesca spat at him

Like most large men, Symons possessed a great deal of untapped strength. It was the only way he could leverage his bulk out of bed so quickly, throwing the covers aside and adjusting his pin-striped pajamas. Rolls of fat tumbled and fought inside the flannel, making Francesca think of a poorly dressed substitute for the gelatin-man in the popular holovid commercials.

"A fair good morning to you as well, dear lady," Symons growled sleepily, just now waking to the fact that he was standing. He grabbed a towel off the headboard, scrubbed his face with it. "Ah, and you have brought the living ice sculpture with you this time. How marvelous."

Francesca wasn't in the mood for sarcastic banter. She set her satchel on the floor, and nodded to Curaitis. "Cut it, *Valerius,* and get dressed. You're checking out today."

"Out?" He stared from Francesca to Curaitis. "But the series isn't complete. Three more 'originals,' you said. We have a deal."

"That deal was contingent on your cooperation with basic security precautions designed for your safety," Curaitis said flatly. "Entering and leaving the building was to be accomplished only at night. No one was to know your location. And under *no circumstances* were you to leave even a hint that Reg Starling was on Upano."

Symons winced as if struck. "All right, so I sold a few sketches of earlier paintings in the 'Bloody Princess' series. But I could have come by those through my contacts back on New Exford." He attempted to sound indignant. "And for what you're paying me for Starling masterpieces, I see no reason why I shouldn't be allowed to seek extra income. I watch the vids. Those paintings are becoming his hottest properties ever."

Francesca gestured for Curaitis to start the clean-up. He dug a canister out of his satchel, went to the bathroom, and then struck the top from the aerosol. He tossed the hissing can into the facilities and shut the door on it.

"First of all," she told Symons, "the few times when Reg created sketches, he *never* allowed them to fall into the hands of collectors. He never let anyone even see them. He burned them as soon as possible. Second, it doesn't matter if you *could* have gotten them legally. You were already in legal trouble on New Exford for forging Reg's work. We can't have your name tied to his, or the whole thing falls apart." She bent down and dug an incendiary device from her satchel, waved it under Symons' nose. "Now, get dressed."

"All right," he said. "But would you mind leaving the room, please?"

"Pull your clothes on over the pajamas," she told him. "We have work to do." Francesca began gathering the canvases together on the floor, kicking them into a loose pile.

The aerosol Curaitis had loosed in the bathroom was already leaking fumes into the apartment. From the acrid scent, it was some kind of petroleum-based solvent. Her nose stinging, Francesca began to breathe through her mouth.

"What is that stuff?" Symons asked, one arm stuck into a shirt.

"It will adhere to and dissolve any oils or other trace evidence you've left around the apartment," Curaitis said. He moved into the kitchen, leaving open the doors to the oven, the cooler, and the cupboards. He pulled out another timed incendiary, set it, and clipped it to the cooler door.

"It is also highly flammable," he added, and Symons began to dress faster.

Francesca had pulled the cloths off every easel, studying the paintings with her amateur eye. The unfinished works certainly looked like Reg's style, but then Valerius had also fooled the art experts on New Exford, so what did she expect? The man was a pig and completely self-serving, but he had talent. No denying that.

"Ah, Reg," she whispered to the painting. "Would you approve of our plan?"

She liked to believe that he would have. Francesca had spent a great deal of time becoming Reg's friend, and was one of a handful of people in the entire Inner Sphere who knew of the neo-gothic painter's former life as Sven Newmark.

As an aide to the late Ryan Steiner, Newmark had helped carry out the assassination of Melissa Steiner-Davion. Francesca doubted she would have liked Newmark, but she had come to like the man he became in fleeing his past. As Reg Starling, he had agitated for full disclosure of events surrounding the Clan war, including Melissa's death. He had also kept the evidence needed to tie Katherine to the assassination plot.

Unfortunately, Katherine's agents got to Reg Starling, helping him commit suicide before he had fully confided in Francesca. Yet, Reg had a long arm and an inimical disposition even from the grave. He'd made sure that the evidence ended up in Francesca's hands—now in Victor's safekeeping—evidence that she and Curaitis were presently working to authenticate. The plan was simple. Convince Katherine that Starling-Newmark was still alive, and validate the evidence through her attempts to cover it up.

Francesca used a touch-release on her solvent, dousing each painting with a good measure.

"That is six months of work you are destroying," Symons yelled. "We could take them with us."

"No," Francesca said. "We can't be seen carrying unfinished Starling works. And if Reg were fleeing, he'd make certain to destroy them beyond recognition."

She struck the top off her aerosol, tossed the spitting canister into the middle of the studio, and placed a magnesium-laced thermite on one of the easels. Curaitis set off another aerosol in the kitchen area, tossed a last incendiary onto Symons' bed, and then hustled the fat man out the door.

Francesca opened another of the solvents and left it

spraying just outside the hall door. Then they hurried not for the stairs but a freight elevator at the back of the building. Francesca pried out the maintenance panel and crossed a pair of wires.

"There was a working elevator in this building the entire time?" Symons complained as the cabin wheezed and labored downward. "You could have told me that."

"We didn't want to make it too easy for you to come and go," Curaitis said, pulling on a transparent glove. "You might have gotten careless." There was no reply to that. He took a spray bottle and doused his fingers with an oily mist, then smeared some dirt from the floor into the mix.

"The button?" he asked Francesca.

She shook her head. "Not quite that careless. The back of the maintenance panel."

Curaitis dusted his gloved hand against his opposite sleeve, then grabbed the maintenance panel firmly by the edge, overlapping both front and back with his fingers. Then he released it and used his cuff to wipe the front of the panel, leaving the false prints behind. He shucked the glove back into his satchel.

"You think anyone is going to find that?" Symons scoffed.

Curaitis turned a cold glance on him. "I would," he said simply.

Francesca checked the boarded-up back entrance through a crack in the boards, then unlocked it, and swung the façade out on oiled hinges. "Looks clear," she said. "I think we made it in time."

"Ah . . . look . . ." Valerie Symons made apologetic noises deep in his throat. "Perhaps I have not adequately expressed my appreciation for your efforts to keep me out of prison. Or for the, ah, employment."

Francesca and Curaitis exchanged glances. Curaitis shrugged, a rare show of opinion from him.

"That's quite all right, Valerius." Francesca patted the man's beefy arm. "And we don't mind the newest work you've handed us, either."

The man frowned. He truly did not understand the

stakes the two agents were playing for. "And what would that be?" he asked.

They led him out into the alley and toward their waiting vehicle. Francesca surveyed the upper windows and rooftops while trusting Curaitis to check the ground. They put Symons in the car first, then Curaitis took the driver's seat while she slid in next to the big man.

"Keeping you alive," she said, pulling the door shut behind her.

8

Atholl, Halfway
Bolan Province
Lyran Alliance
4 June 3064

Painted in lavender and gold, with a brocade wallpaper of vines and flowers as faux wainscoting, the Happy Harlot's master suite was no less garish than the rest of the place. A darkened fireplace went unused in favor of central heating, and the oppressive sent of orchids had permanently leeched into the walls, plush carpeting, and duvet. The suite was not one of the "working rooms," or Victor wouldn't have slept in it no matter what security the place provided.

Waking in a real bed—especially a hand-carved masterpiece from Timbuktu—was an odd experience. For the last seventeen months, his sleeping quarters had been limited almost exclusively to DropShip staterooms, military field cots, a hospital bed, or the chair behind whatever desk in various borrowed offices from world to world. His last semi-comfortable sleep had been on Coventry, during two weeks as a guest of Duke Bradford while planning for the assault-that-never-happened against Alarion. Before that, it was Mogyorod, where he woke up every morning next to Omi Kurita.

His dreams of Mogyorod melted away with the morning light, leaving him with just memories of that far-off time. Eventually, he'd had to send Omi away, for her own safety. But the longing to take their relationship to the next level, to declare it openly, was always present.

Victor tossed back the covers and sat up on the edge of the large bed, his feet not quite reaching the floor. He ruffled his sandy blond hair, feeling suddenly farm-fresh in this pseudo-sophisticated room, then got up and padded into the adjoining bath for his morning ablutions. Half an hour later, he put on the uniform he'd worn the previous evening, smoothing out the worst of the wrinkles with the back of his hand.

A lifetime of pictures hung on the walls. The madam's lifetime. Victor tried hard not to look too closely in case he should recognize someone. A sitting area off the bedroom had a vidstation on one table. He sat down in a surprisingly comfortable straight-backed wooden chair and spent time catching up on the personal messages that always collected during his travels between worlds.

Yvonne, his youngest sister, had recorded one concerning her intention to travel to Tancred Sandoval's side. Tancred, in a longer vid, reported his successes and failures in the Draconis March and said he would attend the Star League conference. He then spent an equal amount of time on how much he looked forward to seeing Yvonne again. Victor wished them both well.

There was a voice-only from Martial Gavin Dow, several of them in fact, all suggesting again that Victor refuse the allegiance of the renegade 244th Division. Victor had to admit he would be due some political hell when and if he was ever able to resume his old post as Precentor Martial. There was also a message from Kai Allard-Liao saying that he would not be allowed to attend the Star League conference in November. Not for the last time, Victor cursed Sun-Tzu Liao. Then followed a lengthy queue from various commanders, nobles, and intelligence agents about their battles or the fight for a particular world.

But nothing from Omi.

A soft rap at the door distracted Victor from the long list of battle reports. "Come," he called out, pausing the latest video playback.

The door cracked open, and a polished boot stuck itself into the slot. Kicking the heavy door the rest of the way into the room, Lieutenant-Colonel Daniel Allard entered with his hands full of Victor's breakfast tray. Dan, who had his father's white hair and inquisitive blue eyes, had also taken over as commander of the legendary Kell Hounds on Morgan Kell's retirement. The front panels of his double-breasted uniform jacket came together to form the unit's trademark red-and-black hound's head, an emblem known and respected throughout the Inner Sphere.

Watching him deliver breakfast, Victor could do little more than stare dumbly.

"Bah, you're up." Dan set the tray on a clear spot in front of Victor with a clatter of silver and china. "I wanted my plaque to say that I served you breakfast in bed here."

Victor held up his hands in surrender. "Don't start. I think Jerry and Tiaret are conspiring to torment me." He looked over the tray. Eggs, quillar on toast, enough sausage to feed three men, and juice. It smelled hot and wonderful. "Who drafted you into the kitchen crew?"

"Actually, I intercepted Tiaret, who was making this morning's delivery, ambushed her with superior position, and took control of the situation as I saw it."

"Spoken like a New Avalon Academy graduate," Victor noted, shaking his friend's hand and nodding him into another chair. "What was your superior position?"

"I'm outbound in an hour and wanted to say goodbye. With a hard burn, I can catch the same JumpShip that Morgan and Phelan are taking."

Victor nodded in regret. "Sorry to make you come all this way for nothing. Especially with what's going on back in the ARDC. Your people are still on top of things?"

"Akira and Scott can handle anything in my absence. Phelan's Wolves respect them, so they can coordinate until your man makes it through." Allard leaned forward, his elbows on his knees and his hands clasped together. "You made the right call, Victor."

"I hope so. It wasn't easy." Victor sampled his juice. "I've been fighting the Clans for most of my professional and political life, Dan. They wave a red flag, and I'm usually ready to jump at it. To turn my back on them now feels like courting danger."

Despite that, Victor knew that his own people had to come first, especially now that he had set foot on the path of civil war. He knew it, but that didn't mean he had to like it.

Allard helped himself to a piece of sausage, shaking it at Victor like an instructor's baton. "If you went chasing them now, you'd be playing right into your sister's hands and you know it. The Falcons want a fight, and we'll give them one. The ARDC will hold. And I think you can rely on this Archer Christifori. He seems a capable man."

"He is. And we're damned lucky to have him."

"It's not luck, Victor." Allard smiled and finished chewing his sausage. "You surround yourself with competent people, you get competent results." He puffed his chest out and buffed his nails against the front of his jacket. "Now you only have to worry about the Star League conference, the brewing trouble in the Isle of Skye, and winning this civil war."

"Thanks. If you're trying to make me feel better," Victor said, pausing for dramatic effect, "it's working." He smiled. With the people he had on his side, he could almost think about the Jade Falcons launching several heavy assaults into Lyran space and not worry. Almost. His smile faltered.

Allard slapped the air. "Damn, Victor. Let it go. You've done your part to turn back Armageddon. Let Katherine worry about the Clans for a change, and let her be in for the shock of a lifetime when she wakes up to what you've done while her back was turned." He looked askance at his friend. "What?"

Victor had paused with a link of sausage held halfway to his mouth, his brain spinning into overdrive. There was an almost-audible snap as a piece of the puzzle he'd been wrestling with fell into place. He'd been so preoccupied with the Falcons and with trying to find that perfect target to get his momentum rolling forward again that he hadn't even once considered the idea of a feint.

"You, my friend, are a military genius," he announced.

"And that's what I've been saying," Allard said.

Victor only smiled, bit into the sausage's spicy meat, and savored his budding plans.

9

The bridge of the DropShip *Arcturus Pride* shook under new weapons fire, and Colonel Linda McDonald grabbed quickly for the edge of a nearby workstation while keeping her feet planted wide on the deck for stability. Recycled air wheezed from a vent behind her like a cold breath against her neck. Dressed only in a MechWarrior's boots, shorts, and sleeveless coolant vest over a halter top in preparation for combat drop, she felt gooseflesh pucker the skin of her arms and legs. Her cheeks felt numb with cold, and she didn't know what had become of her usual buoyant confidence. A ground officer who'd been on garrison duty too long, she felt totally out of her element in the space battle taking place.

Not that anyone noticed. The crew of the *Leopard*-class ship had more than enough to occupy them while running the gauntlet of enemy aerospace fighters to make planetfall on Halfway. Navigation divided its time between computer-projected paths and the real-time battle displayed in the holographic tank. Weapons directed the *Arcturus Pride*'s various fire bays. Directing them all,

Captain Thomas Mickelson shouted terse orders as he coordinated the inbound run of the Eleventh Arcturan Guard's twelve DropShips with the actions of their aerospace brigade. If he spared any time for Linda Mc-Donald, it came in flashes of annoyance that she was still on *his* bridge.

A pair of damage-control petty officers worked at the site of an earlier electrical fire, checking the dead circuits and rerouting power around that workstation. The acrid scent of burnt insulation stung her nose and made her eyes water. Blinking them clear, she stared at the holographic tank. It showed that another pair of fightercraft belonging to the Sixth Crucis Lancers had broken through the aerospace umbrella, rolling in to streak up the *Leopard*'s side, lasers stabbing through armor, venting outboard spaces to hard vacuum. The *Arcturus Pride* shuddered and rolled as the explosive venting of ship atmosphere shoved the vessel around.

"Auxiliary maintenance locker six-tach-one-one has lost integrity," the damage control officer announced over his direct circuit to the bridge. "We're sounding all of deck six for atmospheric leaks." The DCO always sounded so calm, but McDonald supposed that was logical, protected as he was in the center of the DropShip.

Another quake shook the DropShip as a trio of Lancer fighters knifed up over the top, drilling their weapons home and escaping return fire. McDonald had only now identified the earlier attackers as *Stingrays*. Enemy fighters continued to slice through her aerospace picket as if it didn't exist, making high-speed passes she rarely saw until they were right on top of her.

She frowned angrily. If only she had a WarShip, the Lancers wouldn't be feeling so superior. But she didn't. Only one of the *Fox*-class corvettes had accompanied them forward from York, and Maria Esteban had it.

Dividing the assault force into two drives, Esteban had kept the LAS *Robert Kelswa* as her flagship. McDonald had command over the nadir point, while Esteban had jumped in at the zenith point far above the system's elliptic plane. With her were the Alliance Jaegers and a mixed RCT of provincial militia picked up on Carlisle, Alarion, and another half-dozen worlds stretching back to Timbuktu. When they detected no sign of Victor Davion's JumpShips at either point, they assumed them to be hiding further in-system and had commenced their assault on Halfway.

Three days later and still unopposed, their DropShips swung around, pointing their fusion drives inward as they began the long deceleration burn that would finally park them around Halfway and allow for controlled descents. Only today, with the planet growing large on the monitors, had the Sixth Crucis Lancers aerospace brigade finally risen up to meet them. The veteran Lancers controlled the space around Halfway, and unlike her own unit, had apparently kept themselves trained in brigade-strength zero-G combat. Ignoring Esteban and the necessity of tangling with her WarShip, they concentrated hard on the Eleventh Guard. Losses mounted, and there was nothing McDonald could do.

Still, she refused to leave the bridge. Unless the ship reached Halfway's atmosphere and her 'Mechs began combat drop, this was where the battle would be fought. And where it might be lost. She refused to die buttoned up and helpless in the dark of her cockpit, never seeing the final hammerblow.

McDonald preferred to meet her fears head-on, the same attitude that had prompted her to declare for the Archon rather than sit out the civil war in garrison on remote Timbuktu. Those same fires of loyalty burned at the core of the entire Eleventh Arcturan Guard and would eventually consume the traitor-prince Victor.

As if her thoughts had provoked the Lancers' wrath, the deck of the *Leopard* suddenly bucked and then dropped out from under her feet. Her stomach lurched in that instant of free-fall, then the trembling deck slammed back up into her boots as the tortured shriek of tearing metal reverberated through the ship. She could smell the fresh ozone of damaged circuitry, could sense its acrid taste at the back of her throat.

The navigator had a bloody gash over one eye from

hitting his head on the console, and one of the damage-control petty officers lay motionless on the deck, the left side of his face bloodied and bruised while his companion checked for vitals.

"That was the port-forward missile bay," the DCO called over his announcing circuit. "One of the munitions lockers blew out. We've lost atmosphere forward of bulkhead twenty, levels three and four."

"Colonel McDonald," Mickelson said, "I will now request and require you to abandon my bridge for the 'Mech bay."

Slowly, cautiously, McDonald relaxed her death grip on the workstation, and color returned to her bloodless fingers. "How long until insertion?" she asked, talking around her heart, which was still lodged in her throat.

"High-level drop will be possible in ninety minutes, or closer to two hours if we run you down to the surface. We'll need to bleed away a lot more of our forward velocity."

"I can wait," McDonald said.

"You can if you want to try holding your breath through two decks of hard vacuum," Mickelson said, remaining just this side of respectful. "We just lost the main trunk. If the *Pride* takes another penetrating hit amidships, there will be no safe route to get you into that tin monster of yours."

That would be worse than being trapped in the 'Mech bay while a space battle raged. McDonald was a Mech-Warrior as well as a commander. No way would she be left behind while her command lance drop onto the surface of Halfway.

She released her hold on the console, pausing at the captain's station only long enough to trade the traditional handshake and salute. "Get us down there, Tom," she said. Mickelson barely nodded, his attention glued to the battle at hand.

Moving unsteadily across the bridge, she now had the task of reaching the lower 'Mech bay without getting bounced too hard off a bulkhead. Traversing that short stretch between the two nexuses of power on any

DropShip, she felt truly vulnerable for the first time. The feeling continued right up to the point when she scaled the gantry ladder, tossed a casual salute to her command lance, and then finally climbed into the cockpit of the *King Crab* and dogged it behind her.

Unlike most BattleMechs, the *King Crab* had room to spare inside its flat, wide-bodied design. Enough space for two cockpits, one for the controlling MechWarrior and a second traditionally reserved for a regimental commander. That allowed the superior officer a hands-free position from which to command the battle. Until this moment, Linda McDonald could never have imagined riding into battle as an *observer*. She always fought her own machine right alongside her warriors.

Settling into her seat, she pulled the bulky neurohelmet down from the shelf overhead. She fitted the helmet over her head and secured it with a strap, letting it rest against the padded shoulders of her coolant vest. She snaked the thick cable extending from under the neurohelmet's chin through restraining loops in her cooling vest, then snapped it into a socket to the right of her seat. Then she plugged her vest into the coolant supply line dangling to her left, rechecking it for cracks and kinks. Proper coolant circulation would be crucial once ground combat began.

Next, she ran her first safety checks and began the start-up procedure that would bring her hundred-ton assault 'Mech to life. She could feel the deep rumbling of its fusion reactor through her feet, and within seconds, the temperature began to rise toward nominal operation levels. A slug of coolant pulsed into her vest, and she gave an involuntary shiver.

"KGC-zero-zero-zero," the computer intoned, naming the *King Crab*'s design specification. McDonald knew many MechWarriors who named their machines or who changed the factory start-up sequence to a more customized greeting. She had never felt the need.

"Security sequence initiated," the computer said. "State identity." The voice was slightly feminine but devoid of any real color.

"Linda McDonald," she said, digging out neo-leather gloves from a storage bin. She preferred their better grip to bare skin on the controls. "Colonel, Eleventh Arcturan Guards."

"Voiceprint match obtained. Secondary protocol enabled."

Because the technology for faking voiceprints had been known for a millennium, most BattleMech security programs required a key code or phrase that was known only to the MechWarrior. Bypassing this required serious time digging through the hardware of a BattleMech's computer, a skill not easily come by in the technology-precious Inner Sphere.

McDonald flexed her grip around her controls. "Idle minds are Davion tools," she said.

"Security protocols answered. Higher computer functions released." Those, of course, included targeting and fire control.

"Colonel McDonald is buttoned up and active," she said into her helmet mic. Her comm system was tied into the ship's priority frequency as well as to the private channel with her command lance.

"And just in time," she heard Captain Mickelson say, the edge still in his voice. "We were about to get some help from General Esteban's escort forces when the Lancer fighters bugged out, heading for the fifth planet in system. That's probably where they've hid all their DropShips."

Linda McDonald smiled. That meant there was little, if anything, standing in the way of their ground assault. "Good news, Tom. My compliments to the other captains and our fighter pilots. Pass the order that I want all Eleventh Guard machines on standby readiness—we're on the ground in less than two hours.

"And then"—she lowered her voice to keep the mic from picking it up—"we see what kind of defense Victor Davion has for us this time."

"In a word," Maria Esteban said, her delicate hands clasped behind her back, "nothing."

Still in MechWarrior's garb, her muscles tight and trembling from the adrenaline of a battle never fought, Linda McDonald stared at the spaceport tower's large wall screen, her expression souring along with her mood. The three-meter display currently offered a tactical map that showed Halfway spread out like the peelings of a shucked naranji. Flashing icons represented the battalion-strength units deployed across the world. Less than half were grouped nearby, though they were an impressive enough sight out the ferroglass windows of the spaceport tower.

Halfway's largest spaceport occupied ten square kilometers outside of Torrence, the planetary capital. Ten DropShips commanded the skyline, looking like someone had dropped a small city of bulbous skyscrapers onto the landing field. Three regiments of armor and two more of infantry controlled the perimeter. A full 'Mech battalion guarded the tower itself, though from what, McDonald was no longer certain.

Finding the spaceport unoccupied, or deserted, to be more accurate, she had quickly commandeered it as a base of operations while searching for the armies of Victor Davion. And in half a day, there was still no sign of them. Not so much as an infantry squad remained behind.

McDonald paced down one bank of dark monitors. With the arrival of her assault force, normal spaceport activity had been suspended. "We should return one RCT to York," she said. "Maybe we could interdict Victor's JumpShips this time and strand him in place."

Maria Esteban shook her head. Streaks of silver in her dark, coarse hair were all that gave away her age. "He won't return to York," she said. Her voice was soft but full of conviction and what sounded to McDonald like respect.

She nodded. When it came to matters strategic, she deferred to Maria Esteban. The general had over forty years of command experience, twenty-seven of those as commander of the Eleventh Arcturan Guard. Though it was no secret Esteban had hoped to retire on Timbuktu, when her troops began champing at the bit to help put down Prince Victor's civil war, she had calmly accepted.

As soon as was proper, she turned over regimental command to Linda McDonald, while taking the role of commanding general over the whole multi-regimental assault force. Esteban had fooled Victor Davion not once but twice already, on Alarion and on York. Three times, if McDonald counted the way Esteban had secretly diverted the Skye Rangers from joining up with Victor. If he was finally returning the favor, McDonald could not fault her mentor now.

"He'll want to move forward," Esteban said. "If he truly needed a waypoint between Alarion and his next target, he would have held against us here. I had hoped he would, but when we took away York, we apparently forced him into a blitzkrieg drive. He'll move faster now, always attempting to stay one jump ahead of us."

"Will that work?"

Esteban shrugged. "Yes. If he can keep moving fast enough, if he has enough supplies with him to last until Alarion or Coventry shipments catch up to him, and if he doesn't run into heavy opposition."

"Then we should go after him." McDonald thumped one gloved fist into the palm of her other hand.

Esteban's look was disapproving. "Your unit isn't ready to move, and you know it. Leaving the Lancers' aerospace brigade behind accomplished exactly what it was supposed to. They hammered your aerospace units and nearly crippled three DropShips on their way out, convincing us that there was a target on planet worth defending. We've wasted too much time on an empty world. Now we also have to stop for your repairs."

The general's voice dropped almost to a whisper, as if she were speaking only to herself. "He's turned what I did to him on Alarion back on us. Victor learns. We can't ever forget that."

McDonald nodded. She hated crediting the traitor-prince with any virtues, but to think him incompetent would only set her up for failure. Though she always referred to him as Victor *Davion* to divorce him from his Steiner birthright, she knew he was probably one of the most able generals since the time of Kerensky.

And now Maria Esteban was proving herself to be his peer.

"Then I should remain here," McDonald said. "You try to run Victor to ground, and I'll catch up soon as possible."

"Close to what I'm thinking," Esteban said, "but not quite." She gestured in the air with one finger, as if drawing out a map. "I'm betting Victor has passed through Aristotle and perhaps Clinton. Both are worlds where he can expect to be welcomed."

She nodded, smiling slightly to herself. "I'll take half the assault force forward on a flanking track. Unless we get a confirmed position, I'll go no further than Arganda and await you there."

McDonald was impressed at the way Esteban had pulled up those system names from memory. She herself needed a moment to call up a mental image of the Lyran Alliance star map to visualize the move. "You think you know where he is going," she said slowly. "Is it Hesperus?"

Esteban's smile widened, like a teacher happy with her student's progress. "It fits his pattern and his needs. For his first targets, Victor moved to quickly secure important industrial worlds. From Inarcs to Coventry to Alarion—Hesperus would be next in line. And it would be a crushing defeat for the Archon to lose our greatest industrial world."

McDonald heard something in the general's voice. "But you don't think he can do it."

"Hesperus is too close to the Isle of Skye," Esteban said simply.

It took McDonald a moment to reason out the cryptic statement. Then she remembered that Robert Kelswa-Steiner had set himself up in Skye. The Arcturan Guards had always maintained ties back to the Kelswa family, true, but McDonald considered Duke Robert an agitator whom Katrina Steiner would be better off without. Among his many political ambitions, he supported a free

Skye. To think of accepting his help made her think of the old Terran fable of supping with the devil.

"Skye and most of the Freedom Theater is a roadblock in Victor's path to Federated Suns space. Robert Kelswa-Steiner is a powerful man sitting astride that roadblock."

"I'll bring a long spoon," McDonald said, trying to show some enthusiasm.

Esteban pursed her lips. "If it will set some of your fears to rest," she said finally, "ask yourself how I managed to deny Victor the Seventeenth Skye Rangers at York."

That got McDonald's attention. "Duke Robert diverted them?"

Of course he had. Who else would have more pull with the Skye Rangers than Victor Davion? Maria Esteban was giving McDonald a glimpse of the inner workings that had made their recent victories possible, intricacies that might also lead to a final victory. "The Seventeenth will not join Victor at all?"

"Barring some unforeseen—and unlikely—alliance between Victor and Robert, no. The Seventeenth Rangers are bound for the Isle of Skye, and nothing is going to stop them. But Victor may not realize that yet, and even if he does, he may believe that Skye's instability will give him the opening he needs to secure Hesperus. If he thinks he can take it, that's where he'll go."

"And that's where we'll destroy him," McDonald said, completing the thought. Suddenly, she was feeling a lot better.

It could work. It could be the end of the civil war, in fact. Victor was an able general, but he didn't have the resources to match. His support in this civil war was scattered over many individual planets, each world fighting for its own small piece of a larger prize. *That* was his fatal weakness. McDonald saw that, and in that moment began to believe that if she could focus enough strength against Victor personally, she could break him.

For the good of the Alliance.

For the sake of the Archon.

10

Stepping through the front door of the Snord Antiquities Museum, Rudolf Shakov escaped the drenching rain that had socked in Clinton's capital of Jeffda for two days now. The warmth immediately set to work chasing the chill from his bones, and he was grateful. An attendant took his umbrella and offered him a towel, which Shakov declined, asking instead for directions.

Following what he'd been told, he left the entrance and turned down the first hall. Founded and maintained by Snord's Irregulars, the museum was not so well known to ordinary citizens outside Clinton, but it was famous among warriors all across the Inner Sphere. The Irregulars, an elite mercenary unit for many years, also had an infatuation with Star League-era artifacts, especially those of military interest, and they'd been collecting them for many years.

Shakov suddenly stopped in his tracks. Awestruck, he stood before a transpex case containing a document that had changed the course of history. Signed by Jerome Blake, founder of ComStar, and dated 2788, it was described on a nearby plaque as one of the five declarations sent to the leaders of the Great Houses, informing them that Blake had seized Terra, which he intended to hold under his "neutral protection for the legacy of all mankind." This copy had been hand-delivered to then-Archon Jennifer Steiner by an ambassador. Curiously, there was no mention of what service Snord's Irregulars had performed to win this document from the Lyran state.

Shakov had conflicting emotions as he contemplated the ancient artifact, signed with Jerome Blake's precise, economical signature. It had come down through time, at this moment connecting him directly to the founder of the organization to which Shakov had devoted so much of his life. He honored Blake for creating ComStar, which had saved the interstellar communications network from the destruction of the Succession Wars and had protected many other advanced technologies. Yet, it was Blake's implementation of a secret-society mentality that eventually led to the reformation of ComStar as a neo-religious order.

That combination of high technology and religious dogma had created many conflicts, both external and internal, struggles that had weakened ComStar, and made something so logical as Victor Steiner-Davion's nomination to the post of Precentor Martial seem like a threat to the insecure. It was why Shakov and others had left the Com Guard to follow Victor, the exiled prince. They saw in him the same honor and integrity of the previous Precentor Martial, Anastasius Focht. Shakov didn't think such great men came along very often.

Thinking of Victor reminded him that he wasn't here to visit the museum, but to deliver a message to the prince. He carried a noteputer in one hand, and the dedicated verigraph reader was buttoned into his right vest pocket. Turning away from the display, he headed toward the museum's east wing, following the directions he'd been given.

He was anxious to fulfill his mission. The message he carried might finally bring two weeks of waiting and preparation for the next stage of the war to an end.

In anticipation, Shakov had chosen to "look Com-

Star," as Archer Christifori had put it. He wore white fatigues, more serviceable and warmer than a dress uniform. His silver-starburst rank device was buttoned onto his collar, and he wore a flat cap with a kepi that hung down the back of his neck. The Com Guard insignia was missing from the cap, however. He'd torn it off the day the Prince's Men resigned en masse. On that day, Shakov had wondered if he'd live to regret it.

He hadn't so far.

As promised, he found Victor in the east wing, keeping company with Jerrard Cranston and Tiaret in a room dedicated to the fall of the Star League—the original Star League. They were standing near a large display featuring a gnarled wooden throne. Also with them was an equally gnarled old man in a wheelchair.

Well, of course, *he* was here, Shakov thought, studying the old man. He hadn't met Cranston Snord before now, but the insignia worn proudly on his sleeve made him immediately recognizable. Age had not been kind to the famous commander, whose once able body was now confined to a wheelchair. His shoulders sagged and he hunched forward as if about to share some secret. His hands, resting on the chair's armrests, trembled. But no one doubted the strength of mind that lurked behind those flint gray eyes. They stared into Rudolf Shakov like a pair of diamond-cutters.

"One of your pet Com Guard?" Snord asked Victor, but Shakov heard the joking intent and decided not to take offense. The old man seemed to be merely testing the waters for a sense of humor.

Tiaret, however, bridled at the implied insult to her comrade, an uncharacteristic show of emotion from her. She and Shakov had spent a great deal of time together in the past six months, and he took her reaction as a positive sign. For him.

Then again, perhaps she was simply reacting to Cranston Snord and his infamous past as a Clan defector.

Victor smiled indulgently at the old man. "Demi Shakov is one of my most valued officers, Colonel. And I think his arrival means we are about to leave Clinton."

He turned to Shakov. "The latest batched messages are in?"

Shakov brandished the noteputer, which he passed to Jerrard Cranston. "Three days later than they should be," he said, "but yes. We're still staying one jump ahead of the mail. And I suspect some of the local precentors on Alarion and Halfway are deliberately dragging their feet. Probably on direct orders from Gavin Dow."

Victor's selection of Dow to sit in for him as Precentor Martial did not sit well with Shakov and many others of the Prince's Men. Politically, the move was a master stroke—Katherine could hardly come back to accuse ComStar of taking sides when it was her own Lyran precentor promoted in Victor's absence. But Dow was also a political animal and had his own agenda. Shakov did not look forward to seeing what the man would do with the temporary boon of power.

"One bridge at a time," Victor reminded him. "Primus Mori will keep Dow from stepping too far out of line in my absence. Now, let's see what you've got."

Shakov unbuttoned his vest pocket and produced the verigraph reader. He saw hope spark in the prince's blue-gray eyes.

"I'm sorry, but there's nothing from the Combine," he told Victor. "Their communications blackout is still in place. This message originated at Skye, so I'm assuming it's a response from your cousin."

"Third cousin," Victor said absently, as though reluctant to acknowledge a blood relation to the troublesome Robert Kelswa-Steiner. He held his thumb over the verigraph reader to let it sample his DNA. The most secure method of communications possible—next to personally whispering your message in the recipient's ear—the verigraph would only open the attached file if a DNA check matched that of an authorized recipient

While Victor unraveled the encoded message and Cranston examined the rest of the reports, Shakov had a chance to examine the artifact that had so interested the small group before his arrival. Tiaret stepped up next to him, dwarfing him with her two hundred-fifteen centimeters. He glanced up, caught her impassive gaze and tipped her a sly wink. He couldn't help a wicked sense of enjoyment at the consternation that quickly passed over her dark features, followed quickly by an angry glare.

"So, Demi Shakov," Cranston Snord said, cutting in on the silent byplay, "what do you think of our prize?"

Returning his gaze to the artifact, Shakov couldn't help a slight grimace. The throne, whose bottom edge emerged from a tangle of root-work, looked more like it had been grown instead of constructed. Both the base and the back looked worm-eaten and half-rotted. Artistic merit, if any existed, relied purely on shock value. Looking at the thing was the visual equivalent of biting into rancid cheese.

"It's . . . ugly," he said truthfully.

"Gopherwood," Cranston told him, his voice wheezy but strong enough. "It's also several centuries old. Still, it was probably considered high art in the old Rim Worlds Republic, where it was fashioned."

The old man gestured grandly with one trembling hand. "This was the throne of Stefan Amaris."

Shakov nodded, feeling the same sense of awe overcome him as with the Blake document. Amaris was a name cursed by history as that of the usurper and the assassin responsible for the fall of the first Star League. He had betrayed First Lord Cameron, murdered his entire family, and set in motion the final battle that would sunder forever the finest government mankind had ever known. All for personal ambition and what must have been, in Shakov's opinion, no small amount of insanity.

He rubbed at his cheek, aware that the throne, no matter how revolting for what it represented, exerted a fascination equal to the signed document of Jerome Blake. Like it or not, this thing represented a pivotal point in mankind's history. A defining moment. And for just that instant, Shakov could almost sense in his own skin the kind of ambition that could persuade someone to cross the line from man to monster.

He would never say that he was glad he'd visited the museum today. But he would never forget it. Ever.

"Well, it's exactly the answer I was expecting," Victor said, breaking the spell the Amaris throne had cast over Shakov. "Robert is most eloquent."

Shakov was glad to shake off his fascination and turn to the prince.

Jerrard Cranston spoke without looking up. "What did he say?" he asked, still shuffling through the summaries Shakov had compiled for the other messages.

"He said no." Victor handed the verigraph, now blank, back to Shakov.

Shakov swore under his breath. That was it? No? Not even room for negotiation? With four regiments sitting on Clinton, waiting for the "go" order to attack Hesperus, the refusal presented a huge problem. Their situation hinged on plans for immediate combat, as Clinton offered barely enough support structure to keep Victor's force properly fed and billeted. The arrival yesterday of the Sixth Lancer aerospace brigade was taxing resources to the limit.

Cranston finally looked up from the summaries he'd been perusing. "The rest of the war is proceeding in line with earlier reports," he said, ignoring the news from Duke Robert. "Tsamma and Wernke are a toss-up. Tikonov is leaning in your sister's favor again. Kathil's still a meat-grinder, chewing up anything we or Katherine manage to send in there."

He looked down at the hardcopy reports. "Some good news, too. The Fifth Syrtis Fusiliers are declaring victory on Axton, in your name."

Victor had a faraway look, his eyes focused in the distance as if he could see the battles taking place on each of those worlds. "Anything else?"

"Tancred Sandoval sends word that the First Chisholm's Raiders have fallen back to Breed. Apparently, the Combine's Sixteenth Galedon and Twenty-second Benjamin finally threw them out of Kurita space."

That was news, Shakov thought. It made them the second regiment the Kuritas had booted out from those that had jumped the border in unsanctioned attacks last year. It also left at least four important Combine worlds still in the hands of Duke James Sandoval. He noted that Cranston was mentioning worlds and battles in the Federated Suns, reports that Shakov had placed toward the bottom of the message queue.

Cranston's expression softened as he looked over at the prince. "The Raiders brought no news out of the Combine other than those troop movements," he said in a low tone.

His voice drifted off for a moment, then he picked up his thread again, all business. "But, closer to us, the fighting on Giausar and Dalkeith is still heavy. Two of Katherine's regiments have firmly relocated to Bolan," he went on, naming the provincial capital they had decided months ago to bypass, "with transport available for future maneuvers. The garrison militias on Furillo and Dar-es-Salaam are also rooted in place."

Shakov knew what Victor was thinking. All those were worlds with no immediate strategic value, except as strongholds of support for Katherine. Victor glanced first at his intelligence chief and then at his communications advisor.

Shakov shrugged, unsure of what more the prince was looking for. "The Jade Falcons still hold an incredible advantage all along the border," he said.

"But Christifori is making progress," Cranston put in. "Phelan reports that his people have made contact with the Watch, and messages have gone into the Wolf occupation corridor. If Vlad Ward is receptive, he and Phelan could conceivably split the Falcon Occupation Zone in half."

Shakov looked from Cranston to Victor, wondering why they continued to ignore Duke Robert's refusal to support an attack on Hesperus. They all knew it meant the world would be nearly impossible to take. Though he was confused, he knew that his duty was to provide support to Prince Victor, no matter what. And when it came to the Clans, he figured you go to your best source.

He turned to the only Clan person among them. "Tiaret, what are the chances that Vlad Ward will agree to join Phelan in the struggle against the Falcons?"

"There is little respect lost between the Falcons and the Wolves," Tiaret said. "I would guess that it all depends on the advantage to Vlad's Wolves and how Phelan Kell approaches the subject."

Shakov stroked his goatee. Tiaret's evaluation was close to his own.

"Think of it this way," she said. "If the Capellan Confederation threatened Word of Blake strongholds in the Chaos March, what would it take to convince ComStar to go to their assistance?"

Victor gave a mirthless laugh. "Less than it would take to convince Robert to support me or even to turn a blind eye to my efforts in *his* Isle of Skye." He still didn't sound surprised at his cousin's refusal.

"You don't sound too disappointed, Highness," Shakov said, suddenly realizing he was on to an important truth. "So, if you expected Duke Robert to oppose you—"

Victor's face set into an intense, hard expression. "I never intended to attack across the province border into Skye," he said. "But by now, any agents Katherine has inside the task force have reported that I plan to do just that. Robert will also leak word of it to Katherine, which she'll take as verification."

And with the entire task force ready to move, Shakov realized that this bit of misdirection was all Victor had been waiting for before naming their true target. "Then where *will* we attack?" he asked.

"Everywhere else," Victor said. "Including the one place I believe Katherine has not prepared."

Just when he thought the Prince was going to explain, Shakov was even more confounded than before at the Prince's evasiveness. Even Tiaret was letting her confusion show.

Jerrard Cranston stood up, his expression closed and secretive, confirming for Shakov that he was the one other person, minimum, who might know Victor's true mind.

Surprisingly, old Snord didn't seem surprised either. He leaned back in his wheelchair, eyes rolled up toward the ceiling as a slight smile tweaked one corner of his mouth. Shakov was sure Victor would not have confided in the old mercenary—he had guessed! While he, Shakov, hadn't even begun to imagine. For a man who'd spent most of his life privy to great secrets, the frustration of being aced by a retired mercenary commander ate at his pride.

"Maybe you're better suited to ComStar than I ever gave you credit for," Shakov said to Victor, unable to hide the hurt that he felt at being left out.

"I will take that as a compliment," Victor said, but his tone was kind. "Don't worry, Rudolf. All will be made clear. We've just been waiting for the right timing to spring what I've got in mind. And it's going to give my sister fits."

Which would have been enough for Shakov, banishing any doubts in his prince and general. Until . . .

"Now the only question remaining," Victor continued, "is to see what she has planned for me."

11

Snohomish Springs, Furillo
Bolan Province
Lyran Alliance
16 July 3064

Rudolf Shakov tightened his grip on the control stick and throttle of his *Exterminator*, carefully kicking his 'Mech through one of the knee-deep snow banks surrounding the Snohomish Springs arm of Defiance Industries on Furillo. The complex lay in the shadow of the planet's Mont Vert range, where the corporation mined and smelted high-grade ferrocomposite steel for Battle-Mech and vehicle armor. The site looked year-round onto tall, snow-capped mountains. Just now, with the local seasons reversed from a Terran-standard year, Snohomish Springs sat in the grip of a hard winter.

And under the harder thumb of the Prince's Men.

Dirty-white heaps clogged the sprawling industrial yard like manmade bergs floating on a gray ocean, some of them piled as high as a BattleMech's chest. Emerging from the snow bank, Shakov throttled his *Exterminator* into a run for cover behind a storage bunker. Missiles fell in a hard rain around him, pockmarking the ferrocrete that busy snowplows had scraped so clean. Fire, smoke, and gravel geysered skyward.

He made the corner of the reinforced building with

only a light battering from the autocannon of a thirty-five-ton *Garm*. Waiting for him in the lee of the bunker was Adept Bills, his *Raijin* hunkered down on its rear-canted legs. With its forward-thrust cockpit and high, arched back, the *Raijin* had a raptor-like appearance.

"Over the top," Shakov ordered.

Both 'Mechs turned toward the three-story building and triggered their jump jets. Lifting off on fiery plumes of plasma, they made the short flight to the roof of the windowless bunker. Gravity pressed Shakov back into his seat, then quickly released him again as the jets cut out and his *Exterminator* landed easily in a crouch.

A *Beowulf* from the Prince's Men had cut in front of the building, trying to single-handedly hold back a reinforced lance of the Furillo provincial militia. Shakov and Bills added their firepower, all three concentrating on a forty-five-ton *Cobra*. The *Raijin's* PPC ate at the *Cobra's* torso, consuming armor while a staccato burst of emerald fire from the *Beowulf's* pulse laser hit it in the legs.

Shakov had better luck. His long-range missiles arced over to hammer at the *Cobra's* now-unprotected chest, almost knocking the 'Mech off its feet. The *Cobra* answered with two missile spreads from the launchers in its hands, but from the way it limped back unsteadily, Shakov knew he had cracked its gyro housing.

Then his anti-missile system came alive, the rapid-fire weapon eating through several hundred rounds as it spread out a shield of bullets. Only a bare handful of warheads survived to shred armor off his *Exterminator's* left side. The *Raijin* was less fortunate, taking a severe beating from more than a dozen missiles from the Cobra's second flight.

Both 'Mechs lit off their jump jets again, retreating back into the safety of the building's shadow before the militia's two Typhoon assault vehicles could move up. The *Beowulf* rounded the corner to join them.

"Report by team," Shakov ordered, selecting his all-hands channel. He estimated about thirty seconds' grace before the militia got bold enough to come for them.

With the situation heating up, it was all he could spare. He glanced up through his cockpit shield. The sky was clear today, except for the gray vapor trails of two aerospace fighters streaking overhead to carry out surveillance flights over the mountains.

Victor had made it very clear in the planning sessions that he wanted each spearhead to draw a lot of attention. "Make it bright and noisy," he'd ordered Shakov and Precentor Irelon before splitting off with the bulk of the Outland Legion. To where, Shakov didn't know, which bothered him still.

"Get Katherine's attention, but don't get comfortable until you hit your final target on Furillo."

Each of Victor's forces had a final target. The Twenty-third Arcturan Guard, newly arrived from the Arc Royal Defense Cordon, had doubled back toward Aristotle, in preparation for a drive through Gallery and Thuban, a move that took them too close to the spiked gauntlet of Tharkad for Shakov's peace of mind. Colonel Vineman had taken her Sixth Crucis Lancers on a whirlwind path through Soilihull, Drosendorf, and Gypsum, on a path back toward the provincial capital of Bolan.

Of them all, the 244th had drawn the easy run. From Clinton, the Prince's Men had hit Eidsfoss for supplies, followed by Ciotat, but only long enough to smash the mercenary company, Bogart's Men, and to insert Doc Trevena into the local resistance. Now, they were hunkered down on Furillo, the first force to reach their objective.

Victor had asked for "bright and noisy," and Shakov was giving it to him.

With Irelon not quite back to fighting trim, Shakov had led the 244th Division against the sprawling Snohomish Springs factory complex. Reinforced by two 'Mech companies of Prince Victor's Outland Legion, they had easily shoved aside the green garrison battalion of the Furillo planetary militia. Infantry had the more difficult task of clearing every building and factory floor of Lyran battlesuit troops. The task had taken almost seventy-two hours, as both sides were trying to fight without damaging the factory equipment. Neither wanted it hurt.

Not yet.

Beta Team was first to report in to Shakov. "I've got one company of militia, no support, still picking around the edge of the minefield."

Next came his Gamma Team commander. "We're being hard pressed on the northeast, but we're holding."

The Delta commander should have been next, but aerospace commander Demi-Precentor Hassenjoul interrupted the sequence. "This is Echo Flight," he shouted over the airwaves, kicking in the muting circuits of Shakov's comm unit. "Relief column has reached Jasser Pass. Standing by."

Hassenjoul was right to break in out of order. With the 244th controlling the skies over Furillo, the militia, stationed in the west, had decided not to risk a DropShip run over the mountains. The possibility of catastrophe had been spelled out to them in big, bright letters four days ago, when the 244th aerospace swatted down fourteen VTOLs before the militia learned their lesson. Now, the relief force was strung out in a column several kilometers long, slogging their way through the mountains, which were avalanche country.

Shakov swallowed hard, his throat dry from hours of slow dehydration. The temperature outside might be hovering at four degrees centigrade, but a 'Mech in combat was rarely anything less than a sweatbox.

"Demi Hassenjoul, you are clear for Plan Thunder Mountain, at your discretion," he said.

By which, the aerospace commander knew, Shakov meant to spare as many lives as possible. Sonic booms from repeated fly-overs would trigger massive avalanches along the lower slopes on either side of the pass. Any vehicle, including a 'Mech, caught under the tons of cascading snow and debris might be lost for good. It would also trap most of any column until the roads could be cleared, which might not be until spring.

"Demi Shakov," broke in one of the infantry-spotters,

her teeth chattering audibly. Insulated suit or no, lying motionless in the snow for too long would do that to anyone. "The militia is taking you up on your invitation. Fifteen seconds to contact."

"We're clear," Delta commander called in finally. "Don't worry about us."

Pivoting the *Exterminator* to face the northwest corner of the bunker, Shakov prepared to follow the *Raijin*'s charge. The fifty-ton 'Mech had taken a beating, but Adept Bills was holding it together. Shakov saw that a missile hit had left a jagged crater in one shoulder.

"Mark!" the infantry spotter yelled, a bit earlier than expected. From her vantage point, burrowed into one of the smaller snow banks, she was better able to coordinate the first strike.

On cue, Shakov throttled into a forward walk and fell in directly behind the *Raijin* and the *Beowulf*. The three swung out from the edge of the storage bunker, clearing another dirty-white snow bank by a wide berth. His targeting computers painted targets onto his HUD even before he could see them through his forward shield. The *Garm* and the *Cobra* hovered near mid-range, just beyond the furthest snow bank. Pressing closer, however, were icons for a *Talon-Nighthawk* team and the two Typhoon tanks. Newer designs, every one. None of them were older than six years—the benefits of garrison duty for Defiance Industries.

Shakov traded long-range missile fire for the man-made lightning of the *Talon*'s particle cannon. The arcing energy cut an angry wound over his left leg, blasting away most of his armor. With his quartet of medium lasers, he continued to rain down missiles on the militia position. With energy to spare, he had upgraded his lasers to extended-range designs. They stabbed out with brilliant ruby lances, burning into the *Talon*'s arms and chest.

The first hard-hitting wave of heat bled through the *Exterminator*'s cockpit as Shakov continued to close with the *Talon*. He cut back on his missiles, wanting to minimize power spikes from his fusion reactor. In energy weapons alone, he matched the destructive power of the militia *Talon*. The *Exterminator* also edged it out in range, but the militia 'Mech boasted a superior engine that wouldn't allow Shakov any slack. The *Talon* rushed forward, pulling his companion *Nighthawk* along in his wake and forcing the escorting tanks to keep pace or fall behind. Lacking the *Talon*'s speed, the Typhoons trailed, though slightly.

Shakov held his ground for a moment, adding to the hellish energies being traded between the opposing lines. Lasers flashed intense, gem-bright lances, and the two PPCs whipped blue-white lightning over the gray ferrocrete. Missiles poured out thick and heavy as the *Cobra* moved up to join the *Garm*. A pair of warheads detonated against the side of the *Exterminator*'s head, shaking the cockpit with a vicious one-two punch. Shakov clenched his teeth against the violent tremors. He heard a grating screech, like stressed glass, then saw that the detonations had pressed a hairline fracture through the left side of his transparent shield.

Shaken, he nearly committed himself to another volley. Then he shied away as the Typhoons cruised forward. Hard-hitting designs, each of the urban-assault vehicles carried a twelve-centimeter autocannon.

Shakov's tactical heads up didn't identify the machines by name, but if he happened to drift too close, he'd get a violent reminder. That was one of the drawbacks to fighting inside the factory complex. Magres imaging was almost worthless where so many signal returns painted ghost images. His team relied instead on motion-tracking and passive signal interpretation. 'Mechs threw out enough active radar and communication signals that they could usually be profiled and identified by design. It wasn't so easy with vehicles. All the computer offered was speed and probable weapons based on the targeting radar.

In fact, gleaning even *that* much from the HUD's compressed tactical information in a glance took years of experience. Experience Shakov was betting the Furillo militia didn't have.

They were, however, about to get a crash course.

"Second strike, fourth strike, prepare," Shakov ordered, falling away again in front of the aggressive *Talon*. Sweat stung at the corners of his eyes and drenched his bare arms and legs. As his heat scale slowly dropped back down into a safer band, he cut his lasers back by half.

The *Beowulf* had also stepped back, limping from a fused leg actuator. Adept Bills stood his ground. When Shakov checked his thermal imaging, the *Raijin* was glowing a very unhealthy red. It had to be riding close to automatic shutdown, but he had no time to send the adept any warning.

"Second strike, fourth strike, mark!"

As if triggered by Shakov's words, the *Raijin*'s missile ammunition bin cooked off under the extreme heat conditions to which it had been pushed. The right-side armor bulged and then burst outward, split in a dozen places by gouts of flame. Internal detonations continued to shake the 'Mech, which danced like a puppet on tangled strings. As the 'Mech lacked cellular construction, the explosive force tore through the center of the mighty machine, ripping away the fusion reactor's physical shielding. As containment failed, the red-orange flames were pushed aside by golden fire as the erupting reactor expanded to gobble up myomer and armor as new fuel.

For several endless seconds, slow death enveloped the *Raijin*, just long enough that Shakov counted his man dead. Then the cockpit's wrap-around shield blew away on explosive charges, and Bills escaped via his ejection system, rocketing up and away from the disaster. A pillar of golden flame chased him into the sky as the reactor finally let go with its full force, and the 'Mech all but disintegrated.

Shakov could only stare dumbly at the loss of the *Raijin*. He almost forgot that he'd actually given the attack order for this carefully prepared trap. Even so, it was the *Talon*'s PPC, flaying his right side bare of any protection, that again woke him to the battle. He wrestled the *Exterminator* to the left, turning fresh armor toward the *Talon* even as three of the large snow banks trembled, crested, and collapsed in on themselves.

Like feral animals bursting from their caves, two Burke armored vehicles erupted from the piled snow on the flanks of the *Garm* and the *Cobra*. At the western edge of the industrial yard, a ninety-ton Challenger X Main Battle Tank also clawed its way on armored tracks from the center of an even larger drift, its gauss rifle hammering into the rear of a Typhoon. The carefully piled snow had hidden the heat bloom of their reactors, which fired up at the earlier signal of the infantry spotter. Their targeting systems had remained shut down, so that any militia warrior who noticed a magres echo would have written it off as a ghost without the emission signature to verify.

Of course, their targeting systems were active now.

The triple-PPC of each Burke spat argent energy in lethal, arcing whips, scouring armor and probing into the center of the militia 'Mechs with ripping claws. The *Garm* lost its right arm but held to its feet under the blistering salvo, then turned and fled for distance. Molten globs trailed away from where it had stood, the liquefied composite steaming in the cold, moist air.

The *Cobra* was not as lucky, having been nearly gutted earlier by Shakov's *Exterminator* and the *Raijin*. One particle cannon drilled it dead center, spearing into and through the 'Mech to erupt out the back side. Golden fire spilled into the cavity left behind, leaking through the large rents. Then, a large portion of the head blew out, and the MechWarrior ejected on short-lived rocket boosters. At the height of its arc, his seat sprouted a parafoil-style chute similar to the one that now carried Adept Bills. The *Cobra* stumbled to its knees and pitched forward, slamming into the ground just as containment on the fusion reactor was completely lost. The 'Mech disintegrated, the explosive force picking up the nearby Burke and standing it on one end before roughly throwing it down again.

The seventy-ton Typhoon was made of sterner stuff, and the urban assault vehicle might have stood up to the Challenger's gauss rifle if not for the subsequent hammering of autocannon fire and the twin lasers. The tank pounded the rear of the UAV into scrap and apparently reached underneath to savage the drive train. After a few lurching starts, the UAV settled into a final rest. Targeting computers were shut down, and its upper hatch popped to signal surrender.

In all this, Shakov and his MechWarriors pressed forward, challenging the shocked militia. He kept a firm thumb on his laser trigger, firing them as fast as they could cycle. Ruby lances stitched up the *Talon*'s side, carving at its armor but unable to find any critical weakness. The *Beowulf* chased the retreating *Nighthawk* back past the mangled corpse of the *Cobra*, carving more armor from its back side before the militia machine dodged around a snow pile and made good its escape.

The *Talon* also turned to run, but if the MechWarrior thought the eastern snow bank had not produced an armored vehicle for lack of one, he could only watch in horror when Shakov called out, "Third strike, mark!" The gauss-equipped Demon that burst free effectively cut off the *Talon*'s escape.

Shakov toggled for an open channel, hoping the enemy warrior was listening in. "Power down or pay for it," he said, pulling his cross hairs over the 'Mech's outline.

There could be no doubt that the *Talon* would never make good its escape. The militia MechWarrior powered down. Flanked by two gauss-toting vehicles and lacking the speed to break free, the crew of the remaining Typhoon decided that the same applied to them and they also surrendered.

Watching Bills glide to safety on the parafoil, Shakov made a quick tally. No lives lost and one 'Mech destroyed in exchange for the capture of a pristine Typhoon, a scrapped *Cobra*, and a *Talon*.

"Several hundred tons of new technology," he transmitted on a closed circuit to the rest of Alpha team. "The kids had no idea what to do with it." It was true what Jerome Blake had always said. Technological advances did not directly relate to greater overall intelligence.

Raymond Irelon's gravelly voice came over the comm system so clear that he might have been sitting alongside Shakov in his cockpit. "If you're done congratulating yourself, you might go lend Gamma team a hand," Irelon said. He had remained in orbit, working with the technicians to break the militia communications net.

Shakov selected for a private frequency. "I don't like to leave our southern approach without 'Mechs. I'll send the MBT and the two Burkes."

"You should lead them around to the northwest on a flanking maneuver," Irelon replied. "You won't have to worry about another push from the south."

"What do you know that I don't?"

"Where shall we begin, Demi Shakov?" Irelon growled. "We intercepted the militia working their way through the satellite net. They are to fall back."

"About time they figured out they don't have enough here to retake Snohomish Springs." But why would that be cause for Irelon's concern? "They've discovered that their relief forces are trapped at Jasser Pass?"

"Thunder Mountain hasn't even begun yet. Demi Hassenjoul is waiting for a few stragglers to clear the slide zone." Shakov could hear the frustration in Irelon's voice. "The militia has just received a transmission from the LAS *Robert Kelswa*."

The WarShip! One of the two that had chased Victor's assault force off York. "How long till they get here?" he asked.

"About four days at a one-gravity burn. They're not tracking on an intercept for Furillo. Looks like they mean to interdict our transport, but we'll be long gone before they get close. We have one day," Irelon said, "and then we clear off Furillo."

Shakov nodded. The weight of the neurohelmet suddenly felt incredibly heavy where it rested on the padded shoulders of his cooling vest.

"Bright and noisy," he murmured, but the words were loud in the tight confines of his helmet.

"We got someone's attention all right."

12

Castle Sands, Dar-Es-Salaam
Bolan Province
Lyran Alliance
24 July 3064

Victor was tired of slogging his way through the Lyran
Alliance, though it looked like the various spearheads
launched from Clinton had accomplished their aims, creating confusion in Katherine's military machine. Here at
Dar-Es-Salaam, however, the local militia had finally
tumbled to the fact that his Outland Legion was nowhere
near large enough to take and hold the planet. The in-
creasing number of their strikes and ambushes proved it.

The crusted, sun-baked ground of Castle Sands
cracked under the metal-shod feet of his *Daishi* as he
pushed it forward at a straining fifty-five kilometers per
hour, leading a charge to rescue an Outland Legion assault lance and bring them down out of the coastal ranges
of Dar-Es-Salaam. The local militia's command lance had
reportedly trapped a pair of Legion scout 'Mechs against
the ocean, and at two-to-one odds, should have rolled
over them like a juggernaut.

As the sparse, scraggly brush and light brown soil gave
way to gray sand and sword grasses, Victor could smell
the salt tang as his life-support system pulled fresh air

from outside. The ocean, however, was still hidden behind one last hill of dark, sea-stained rock.

"Anything?" he asked Jerry Cranston, who piloted the *Devastator* running at his *Daishi*'s back. His heads up flickered with possible threat-contacts, but the old communications bands were still full of static. The technicians had barely had enough time to add a single new frequency that would allow the lance to talk.

"Whoever is jamming us knows what they're doing," Cranston shot back. "I don't like this, Victor. Tread carefully."

With both of them at the controls of one-hundred-ton assault 'Mechs, the comment might have been amusing at another time. But in a race to save lives, Victor accepted the caution. He knew what worried Jerry. Instead of rolling over Victor's men, the enemy commander had toyed with them, keeping them on the ropes and obviously using them as bait.

And you didn't need bait unless you had a trap.

The trap sprang on Victor's four assault machines just as they lumbered around the last rock outcropping, which opened up on the long beach where the plains of Castle Sands met Dar-Es-Salaam's Great Ocean. Three assault machines—older designs, but still lethal—waited with the swelling ocean at their backs. Further out, creating artificial reefs over which the waves broke in a fury of mist and white froth, three more battlements stood half-submerged. Their number told Victor that his scouts had sold themselves dearly, bringing down a militia assault machine with them.

Hardly a fitting epitaph, but all he had time for as a *Banshee* opened up on him. One of the 'Mech's two PPCs whipped its blue-white lightning within a meter of Victor's ferroglass shield, the ghostly afterimage drawing a blue scar across his vision. Both cannon sliced across the *Daishi*'s chest, and the 'Mech rocked back on its heels, shedding armor like a molten sweat. A 9S *Zeus* added its energy cannon and lasers to the attack, while an enemy *Victor* drilled a gauss slug into the armor over the *Daishi*'s knee. The militia knew who their target was, and meant to bring Victor down fast.

The *Daishi* shook violently, teetering on the edge of complete gyro failure as Victor leaned forward, using his equilibrium to help compensate for the hard-hitting attack. Cranston and the two Legion MechWarriors moved up to shield him from the concentrated fire, their own weapons answering the assault.

As the militia eased back into the surf to buy themselves distance and time, Victor took the opportunity to catch his balance. Then he dropped his cross hairs over the *Banshee* and pulled into a long burst from his twelve-centimeter autocannon. The slugs, tipped with depleted uranium for knock-down power even against a BattleMech, ripped jagged holes through the *Banshee*'s armor. Then, his trio of pulse lasers stitched deep across the other 'Mech's torso, one of them widening an existing wound in the left side. The gauss rifle's ruptured ammo bin let three melon-sized slugs tumbles free of the bin.

Only in that moment did Victor realize that the *Banshee* had not fired its gauss rifle in the earlier attack. It must have taken serious damage before his arrival, and that didn't make sense. Three militia 'Mechs to his four, one of them partially crippled? And unless one of the three half-submerged corpses was a *Berserker*, what had happened to Colonel Hubble? This was too easy.

Something was wrong.

"Back off, back off!" he shouted, throttling into a backward walk. "Everyone fall back! Something's not right."

Each man reacted in his own way. A samurai from the Draconis Combine, conditioned to following orders implicitly, halted his *Sunder* dead in its tracks and started a retrograde maneuver similar to Victor's. An *Emperor* piloted by a lieutenant from the First St. Ives Lancers split off wide, less certain of Victor's command or of the danger. Jerrard Cranston held into his advance a bit longer, using his paired gauss rifles to deadly effect as he completely crushed the *Zeus*'s right arm.

That also left Cranston's *Devastator* just inside the

reach of the three half-submerged battlements, which now rose from the ocean like titans. The *Berserker* drew an angry weal across Cranston's arm with its PPC while a C1 *Catapult* and an *Orion* spread half a hundred missiles into the air. Reacting quickly, Cranston managed to backpedal away from the deadly wall of fire that hit where he had stood not seconds before. Blackened sand and fire erupted in dry geysers.

If Victor was left with any advantage, it was the time it would take the ambushing machines to wade clear of the ocean's rough grip. He stabbed out with the ruby lance of his extended-range laser even as he continued backing up to gain distance and time. "What do you think, Jerry?"

Cranston was in trouble, soaking up the concentrated barrage that had been meant for Victor. Unable to hold up, his *Devastator* toppled slowly to the left, collapsing on a small dune. Immediately, Cranston worked to right his machine and get it back on its feet.

"I believe we've finally worn out our welcome," he said, a wince of pain in his voice. Riding a hundred tons of metal and myomer to the ground was never a pleasant experience.

Victor agreed. It was time to leave, though this probably wasn't the best time to have reached that decision.

"You to safety we must see, Prince Victor," said *Chusa* Agami, his Combine accent thick enough to make Victor worry that his new frequency was being jammed. "You go, *hai*?"

"We all go," Victor said, keeping a firm grip on his controls as a gauss slug from the *Victor* smashed again into his leg, worrying the armor down to its last few plates. Another one of those, and the possibility of escaping back into the coastal range would be moot. He wrenched his targeting reticle toward the *Victor*, pairing up his extended-range lasers and slicing at its legs. One missed low, scoring a dark, glassy trail in the sand instead.

"Not practical and you know it," Cranston told him. "They'll catch us."

The same dread that had plagued him on York settled over Victor again. He remembered Demi Hullinger's sacrifice. How many more good men would he lose? Who else would have pay the toll to get him to New Avalon? Damn it anyway, Victor told himself, if he wasn't willing to risk the same as his men, why should they continue to fight for him?

He opened his mouth to argue, but was cut off by a shout of "Banzai!" as *Chu-sa* Agami rushed his *Sunder* forward into the militia's blistering assault, his gauss rifle hammering out one devastating blow after another. The *Sunder*'s PPC arced and spat argent fire. The *Banshee* went down as Agami's fire cored through its left side, damaging the reactor and forcing the dampening fields to fall into place, shutting the 'Mech down.

Agami had already turned to a new opponent, standing up against a counterfire that should have toppled his *Sunder*. Watching him, Victor slammed one fist against the arm of his command chair. He was *not* going to allow a replay of what had happened on York. Agami had already bent the odds back closer to even. Victor would see what more he could do on that score. He reversed his throttle, powering up into a forward run as his lasers lanced out with brilliant force.

"Victor!" Cranston screamed.

"Not this time, Jerry." Heat bled up through Victor's cockpit deck, but hardly enough to worry him. The *Daishi* had dissipation ability to spare so long as he relied only on his extended-range lasers. "Colonel Hubble will be getting his world back, but not before we slap a higher mortgage onto it."

But as fast as he could advance, Hubble's *Berserker* was quicker, and Victor would not be in time to save Agami. He tied in his pulse lasers as soon as he could, stabbing out with gem-bright energy, trying to deter the hundred-ton *Berserker*, which had engaged its myomer acceleration signal circuitry. MASC allowed for short bursts of incredible speed from the assault-class machine. The 'Mech waded ashore, kicking huge sheets of water to either side, its giant titanium hatchet raised overhead for a vicious downward strike. PPC and pulse lasers chewed at Agami's *Sunder*, which had been intercepted by the *Zeus* as well and was looking none too steady.

The giant hatchet rose and fell. And again. The massive blade caved in one of the *Sunder*'s shoulders, rendering the gauss rifle worthless. But the wound was not lethal. That came with the second stroke, as the hatchet's sharp edge sliced into the small crevice that separated the cockpit from the overhead missile rack. Supports sheared and ferroglass shattered as the "head" of the machine crumpled inward beneath seven tons of titanium blade.

Screaming in frustration and anger, Victor finally traded one of his extended-range lasers for the assault-class autocannon to hit the *Berserker* with every ounce of destructive power at his disposal. Flames leapt from the twelve-centimeter barrel as high-velocity metal cut a savage wound across the *Berserker*'s chest and right arm. He followed up with a six-pack of short-range missiles. They spiraled in under the BattleMech's missile-defense system to crater its legs with holes that filled up with the rivulets of red-running armor composite as Victor's lasers also slashed at the 'Mech's main body.

Relying on MASC again, Hubble's *Berserker* spun away from the falling corpse of its previous victim and raced toward the *Daishi*. With a back-handed slash, the *Berserker*'s hatchet gored the left side of the *Daishi's* chest, cracking armor and bursting one of the heat sinks. Gray-green coolant spurted out in a brief wash, like blood spraying from a wound. Pulse lasers stabbed out from both machines, splashing armor into a molten mist. As the *Daishi's* reactor spiked, alarms warned of a potential shutdown. Victor slapped at the override, then answered the *Berserker*'s PPC with devastating effect from his autocannon.

The hatchet came down again in an overhead cut. Metal shrieked and tore as the blade bit into the *Daishi*'s left arm, slicing through the titanium humerus and knocking the autocannon to the smoking sand. The *Daishi* rocked over onto one foot as Victor twisted back to the right to compensate. He brought up his right arm, which pulsed emerald blasts into the haft of the *Berserker*'s hatchet. The weapon bent, then snapped off as the metal was stressed beyond its limits.

Victor could hardly breathe, the scorched air in his cockpit like hot coals in his lungs. He tasted the ozone of overheated electronics. The forward shield misted over as his evaporating sweat condensed on the cooler ferroglass. The *Daishi*'s temperature had shot too far into the red, but he wasn't about to back off.

From memory, Victor used his throttle-hand to reach over and toggle off an automatic shutdown. He also dumped his missile ammunition onto the beach before it cooked off and gutted his 'Mech from within. His thumb never left the firing stud to which he'd tied all his lasers, and this time his aim was true as they burrowed in directly over the *Berserker*'s heart. Megajoules of energy pumped past blackened armor and cut at the reactor shielding, probing for the fusion chamber itself.

Victor thought he might have seen a brief flash of golden fire, but Hubble had already dropped his dampening fields, putting the reactor into crash-shutdown. The *Berserker* toppled over backward, then lay sprawled over the damp sand, washed by the tailing edge of incoming waves.

It didn't seem fair that the battle could be over so quickly. Gasping for breath, his eyes burning from the sweat pouring off his brow, Victor twisted the *Daishi* at its turret-style waist, searching in vain for a new target. The *Zeus* and the *Victor* were down, both missing legs. The *Orion* and the *Catapult* had quieted their targeting sensors, and were wading in slowly under the watchful gaze and ready weapons of Victor's surviving lancemates. He imagined that his *Daishi* probably looked as bad as Jerry's *Devastator*, ruined armor, missing arm, and all. But they were both still standing. Agami had not died in vain, and he had died in victory not retreat.

Again, it wasn't much of an epitaph, but Victor believed it would have pleased the Combine samurai.

"Now," he said, loud enough to be picked up. "Now we're through with this world."

And, he added in silent afterthought, with the Lyran Alliance.

13

Ronde Tableau, New Avalon
Crucis March
Federated Suns
26 August 3064

Leaving the executive VTOL fanning the air behind her, Katrina Steiner-Davion walked the short distance to the waiting platform in the company of Richard Dehaver and a small, uniformed security detail. A select gathering of the press corps stood attentively, some of them filming her arrival. Most of them looked miserable, dressed for the warmth of a press room rather than a morning excursion to the high desert. Only a few—most of them women, Katrina noted—had been foresighted enough to wear boots and warm coats. Katrina herself had opted for wool slacks and a heavy wool overcoat of dark blue. She'd wrapped a gray scarf around her neck and left her golden hair loose to warm her ears.

Smiling at the press's discomfort, which she saw as poetic justice, Katrina exhaled sharply. Her breath fogged in the crisp morning air, a promise that winter would come early to New Avalon's southern hemisphere. With local seasons a few months off the Terran-standard year, the Ronde Tableau was in the dying grip of autumn. Not that any trees stood on the painted desert to testify with falling leaves. The only vegetation in this place was some scrub brush and the occasional cactus. Still, the local colors were right. Rust, ochre, and sienna layered the petrified dunes, and the painted rock fairly glowed in the morning sun.

"You are certain of this information," Katrina asked Dehaver as they approached the low stage. It wasn't a question. Not exactly.

"No, Highness. But Jackson Davion is, and in matters military we've always deferred to him in the past." Richard Dehaver stopped just short of the platform, turning his back on the press contingent. His eyes swept the empty desert, as if searching out the ghosts of the First Davion Guard. "There has been no new attack by your brother's forces in three weeks. It's enough for you to claim some momentum toward eventual peace."

Katrina smiled. "I like that." Vague and hopeful at the same time. She'd work that into her brief speech if she could.

The platform onto which she stepped was not quite a full stage but more than a dais. It gave her thirty centimeters over the standing press, many of whom were shifting from one foot to the other trying to generate some body heat. The platform also raised her so that the burnt-orange face of a nearby bluff formed a complete backdrop. No podium today—nothing to disrupt the image of Katrina against the restored desert. She clasped her gloved hands in front of her at waist level.

"Eight months ago," she began, then paused for any final holocameras to begin recording. "Eight months ago, a tragedy occurred on this spot. The First Davion Guards, incited by my brother's call for rebellion, led our nation's loyal forces on a chase that finally ended up on the Ronde Tableau. This peaceful, beautiful area, set aside as a park and a monument since the founding of New Avalon, became a war zone. Infantry dug their position into the petrified dunes. Armored vehicles crushed rock beneath their tread. BattleMechs sighted in their targeting computers on the bluff behind me. Major General Wendy Adams drew a line in the dirt, here, and forced us to come after her.

"We know what happened. We all saw images of the devastation visited on this once-pristine wilderness." Katrina shook her head sadly. "The Third Robinson Rangers, the Tenth Deneb Cavalry, and the local Crucis March Militia forces did their duty and ended a threat to New Avalon's security. That they were forced to do so here was a crime, as hard on them as the rest of us. Which is why I have invited many of their senior officers here today, to serve as my escorts."

She nodded to both sides of the platform, where her security detail had drawn up into two stiff-backed squads. "To tell them again that what they had to endure was important and necessary, and to show them what we have accomplished in restoring the natural beauty of this place.

"Months of hard labor, much of it carried out by volunteers out of all three military units, have polished away the scorched facings and filled in craters. We have scoured and continued to sweep away the fragments of armor and the stains of blood. And where General Adams' BattleMech fell, at a site not far from here that we shall visit later, we have used armor from her 'Mech to erect a memorial. A place dedicated to everyone—soldier and civilian—who lost his or her life in this vain excuse for a civil war.

"Would that the pain their loved ones know could be appeased by the same labor we used to restore the Tableau."

Katrina paused for effect, so that everyone listening, both live and via transmission, would associate her strongly not with a military victory but with the efforts of salvage and salvation that followed. That was an important distinction that her brother would never understand. No matter what his claims and charges, he would be forever remembered as nothing but a rebel leader who dragged two nations into a civil war. Histories—especially the ones Katrina would sponsor—would not treat him kindly.

The ruthless savages masquerading as "ladies and gentlemen" of the press corps had apparently forgotten their misery in listening to Katrina's oration. Camera crews did their jobs. The reporters hung on every word, listening for sound bites, taking notes when necessary on noteputers. No one noticed the frosty clouds wreathing their heads or, if they did, they no longer cared. Katrina felt the touch of cold on her cheeks, but the heating elements built into the platform kept her from shivering under the high desert's chill touch.

"But perhaps," she continued, "just perhaps, we can finally see the dawn at the end of this cold, dark night. And I think it appropriate to say here that, though fighting rages on many worlds in the Federated Suns and Lyran Alliance, hope springs up. Following defeats on several Lyran worlds, including a failed attempt against the province capital of Bolan, my brother's army has fallen silent. I am informed that there have been no new attacks in three weeks' time, and we hope to build on this momentum toward peace and for the end of this civil war."

And that, Katrina honestly wished to see. For her people, who suffered. For her two nations, growing further apart with each new battle. For herself, plagued by a brother who seemed to value nothing so much as war and the force of arms. Could Victor never admit that he had lost?

"I will pursue such ends to the limit of my strength," she promised. "From New Avalon, in the Alliance, and at the upcoming Star League conference on Marik. There, it is my hope that I can win—not only for us, but for the entire Inner Sphere—a promise of peace." She did not reveal her bitterness that the conference had to be moved from *her* capital of Tharkad to a world of the Free Worlds League because of her brother's war.

"I know your thoughts go with me," she said in closing. "Know that my thoughts are forever with you."

The question-and-answer period, the walk to the new memorial, the moments spent in silent contemplation for the benefit of the holocameras—it all took time Katrina knew she did not have. Now that she had called into question Victor's ability to prosecute this war to its fullest extent, she knew he would find a way to respond.

If he wasn't planning something already.

Armstrong One leapt into the air on thumping rotors, picking up an escort of additional militia VTOLs as it turned and sped for distant Avalon City. Through copper-tinted windows, Katrina watched the landscape flash by, trying to divine her brother's plans. After ten minutes and a small glass of champagne to relax her, she handed half of the fruity beverage back to a servant and turned to Dehaver, who was sitting next to her.

"So where is he?" she asked abruptly.

Dehaver rubbed at the side of his freckled nose. "We don't know. From Clinton, he struck in four directions with the obvious intent of distracting us. And then, nothing. The 244th Com Guard made it off Furillo half a day ahead of Esteban's strike force. Then Victor, if he truly was there, abandoned Dar-es-Salaam. Within the next week, we lost contact with the Lancers on Gypsum and the Arcturan Guard on Thuban. Except for the Guard battalion Colonel McDonald managed to strand on Thuban, they've all disappeared."

"Thank you for that review, Richard. Allow me to rephrase." Katrina's voice was shot through with dry sarcasm. "Where do we *think* he is?"

"Opinions differ. Simon Gallagher believes Victor may have fallen back to Alarion, to rest and refit for another stab through Bolan Province."

She shook her head. "Even I know better than that. Victor would not fall back so far in a voluntary retreat. He doesn't like to fight the same battle twice."

"Jackson Davion agrees with you. So does your aunt," Dehaver said. "Nondi Steiner believes that Victor will strike at Hesperus. It has all the markings of his earlier targets, offering needed manpower and equipment. It's also our greatest industrial world. With Coventry and Alarion already under his control, taking Hesperus would be the single-most powerful blow Victor could strike at you. Except for taking Tharkad, of course."

Katrina considered that for a moment. "Can he take

Tharkad?'' she asked, knowing that Dehaver never made casual remarks. She would have preferred to dismiss the thought without voicing it, but she couldn't let her emotions interfere with a proper military analysis.

"I found it especially poignant that no one else considered the possibility that Victor could be hiding in the Arc Royal Defense Cordon," Dehaver said. "So I had it drawn up as a war-game evaluation. It would take your brother's whole escort force along with the Kell Hounds, the exiled Wolves, and a number of elite regiments to take and *hold* Tharkad. It would also leave the ARDC open for complete domination by Clan Jade Falcon." He spread his hands. "In my opinion, he might be consider that a worthy trade."

"But you aren't an ally of Morgan Kell, who would be hurt by such a strategy," Katrina said. "And I find it hard to believe Victor would willingly give up a single Inner Sphere world, even for Tharkad. So, while the Jade Falcons attack us, Tharkad is safe. That is a statement I never thought I'd make." It was also another argument against delaying contact with Vlad Ward, to seek assistance from the true Wolf Clan.

"So," she said, turning back to her original question, "that leaves Hesperus. Politically, it would be a dangerous target, forcing Victor to go up against Robert Kelswa-Steiner and the Free Skye movement." She smiled thinly. For all her scorn concerning Victor's political acumen, he had apparently learned quite a bit over the last several years. "Especially as Victor had Robert's father eliminated."

"Which resulted in Robert's rise to Duke and leadership of the Free Skye Movement," Dehaver reminded her. "It's true that he leaked you the information that Victor had contacted him about an attack on Hesperus, but I would remind you that Duke Robert is not an ally."

"As if I could forget, Richard." Katrina face tightened with anger for a brief second. "It's Robert's meddling that has forced me to strand so many good units within the Skye Province." She thought a moment. "What about Jackson Davion? What does he think?"

"He doesn't say. When Victor first struck out in four directions from Clinton, Jackson still thought Hesperus was the true target. Now that all four spearheads have disappeared, save for a battalion of the Twenty-third Arcturan Guards stranded on Thuban, he just wants to wait and see."

Katrina easily read the distrust in Dehaver's voice. "You think he's falling into Victor's camp? I'd sooner believe that Victor has simply given up. You don't understand Jackson. His pledge, once given, is ironclad."

"You've seen my report that Jackson Davion supplied information to Tancred Sandoval last year—information that helped Sandoval turn several nobles against his father, and into Victor's camp."

Katrina frowned. "That is a distortion, Richard. Jackson supplied the information to Mordecai Rand-Davion, one of our distant cousins. He also informed me before you did that the information had found its way to Tancred, and he offered to resign."

"Three days ago, Jackson Davion traveled to Galax to inspect the shipyards. While there, he attended a gallery opening."

"And?"

"The largest draw at that gallery, advertised beforehand, was a new painting by Reg Starling."

It was the first time Dehaver had mentioned Starling since their talk three months ago. Hearing the name hit her hard, like a blow to the gut. "That was supposed to remain beneath my notice, Richard. By now, you should have proven that Starling is, in *fact*, dead."

He stared back at her with his soulless eyes and not an ounce of apology. "I can't. We checked his cremated remains and managed to pull out DNA. The remains aren't his. And I've had this latest painting examined professionally. Not only is it verified authentic, the paint is a special mixture invented after his death. Starling could not have painted it anytime before March of 3063."

"What else?" she asked, hearing the odd note in his voice.

"I have a current fingerprint."

Katrina steeled herself. "And where did that come from?"

"Upton. His studio was incinerated, but Lyran Intel rescued one good set of prints from Starling's escape route. He made it out just hours—maybe a day—ahead of our agents. We're looking for him again, which means we have to track backward from the main gallery for his work on New Exford. That's the one he was using at the time his suicide was reported."

Which should have put an end to Sven Newmark alias Reg Starling, Katrina thought. "This pleases me not at all, Richard. In two months, I have to bury Victor at the Star League conference and secure the First Lordship. *Nothing* is more important than that. I do not need a new political nightmare cropping up at this time. You said you could handle this." She waited for his affirming nod. "Then do so. Quickly. Quietly.

"And close that gallery on New Exford. Permanently."

14

Linda McDonald high-stepped her *King Crab* over a venting crevice, and crossed through the scalding curtain of steam. The only effects were some condensation on her ferroglass screen and a brief surge in temperature. Her heat sinks dealt easily with the heat, though that hadn't been the case during the combat only recently ended. Then, her cockpit had been like a sauna, and she'd gasped for breath in the sulfur-tinged air. Wiping away the sweat dripping into her eyes, she'd vowed by the Unfinished Book that if she ever met an engineer responsible for cockpit life-support systems she would buy him a drink. Several drinks.

That had been high up on the side of Scorpius Mons, Thuban's impressive volcano. It was there that her command lance had tracked and demolished the final three BattleMechs of the Twenty-third Arcturan Guard amid steam funnels and drifting clouds of ash. A better image of Hell she was unlikely to ever find, and she was the demon calling the Twenty-third to a final accounting for their sins. Those three—and one of her own—would not be coming down again under their own power. Salvage crews would get to them eventually, once they were finished here on the lower plains.

Where she had returned to face her own demons.

Scorpius Planus—the Scorpion Plains—spread out west from the volcano—flat, gray, arid, and acidic. This was where most of the fighting had taken place in the last weeks, and where the mixed battalion belonging to the Twenty-third Guard had made their next-to-last stand. A natural cloud cover, dark with the promise of rain, reminded her of the giant ash clouds of previous days. Ash touched everything here. It drifted like dry, gritty snow on the ground and was carried by the winds. When the rains finally came, it would turn into a thick, sticky mud and later dry into a cement-like glaze.

Very few of the hardy creatures able to survive here were not poisonous, which was why the salvage crewmen wore heavy gloves and leather arm shields as well as filtered masks to help them breathe the ash-choked air. McDonald throttled back to a slower walk, then eased into a wide-legged stance. She watched the crews work, recovering armor and actuators from the two lances of ruined 'Mechs. At times, they would harvest complete arms and legs or use cranes to haul entire 'Mechs up onto flatbed haulers.

Armored vehicles got less attention—and yet more. There were almost three times as many. However, they were completely ruined or so near that state that it wasn't worth the time to tear into the mangled wreckage for parts. Only if lacking treads or a hovercraft skirt or maybe a turret was the entire vehicle salvaged for repair.

There were also more bodies to recover out of a tank crew. They were zipped into black bags and loaded with some amount of care into a waiting Karnov VTOL transport. These gave McDonald the most trouble. They were Lyrans, each and every one, ally or enemy. And not just Lyrans, but members of the Arcturan Guards! The Frost Giants, a sister regiment to her Eleventh Golden Lions. Each bag that was zipped, taped, and then carried off held one of her people or someone she would have once called a comrade. And the prisoners wouldn't be any easier to deal with—three men or women captured for every one sealed and officially stamped KIA.

Was that why General Esteban had ordered McDonald here, why she had been pulled off the trail of the Com Guard 244th Division and Furillo given to the LAS *Katrina Steiner* while McDonald trapped and hunted down a mixed battalion of the Twenty-third Guard on Thuban?

The message was clear, all right. She didn't need anything more to show her the trials and terrors Victor Davion was putting the Lyran Alliance through. And she was tired. Tired of the damage he left in his wake. Tired of his baseless accusations against the Archon Princess, especially that she had somehow arranged the assassination of their brother, Arthur. If Victor had proof—not some quaint little conspiracy theory—why didn't he bring it before the Estates General? Or its Federated Suns equivalent, which she imagined as some kind of Arthurian court of honor where things were settled by 'Mechs jousting at a hundred paces, or some such. Victor could even hand it over to the media, or the Star League council.

But he didn't. And to Linda McDonald, that made all the difference. Katrina Steiner-Davion worked selflessly in the interests of billions of subjects while this war served the interests of only one man, Victor Davion. Apparently unable to ever prove his case, he resorted to the very tactics he swore to abhor, but at which he proved time and again to be so adept. Violence. Destruction.

McDonald flexed her left hand, tightening it into her neo-leather glove, then returned it to the throttle, which she pushed forward for a slow walk. The *King Crab* lumbered forward, stirring ash with each step, rocking in its shoulder-swaying gate.

Well, in the Eleventh Arcturan Guards, Victor would find his match, with General Maria Esteban to devise strategy and Linda McDonald to carry out tactical maneuvers. It was a team that had so far turned Alarion into a liability, hurt Victor at York, and now had chased his forces into hiding. A team that would pursue him all the way to New Avalon, because in the end, it came down to a choice between a Steiner or a Davion sitting on the thrones of two realms. No matter that they shared the same bloodline and a common name, their dispositions were plain enough for anyone to see. And while Davions *might* be superior military leaders, the Steiners had always shown more ability at ruling with a fair and even hand.

And again, to Colonel Linda McDonald, that made all the difference.

Ecol City, Thorin
Freedom Theater
Lyran Alliance

The granite fortress, rising out of the southern suburbs of Ecol City, was a source of pride for the citizens of Thorin. Built three hundred years before, it was a true relic of the original Star League. Though turned to ruins during the First Succession War, it was later rebuilt as a monument and then, with the rebirth of the Star League, pressed back into service as a garrison post. Though small, by Star League standards, the fortress housed a full battalion and provided a strong point close to Thorin's largest spaceport and the world capital.

Rudolf Shakov's first thought, upon seeing it initially five days ago, was to wonder how Cranston Snord might somehow find a way to transport the magnificent structure back to Clinton, where he could rebuild it as a new wing to his impressive museum.

"I still do not like this," Tiaret said to him now, her voice strong and deep even in a whisper. The two of them stood against the wall in one of the fortress' conference rooms, Tiaret by preference and Shakov because all the other chairs were taken up by senior officers and local nobility.

"I think we're all right," he said, letting his gaze roam

over the room. "That Count Parkinson looks a bit shifty to me, but I think you can take him."

Tiaret did not recognize the humor, or else chose to ignore it. "I am referring to our presence here. This fortress is an obvious target." She stared him down with bright, blue eyes, daring him to make fun.

Shakov sobered. Tiaret's concerns were no laughing matter. She had proven herself extremely valuable with regard to security procedures. Still . . . "No one knows we're here on Thorin. Not yet. Our diversionary attacks still have Katherine's forces scrambling to protect Bolan, Giausar, Tharkad, and especially Hesperus." He paused in thought. "The population is for Victor. Precentor Irelon and I have also guaranteed that the local ComStar stations are with us, so any leak through Gavin Dow should at least be slowed. I think we're covered." He looked over to Prince Victor, seated at the table and currently deep in discussion with Jerrard Cranston and General Nadine Killson about current logistics problems.

He dropped his voice a few decibels lower. "Besides, if we try to pry Victor out of a Star League-era fortress to install him in another brothel, I think we'd both be out of a job."

A sharp glance from Precentor Irelon warned that their voices had grown a touch loud. Shakov nodded an apology for them both.

"What—exactly—have we got coming through?" Victor was asking Jerrard Cranston.

Cranston scratched at the underside of his blond beard. "Thanks to Archer Christifori's earlier work here, we have local contacts for most of the basics. Ammunition. Armor. Foodstuffs. It's the larger equipment and replacement parts that will draw up short, and soon. Duke Bradford is promising to establish supply lines between Coventry and Thorin at once. Alarion will be more of a problem, with Maria Esteban sitting between us and them."

"So at the moment," Nadine Killson said, "we have to make do with what we carried with us. Not a problem for my Twenty-third Arcturan, Highness." She glanced away, as if ashamed to admit it. "With the loss of our Zeta battalion on Thuban, we're flush. We could help out some of the others . . ."

"The Sixth Lancers are holding fine," Patricia Vineman said.

Cranston nodded. "The Outland Legion could certainly use more in the way of repair equipment." Shakov knew that many of the foreign troopers had rallied to Victor even against the displeasure of their governments. They had brought little with them but machines and determination.

He watched Victor weigh the problem. They'd used up much-needed resources moving so fast through the Alliance and then carrying out multiple feints, but the distractions *had* opened a door through the region around Skye. Victor's force had slipped unnoticed through less-important or abandoned systems to rendezvous on Thorin, only one jump from the Terran corridor and within easy reach of the Federated Suns.

One jump from Terra itself!

Shakov couldn't help thinking about the chance handed to them, right now, to strike and liberate mankind's birthworld from the Word of Blake. That thought had reigned supreme among most of the Com Guard for some years, ever since the Blakists had seized Terra from ComStar and turned it into their own armed camp. But it was also a dream he'd given up when he'd joined Victor's campaign to end Katherine's rule. He told himself he no longer had the right or the responsibility to concern himself with the Com Guard agenda.

Old loyalties died hard, but Blake help him, he knew he must put them aside. The task force would not strike at Terra. They would, in fact, avoid it, slipping past through uninhabited systems, then erupting into the Federated Suns like a lance to Katherine's boil. This was the dramatic event they'd agreed was needed back on Halfway and that they'd set up by the feints out of Clinton. *This* was why Rudolf Shakov and the rest of the Prince's Men were here.

A light tap at the door warned Tiaret that someone waited outside, and she quickly nodded Shakov into the hall. Waiting there was a technician adept from the Prince's Men, one of the 244th Division's support personnel responsible for the communications network that followed Victor from world to world. The message the adept gave him was so urgent that Shakov barely waited for him to finish speaking before turning back to the conference room. Tiaret let him in, and he walked over to Victor's side in three purposeful strides.

From the look on his face, Shakov saw that the prince thought the message might be the personal one he'd been anxiously awaiting. He shook his head, then bent down to speak in Victor's ear. "We have an HPG transmission from Thomas Marik," he whispered, more for the illusion of privacy than any real attempt to keep the information secret from nearby officers.

Victor nodded. "I'll view it later," he said, sotto voce. The hope in his eyes died, and all the life seemed to drain from his face.

"No, Highness," Shakov said, still bent toward Victor's ear. "You don't understand. It's not a message, it's a *transmission*."

Victor looked confused for an instant, then understanding dawned on his face.

Shakov nodded. "Yes, my Prince, the Captain-General of the Free Worlds League is holding, *live*, in the next room."

Victor kept to a dignified pace, eager for the confrontation but needing a moment to mentally prepare. He would take only the time he needed. There would be no games of making Thomas Marik wait. Real-time HPG transmissions were as problematic as they were extraordinary, and so were reserved for only the most urgent situations. Besides, no one had known that Marik's Free Worlds League had tapped into Katherine's command circuit of HPG stations.

That in itself was worth Victor's immediate attention. The fortress's communications center was a small room, designed for the more advanced equipment known at the height of the original Star League. Equipment now spilled into a second room as well, with a connecting door broken through the wall. The center had a close feel to it, serviceable but cramped. With so much electronics stacked into such a small space, the scent of ozone was strong. It left the acrid taste of electricity on Victor's tongue.

He didn't ask about security precautions. He assumed that the Prince's Men were on top of such standard precautions as basic encoding. Anyway, without a dedicated encryption key in the hands of both parties, there could be no guarantee of high-level protection. He made directly for the holographic screen, where he met the eyes of the man who gazed back at him from hundreds of light years away.

"Captain-General Marik," he said.

The leader of the Free Worlds League had a commanding presence, even through HPG transmission. The right side of his face was scarred from a long-ago tragedy, but he wore it as a badge of honor rather than a crippling injury. His brown eyes showed only determination and intelligence. Victor knew how easy it was for ComStar to demonize Thomas Marik as Word of Blake's "Primus-in-exile." He overlooked it, even knowing darker things about Marik that so few others did.

"Victor," Marik said, less formal but not particularly friendly. That he used neither a title or a rank in addressing Victor implied that he was not prepared to accord him anything approaching equal status. "I'll keep this brief, since we are never certain how long a connection like this will hold. I have received your petition to attend the Star League conference to be held on Marik." He raised an eyebrow, the one not cut with several glassy scars. "Why do you seek this of me?" he asked bluntly.

Victor clasped his hands behind his back in a position of military rest. "Captain-General, I ask this because it is your realm and it is your support that I eventually hope to win. Theodore Kurita would vouchsafe me, of course, if I asked. But I do not want to arrive as part of the Combine's delegation. I want—I need—to attend as an independent party."

"I have not recognized your civil war, Victor, and I do not intend to do so at this time." Thomas Marik did not hide his frown. He rubbed one hand along the scarred side of his face. "I've seen the horrors of similar wars."

"And I would not wish that on any realm, except in the gravest of circumstance. You know that I once held off trying to depose Katherine for the greater good of the Inner Sphere. We talked of that at the Star League conference of '58. You must believe that I would not take this step, now, unless it also was for a greater good."

"Whose greater good? Your people's or your own?"

"Unless SAFE's resources have been severely crippled of late, you must know something by now of how Katherine stole power from Yvonne while I was away. And the questionable lengths she has gone to since then to maintain that control."

Thomas Marik let out a long breath, then conceded the point with a nod. "Still, you have no official standing, Victor. I will not endorse you as the 'loyal opposition' to Katrina's rule. I don't think First Lord Kurita could do so either, considering the Combine's recent troubles with the Federated Suns. The decision would seem self-serving."

Victor gave a tight smile. "I intend to let *Katherine* endorse me," he said, stressing his sister's true name. "She is certain to make this civil war an issue before the council. You and I both know it. How unbiased will the Star League appear if I am not allowed to answer any of her accusations?"

"And if she makes none?" Marik asked after another slight pause.

"I wish to be present *only* in the position of witness or in the event Katherine makes unjust claims. You have my word on that."

The Captain-General thought for a moment. "Trust is

a hard thing to come by, Victor, for the man who once held my son hostage and then tried to place a double in his stead."

"Which is a mistake I have owned and paid for, Thomas. You know that our responsibilities sometimes push us to decisions we are not proud of, and actions that would be best if they never came to light. At some point, you and I need to look past the facts of that incident, and judge each other on the merits of our individual actions."

Which was about as close as Victor had ever come to telling Thomas that he knew the truth about him. The truth that Thomas Marik himself was an impostor, surgically altered by ComStar and placed on the throne of the Free Worlds League in a grand deception. The schism surrounding Word of Blake's split from ComStar had buried any knowledge of the plot, and Victor's aides had uncovered it mostly by chance. If Marik were not such a fine ruler, if the Inner Sphere didn't desperately need such leaders, Victor would have denounced him long ago. But he was, and it did, so Victor had not.

Marik's stern, twisted expression seemed to soften. "All right, Victor. You gave me your trust once when the only reason you had for doing so was the stability of the Inner Sphere. Though the threat that concerned you never appeared, at least not in any form that endangered my Free Worlds League, that you offered your trust beforehand is worth some consideration."

Spoken like a true statesman, Victor thought, and reaffirmed his decision not to reveal Thomas' secret. Though Thomas Marik was not above also securing some personal considerations.

"I have conditions, Victor," he said, then waited for Victor's nod. "You may not bring any Clansmen, either captured or allied. The same goes for your renegade Com Guard division. They do not enter my realm."

Victor glanced sidelong at Precentor Irelon and Demi Shakov. They were displeased, but not surprised. He didn't look at Tiaret, who would not take such a condition lightly. He would argue it with her later. She would have to concede that if Thomas planned treachery, her presence would not make a difference.

"Agreed," he said.

"And I will hold you to your pledge. No interference unless requested or warranted by Katherine's actions. For that, you have my promise of safe travel and *limited* sponsorship."

"Thomas," Victor said, "I could ask for nothing more."

Marik nodded, and the holographic display immediately dissolved to the Word of Blake insignia, a broadsword-and-star pattern. It faded quickly to a snow of gray static as the HPG circuit fell apart. Victor clapped his hands together and rubbed them briskly. Then he brought the tips of his fingers to his chin and stared over at Jerry Cranston.

"We're ready," he said.

And then he realized that Thomas had, in fact, given him something more. He would never make such a slip accidentally, and it almost meant more to Victor than his pledge of limited support.

Thomas Marik had called Victor's sister *Katherine*.

*   *   *

//route >Thorin-Dieron; through to <Luthien>; receive >Omi Kurita //encode text//

My Dearest Omi,

Six months without word from you has made our time apart interminable. It has made me question ever sending you away at Mogyorod. Yet, concern for your safety remains greater even than my need to see you, to hear from you. And were you here, traveling with me, perhaps I could not concentrate on my tasks to the extent the people of the Lyran Alliance and the Federated Suns deserve. As we have always maintained—our duties first, ourselves second.

Still, on the eve of the third Star League conference, with a thousand things on my mind, you remain foremost in my thoughts. I so look forward

to seeing you on Marik, my love. If it were feasi-
ble, I would schedule a grand council every year, if
for no other reason than to arrange a time when
we could be together. But I'm afraid that the Inner
Sphere could not stand up to so much 'noble government,' and in this still-fledgling time of the Star
League, it is better to proceed slowly and to build
foundations that will last for lifetimes.

Which is what I hope we have been able to do
with each other—build a foundation strong
enough to weather even the greatest storms that fate
might throw at us. Looking back at the trials we
have already endured, I truly believe we have done
so. And I dream of the time when we can speak
again of that promise you made on Mogyorod. For
you, I will always be willing to complicate my
life, however many ways you might find to do so.

With my love,
Victor

*—TRANSCRIPT OF MESSAGE CS-THRN-10/10/64-
1D91F; UNDELIVERED; PROVIDED ON THE ORDER
OF PRECENTOR-MARTIAL PRO TEM GAVIN DOW*

The Snows
of November

15

Two Word of Blake infantrymen, cloaked in the dark, archaic robes that served as their dress uniforms, led Victor Steiner-Davion's party through the Marik Royal Palace to the east entrance of the ballroom. The passage was reserved for functionaries and minor aides to the greater nobles gathered here for the meeting of the Star League Council of Lords. It was just one more of a dozen subtle demotions that Victor had borne stoically, reminded that his place here on Marik was purely that of observer. A friend of the court, so to speak. It was no less than he had requested, and certainly no more.

A chamberlain stopped him at the door with a raised hand, waiting for an announcement from the ballroom's main entrance. For a moment, Victor thought he would be announced. Then, he heard the stately voice of the master of ceremonies.

"Presenting his Excellency, the Duke of Castrovia, Grand Duke of Sian, and Chancellor of the Capellan Confederation, Sun-Tzu Liao," the man proclaimed grandly.

There was no telling if this insult had been ordered by

Thomas Marik or simply arranged by the Word of Blake without the Captain-General's permission. Regardless, Victor was forced to wait and watch as the Capellan party descended the long stairs at the head of the ballroom. Wearing a Nehru jacket and trousers of obnoxious green and gold, Sun-Tzu went first, a bored expression on his face. Almost as if he intended to show contempt, or at the very least indifference, for the entire proceedings.

Duchess Candace Liao followed, also announced, and made up in Capellan dignity what her nephew surrendered. Her emerald gown and regal bearing belonged to a queen, not the figurehead of a conquered province. More surprising was that Morgan Kell chose to make his own entrance with Candace on his arm, a show of support for the subjugated St. Ives Compact that surely would not please Sun-Tzu at all.

Yet, Victor knew Candace well enough to read the lines of worry on her face and a depth of sadness in her gray eyes that he had never seen before. She was finally beginning to show her age. It was surely the result of Sun-Tzu's Xin Sheng campaign to reclaim her Duchy of St. Ives as a part of the Capellan Confederation.

"Returning the favor?" Cranston said, nodding toward the couple.

At the first Star League conference, Candace Liao had thwarted Sun-Tzu's attempt to exclude Morgan Kell from the meeting by proposing marriage to him. Although that was pure politics and no marriage had taken place, it was conceivable that the two had formed some sort of bond. Victor had learned through his own experience with Omi that love could spring up in stranger places.

"Maybe," he said, as his own small party finally entered the ballroom. "They make a good match, though, don't they? And I can't think of two people who more deserve some happiness in their lives."

Cranston looked sidelong at his prince and friend. "I can," he said simply.

The words touched the hollow in his being, an emptiness that began with a message from Hohiro Kurita that had awaited Victor on planetfall. Hohiro advised him that Omi would not be attending the conference. Victor had looked forward to talking with both Hohiro and Theodore again, but it was nothing compared to his longing to see Omi.

"Another time, Jerry," Victor said. "Another time."

As they entered the crowded room, Victor and Cranston separated from their group and headed for the receiving line. He was still getting used to Marik's increased gravity, and noticed that his movements were slower. While he and Jerry took their places in line, his officers and aides would be doubling today as intelligence agents. Moving through the room, they would pick up tidbits from the hundred various conversations to bring Victor news of any political undercurrents. Victor let a few other nobles drift in between him and the Capellan party, wanting to keep a good distance from Sun-Tzu Liao.

The wait was not long before he and Jerry finally stepped forward, coming face to face with the Captain-General of the Free Worlds League.

Twenty centimeters taller than Victor, Thomas Marik stood at stiff attention in his military dress uniform, a white twill jacket with purple piping and a sash running down from his right shoulder to left hip. The League eagle, the symbol of House Marik, rode in the place of honor high on his right shoulder. Victor admired that Thomas did not turn away to hide the scarred right side of his face.

"Victor," Thomas said, his voice neither hot or cold, "I trust the quarters provided to you in Malkent are satisfactory."

"It was kind of you to put my people up at your military stronghold there. We feel very . . . secure." Victor smiled as if his host were the most thoughtful of men for assigning him to an officer's barracks at the sprawling complex that housed the League Central Coordination and Control. Nothing like being surrounded by armed soldiers all day. And the military valet Thomas had given him must surely be a Word of Blake agent.

"As I had hoped you would." Thomas half bowed—

more of an exaggerated nod, really. "Victor, you remember Sherryl," he said, turning to the woman at his side, his second wife.

At that moment, Duchess Sherryl Halas was occupied with her four-year-old son, busily trying to straighten the jacket of the young heir to the throne. He was the first of their two sons, and it was Victor's first time meeting the child.

Victor nodded to Sherryl, then smiled at the small boy. "And this is your eldest son, Thomas?"

Thomas frowned, drawing in on himself. "It is," he said. "A very healthy boy, young Janos."

The words, Victor knew, were meant to remind him of another of Thomas's sons, the sickly Joshua Marik, who had died in a Davion research center. When the doctors were unable to save his life, Victor had approved an ill-fated plan to *temporarily* place a double in Joshua's place so that peaceful relations between the two powerful nations could proceed in the face of the Clan threat. He didn't need any reminders of how costly that mistake had been for him and his realm.

"I hope you will accept my congratulations on a fine heir, Thomas, and all my best wishes for your entire family."

"I'll accept that from you, Victor," Thomas said, a hard glint coming into his brown eyes. "And I owe you a debt for the hospitality you have showed Isis. She has written to us at length about the kindnesses you and Omi Kurita have shown her. I admit I was displeased with her decision to visit you after being dismissed by Sun-Tzu, but, this time at least, I am happy to be proved wrong."

"I was glad to be of service," Victor said, extending his hand.

Thomas shook it with formal solemnity, but he was already looking to the next person in line.

"All things considered," Victor said to Jerry as the two of them moved away from the line, "that didn't go too badly."

Cranston shrugged. "That he invited you here at all

shows progress." The ghost of a smile crept over his lips. "Though, after all these years, I have to wonder, can't you ever attend a diplomatic function without causing *some* stir?"

Victor laughed. "Are you so certain it's me, Jerry? I seem to recall *your* presence at most of those events as well. And there was that time on Solaris VII when you and Kai picked a fight."

"In your name," Cranston reminded him, dropping his voice to a near whisper to keep from being overheard.

"Sorry," Victor said, contrite. Not many would catch the references, but the few who did would know that it was Kai and *Galen Cox* who'd been involved in the incident. Galen had later "died" in a bomb blast, another casualty of Katherine's quest for power. In his place, Jerrard Cranston was born. One more lie to keep track of as both men worked to bring Katherine to some form of justice.

Cranston nodded. "Too many secrets, right? Don't worry about it, Victor. The real test won't come for three days when the Council starts to deal with official business. That's when we start tripping over the obstacles your sister has set in our path." His gaze darted toward a far corner. There, Katherine held court with several Lyran nobles who were attempting to curry favor while working tirelessly to keep any Federated Suns nobility from crowding too close.

Victor had little use for Katherine today and she even less for him. Instead, he worked his way through the crowd toward Morgan Kell and Candace Liao, who were waiting for him just off the reception line. He was stopped twice before reaching them, once for a handshake and another for a salute straight out of the House Davion military handbook. Victor was a lodestone for such attentions, as he had come wearing the old dress uniform of the Federated Suns. With its golden sunburst pattern radiating down from his left shoulder, the uniform stood out even among those of the other House militaries.

As did Morgan Kell's, though for different reasons.

Instead of the Kell Hound uniform to which he was certainly entitled, he wore paramilitary garb that approximated the standard Lyran Alliance dress uniform. He had also affixed every decoration and campaign ribbon he owned to the simple blue tunic, including the Lyran "general's star" rank insignia that came with his noble appointment. He was here as the Grand Duke of the Arc Royal Defense Cordon and not simply as a retired military commander. And with Candace Liao's hand resting comfortably on his left arm, he could hardly look more impressive.

Candace came forward first, taking both of Victor's hands in her own. "It is good to see you well, Victor."

"And you, Duchess." Victor couldn't help but glance over at Sun-Tzu, who was pretending that he wasn't keeping an eye on his aunt. "I'm sorry about the loss of your Compact," he said. "If only I could have done more."

"We all do what we can. Your help was appreciated." She smiled, and it lessened some of the sorrow in her eyes. "Between my children's efforts and the mediation of Anastasius Focht, I can at least say that St. Ives has endured and will continue to thrive, albeit under Confederation rule." She squeezed his hands once more, then let them drop as she traded familiar nods with Jerrard Cranston.

"Is Kai well?" Victor asked.

"Very. And he asked to be remembered to you. He would be here if he could."

Victor knew that Kai Allard-Liao would not be here, but the absence of his old friend pained him nevertheless. Much as he counted on Omi's love, Victor had come to rely heavily on Kai's skill and steadfast loyalty over the years. Now it was one more support stripped away from him.

But some still remained. "Morgan, I'm glad you made it here at least," he said, turning to him as Candace greeted Tancred Sandoval and Yvonne, who had just walked over to join them.

"Victor," Morgan said, extending his one good hand.

He was wearing his prosthetic arm today, but generally kept it down at his right side. "I can't say I'm pleased to be here, but it's a necessary evil." He saw Victor's frown, shook his head. "If not for Candace's insistence, I wouldn't have come. I don't like being away from the Cordon while the Jade Falcons continue to attack."

"Then we all have something in common," Tancred Sandoval said, edging in, trading handshakes first with Morgan and then Victor. "I shouldn't have left the Draconis March, and Victor should be attending to the rest of the civil war. But here we all are."

"Waiting for the other shoe to drop?" Yvonne asked, her voice soft even as she stared daggers over at her sister. Katherine had abandoned her entourage and was deep in a new conversation with March Lord George Hasek. "Now what does he have to say to her?" she wondered aloud.

"A very good question," Cranston said, moving off. "If you'll excuse me, I'll try to find out."

Victor watched his friend leave, then picked up the earlier thread of conversation. "I wasn't arguing your priorities, Morgan. But your calling the conference a 'necessary evil' underscores the sense I have that the Star League conference is somehow losing its stature. This reception is half the size of the last two when my sister hosted the conference on Tharkad. And it's not for lack of invitations, I'm certain."

He nodded toward Candace. "Kai, Cassandra, and Kuan-Yin all stayed behind. Omi remained on Luthien, still coping with her mother's death. And the turnout by nobles from the Lyran Alliance and the Federated Suns is dismal, at best."

Tancred rubbed at one cheek. "Well, in their defense, there *is* a civil war raging, even without our presence. But I know what you mean. The glamour is wearing off, and the Star League is starting to seem like just another government, less of a spectacle."

"But it *should be* a spectacle. It should be grand and exciting to us all." Victor shook his head. "I'd hate to think that we've become so jaded that we find even our greatest triumph, resurrecting the Star League, simply one more obligation."

Morgan exchanged glances with Candace Liao. "I was actually referring to the necessary evil of dealing with your sister, Victor. Though perhaps you're right. It hasn't helped that Sun-Tzu used his powers as First Lord used his powers to prosecute a war of his own. *Or* that Theodore Kurita recently acted as Coordinator *before* his role as First Lord when he annexed Lyran worlds. That hurt public opinion."

"I *am* concerned with what will happen when Theodore and Katherine square off over the Lyons Thumb and the so-called reprisal attacks against the Combine," Victor said. "I'd rather see the First Lord triumphant rather than victimized by her accusations."

Tancred Sandoval frowned. "Unless Katherine can prove that the Combine was somehow responsible for Arthur's death, I don't see how your sister can win that argument." Considering that Tancred might one day soon represent the Draconis March, Victor thought it a good sign that he did not immediately assume the Combine's guilt.

"It makes no military sense for the Combine to provoke such a response, not after the struggles with Clan Ghost Bear." Victor paused, glanced guiltily at Morgan and Candace before continuing. "Tancred, I hate putting this to you, and there's no easy way . . ."

Tancred was ready for him. "You want to know if I think my father capable of ordering Arthur's death to provide the impetus for attacking the Combine?"

Yvonne appeared scandalized that they could speak to each other this way. Morgan and Candace, long familiar with the darker side of politics, seemed unperturbed.

"I've tried to reason it out more times than you can imagine," Tancred said. "I even all but accused him of it to his face. And I can only say, I don't know. He wanted this. The timing was perfect for it, with the Combine weakened and its back turned to the March. But kill Arthur?" Tancred shook his head. "Every man has a price, Victor. I can only hope that my father did not buy his pursuit of the Dragon with that kind of coin."

"Government is rarely a clean business," Candace said. "We try to insulate the public from that, but it's true. And with a machine as complex as the Star League, there is no way to adequately police ourselves. One party will always try to increase their power at the expense of others."

"It will take time to regain the public support we had on signing the Star League treaty," Morgan said, "but I believe we're on the way to doing so. After all, part of our deliberations this month will include petitions for new memberships to the Star League council. Sun-Tzu is certain to press for admittance of the Magistracy of Canopus. The Word of Blake had also petitioned."

"All positive signs," Tancred said. "So maybe the question, Victor, is whether you think the Star League is truly ill, or if you are simply worried now that it has passed from our hands."

Victor gave a slight shrug of surrender. "I can't answer that. And maybe I do feel a bit proprietary. I guess we'll have to wait and see what develops. Perhaps the Inner Sphere *has* grown up enough that it can take care of itself. That would be a nice change."

He was about to smile when the heaviness of reality seemed to weigh down his shoulders even more than Marik's extra touch of gravity. "One thing we can all agree on," he said. "No matter what, we must keep the reins out of Katherine's hands.

"Or I'm afraid there won't be anything left."

16

Katrina Steiner-Davion rested her folded hands on the marble table's cool surface, one long, white-painted fingernail tapping in time with the step of the soldiers who paraded a slow circuit around the hall bearing the flags of each *voting* Council member. Five flags. Five votes. And that was why she was here. Her one and only concern was to win enough of those votes to become the next First Lord. By her count, surveying the room, she already had the election won.

She noted that Thomas Marik had done little to change the room for the meeting of the Star League Council. The hall was slightly smaller than the ballroom she had converted on Tharkad, its architecture more functional than the soaring buttresses and vaulted ceilings she was used to. Of course, the whole Marik Royal Palace was unremarkable except for its bunker-like design.

Eight long tables were arranged in an octagon, with the banner of the appropriate nation or organization hanging from the ceiling above each of the six occupied tables. The empty table closest to the door held only a speaker's podium. The other empty table would be occupied later when the Star League accepted its first probationary member.

To the right of the podium table, under the rearing dragon of the Draconis Combine, sat Theodore Kurita, who presided over this Council as the outgoing First Lord. His son and heir, Hohiro, was present as the current commanding general of the Star League Defense Force. Two other officers accompanied them. Seated at the next table, under the eagle of the Free Worlds League, was Thomas Marik. Also with him were his wife and some high-level Word of Blake precentor. Then came a table for newly elected Prince-regent Christian Månsdotter and his party, representing what was left of the Free Rasalhague Republic. The Clans still occupied most of the former Rasalhague worlds, and ComStar protected the rest.

Katrina had been assigned the table directly across from the podium, under a long banner displaying the emblems of both the Lyran Alliance and the Federated Suns. She had considered returning to the insignia of the Federated Commonwealth, the symbol that had once united the two realms. With Victor fighting the civil war in a Federated Suns uniform, she thought that claiming the Suns emblem for herself would make a strong statement. In the end, she opted for acknowledging both realms individually. She had permitted only Nondi Steiner, as General of the Alliance Armies and her regent in Lyran space, to join her at the spacious table.

To her left was the other empty table, and next to it the Capellan section. Two of the leaders sitting with Sun-Tzu eyed the vacant seats hungrily. The Capellan section, seating six people, was so crowded that it made the room look a bit lopsided. Besides Candace Liao and Morgan Kell, the Chancellor had invited one of his Warrior House leaders, Naomi Centrella of the Periphery's Magistracy of Canopus, and Grover Shraplen of the Taurian Concordat.

The ComStar delegation was seated at the table to the left of the podium. The closest thing the Inner Sphere could claim as a neutral organization, ComStar was nominally a non-voting member of the Star League and would chair any discussion where Theodore Kurita represented his own nation versus his position as First Lord. ComStar had the deciding vote in the case of a tie, which was unlikely this year with five voting members. Gavin Dow sat under the ComStar banner, very much at ease with the boost in political power Victor had handed him. He was accompanied only by Gardner Riis, who represented ComStar as Precentor Orestes of the Free Rasalhague Republic. An interesting choice, Katrina thought, making a note to watch carefully whatever game Dow might play.

She would watch them all, of course. Nothing could be allowed to interfere with her election this time. Not Dow. Not her brother, who was seated in the gallery arranged in long rows behind her table. She didn't believe Victor had a prayer of obstructing her this time, however. He had no standing in the council, and Katrina would move to block any effort by Theodore Kurita to grant him access. Victor had managed to thwart her election twice. Now he would sit as witness to her victory.

Five votes. Out of which she only needed three to carry the election. Theodore would oppose her, of course. Månsdotter was an unknown, but that didn't matter, not so long as she maintained the support of Thomas Marik and Sun-Tzu Liao. Both of them were tied to her in different ways, ties she would reaffirm in the coming week until their votes were a certainty.

Katrina smiled as the flag-bearers finally retreated to the back of the gallery, and Theodore Kurita rose to formally open the first day of the Star League conference.

It was time to get down to business.

As it happened, nothing required her personal attention until the afternoon session. Theodore's State of the League address was brief and perfunctory, outlining several topics of discussion before turning the floor over to

General Edwin Amis, Hohiro's primary aide in the Star League Defense Force. Amis' readiness report was nothing Katrina hadn't heard from her own military counselors, except that the SLDF was rotating the Seventy-first Eridani Light Horse into Clan space to relieve the 151st at the Star League outpost on Huntress.

New, but hardly troubling.

"If there are no questions for General Amis," Theodore Kurita said, his dark, sad eyes sweeping the gathering, "we can move on to our last order of business for today. The petitions for the admittance of new members to the Star League."

Katrina watched him intensely, saw the signs of strain that he tried so valiantly to hide. The last year had not been kind to the aging Theodore, with vicious attacks on his realm by Clan Ghost Bear and the Federated Suns as well as the death of his wife. Still, it had hit him harder than she would have thought. Katrina wondered if she might use that fact to sway him away from her brother, but she knew that was an idle thought.

"I have allowed three petitions for membership to come before this Council," Theodore said. "One from Word of Blake, championed by the Free Worlds League, and one each from two Periphery realms, both sponsored by Sun-Tzu Liao and the Capellan Confederation."

Nondi Steiner leaned toward Katrina. "Hangers-on and parasites," she whispered. Katrina did not miss the sidelong glance from Christian Månsdotter, who had overheard.

She didn't agree with her aunt, who looked at the entire universe with a fanatical pro-Steiner bias. "The probationary members of this Council will be the swing votes of the next," she reminded Nondi, more cautious with her volume. The new members could also leave Sun-Tzu with an impressive power bloc of three votes out of a potential eight. Not enough to automatically win any resolution he might propose, but enough to defeat anything that wasn't unanimous. Katrina knew that the power to deny was often greater than the power to grant, a maxim that had served her well when using shipping shortages to bring some of her recalcitrant nobles into line.

Sun-Tzu stood and was recognized. He had dressed carefully today, no doubt in anticipation of arguing his case. He wore a midnight-blue suit cut in Asian style, with dragons embroidered in gold up the sleeves. His green eyes glittered as he addressed the Council.

"We all remember Anastasius Focht as the honorable and long-standing Precentor Martial of ComStar," he began, and Katrina smiled. In one breath, Sun-Tzu insulted Victor's brief tenure as the Com Guard Martial and all but dared Gavin Dow to keep the position. "Could we have stopped the Clans without Focht? And where would my realm be now? Precentor Martial Focht came to the Confederation last year and worked diligently with me to arrange the final reintegration of the Duchy of St. Ives into the Capellan Confederation. For that selfless act, I cannot thank him enough. I wish him well in his retirement.

"But there remains a promise he made to me and my allies in the name of the Star League. First Lord Kurita agreed to stand by that promise, and now I ask the same of you all. You know of my formal alliance with two Periphery realms, the Magistracy of Canopus"—he nodded down toward Naomi Centrella, daughter of the Magestrix—"and the Taurian Concordat." Protector Grover Shraplen sat up at stiff military attention in acknowledgment. "In joining with me in the Trinity Alliance, both have demonstrated a desire for stronger ties with the Inner Sphere. Both will make strong member nations of the Star League." Sun-Tzu paused and looked over at Katrina. "Yes, Princess Katrina?"

Katrina had risen to speak, and it galled her that Sun-Tzu had dropped her Lyran title, reinforcing in the minds of his allies that she was the daughter of Hanse Davion and ruler of the Federated Suns. Though it would benefit her later in battles related to Victor's war, such associations hurt her now. The Magistracy of Canopus, and to a greater extent, the Taurian Concordat, were no allies of House Davion. The Concordat, in fact, was known for its fear of Davion expansionism.

This would have to be handled with delicacy.

"With no slight intended to your allies, Chancellor Liao, I must disagree with your assessment on one particular."

One of Sun-Tzu's thin eyebrows lifted slightly. "And that is?"

"Both of them will not be members. Not at this time. Whatever you may have promised them, our procedure on this is quite clear. You may not call for a vote on more than a single petition. I believe that was even one of your own concerns when we drafted the bylaws, so that no one nation could ever exert undue and over-powering influence."

"Ah, that is true, Princess Katrina. With the possibility of a further splintering of the Federated Commonwealth, my nation was concerned that the Steiner-Davions and their friends might suddenly be in power over three or even four different realms."

It took all Katrina's will to keep her voice civil, though she couldn't hide a touch of frost. "I am pleased to prove you wrong," she said.

"I am certain that you are." Sun-Tzu half-bowed to her, steepling his fingers in front of him. "But this is still of no concern. I did not mean to imply that I would endorse both nations to the Star League for immediate admittance, simply that I approve of each as potential members." He looked to First Lord Kurita. "Our arrangement, if memory serves, was that you would second either of my allies as new members."

Theodore nodded, and Katrina began to sit down again. Despite Sun-Tzu's obvious manipulations, she had at least forced him to back down to a single nomination. She assumed it would go to the Magistracy, his stronger ally and the lesser of two evils. Seeing Sun-Tzu place his hand with familiar ease on Naomi Centrella's shoulder confirmed her thought.

"I therefore nominate the Taurian Concordat for probationary membership to the Star League," Sun Tzu said.

The words caught Katrina half-seated and half-standing, freezing her in place for a long heartbeat as the entire scene impressed itself indelibly into memory. The confident aura surrounding Grover Shraplen. Sun-Tzu's stoic calm and the strength with which he held Naomi Centrella in her seat. And, perhaps more interesting was the look of calculation that quickly replaced the young Centrella's initial shock. As if she were mentally reasoning out the Chancellor's change of heart.

Katrina wished her more luck than the last woman who'd thought to try. She continued to lower herself into her seat with a casual grace she did not feel.

"We can't let that pass," Nondi said.

Katrina shook her head lightly as Theodore called for the vote. "We can't stop it."

Sun-Tzu would know her initial reaction, would have planned for it. If he were nominating the Concordat, it was because he knew he had the votes. His own. Thomas Marik, who would rather see the Taurians ascending at Katrina's back than the Magistracy behind his own. And Theodore, who would not go back on his word and would consider it another opportunity to pay the Federated Suns for the attacks against his worlds.

"He has the votes," she whispered as the call passed to her from the Capellan contingent. She stood. "I fully support the probationary admittance of the Concordat," she said calmly. Sitting, she nodded congratulations to Sun-Tzu for a hand well played. The young Chancellor bowed again.

It was a unanimous resolution, and Grover Shraplen made a point of moving immediately to the empty table dividing Katrina from Sun-Tzu. A military aide came up from the gallery to join him, and the two acknowledged a smattering of polite applause.

Thomas Marik rose while Katrina was still putting her thoughts in order. "First Lord, shall we also put to the vote Word of Blake's petition?" he asked.

"I'm sorry, Captain-General, but I would like to postpone Word of Blake's petition until we have completed the fact-finding meetings I have scheduled for this week.

Perhaps you would be available to meet with me in lieu of our afternoon session on the tenth?" Theodore waited just long enough for Thomas Marik's reluctant nod. "Good. In that case, I suggest we adjourn for the day."

Katrina did not wait to hear Sun-Tzu's explanation, though he was so obviously waiting to discuss his move with her *after* the fact. She would speak with him soon enough. First, she needed time to think through this opening day's events. Now more than ever, she needed to be certain. To be ready. So that when she made her move, nothing would surprise her.

Not this time.

17

Crescent Harbor, New Exford
Arc Royal Defense Cordon
Lyran Alliance
6 November 3064

From her third-floor lookout, Francesca Jenkins watched through a starlight scope as a pair of black-clad figures crept through the shadows across the street toward New Exford's State of the Art Gallery and Café. She swung the spotting instrument in a short arc to find at least two other teams. They were not dressed for the November chill or the rain-slick pavement, yet not one faltered, slipped, or shivered. Professionals, every one, no doubt wearing the latest in insulated sneak suits.

"You said I'd never see you again," Mr. Archie complained from behind her, but she ignored him.

The Lyran agents below continued to move in on three sides of the gallery. She knew they would be keeping an eye on the surrounding buildings, including the office complex where Francesca and Curaitis were positioned, but that wasn't enough. Not when the opposing team was waiting and ready.

She backed away slowly from the open window, out of what little light fell into the room from New Exford's brilliant night skies. Curaitis came up to the left of the window, a pneumatic rifle held vertically in his strong grip as if for inspection.

"Three teams," she whispered. "Standard two-man posts north, east, and south. Infiltration occurring from the harbor side on the east." She thought a moment. "Your best shot will be the pair at the mouth of the service alley, two o'clock low."

Curaitis nodded, shifted to bring the rifle into firing position before swinging it toward the window. The end of the barrel never moved past the frame, making him nearly impossible to spot from outside except perhaps by infrared snoopers.

"We had an *arrangement*," Mr. Archie whined. This time Francesca spared him a glance. He stood near the open door of the darkened room, a gray man in a gray suit, almost a shadow in the darkness.

"You would have preferred that we not come back?" she asked. "I don't think those agents out there are looking to invest in some of your collection."

Mr. Archie shifted uncomfortably. He was an art expert, not a cloak and dagger agent. Much of his position as the final arbiter of what was and was not art on New Exford he owed to his "discovery" and exclusive deal with the artist known as Reginald Starling. He had agreed easily enough to participate in the scam to keep Reg Starling alive, but that had been about money and prestige and involved nothing more complicated than lying to the press and the art-viewing public. *That* he had done for years.

"But to let them destroy my gallery?" His tone rose a notch too loud in self-righteous indignation, and Francesca backed his volume down with an icy glare. "I have the life's work of some great painters in there."

Curaitis was still waiting, hovering just inside the window like some dark, avenging angel. Francesca counted silently to ten, stilling her own nerves. "If you can look me in the eye, Arch, and tell me that you haven't moved most of those paintings and replaced them with copies for a nice little piece of insurance fraud, *then* we'll talk about what this is costing you."

Silence. Then, "I think I'll wait in the next room," Archie said. He disappeared into the reception area.

"Good idea."

The sound of breaking windows and the flare of orange light cut off any further conversation as the art gallery across the plaza exploded in fire and broken glass. Francesca was back at the window in a quick leap, right behind the double-cough of Curaitis' weapon as he took down the first two Lyran agents with tranquilizer darts.

"There was no exfiltration," Curaitis said, his voice barely more than a deep growl. "They must have exited on the west side."

Which meant the observation teams would be scattering quickly. Francesca checked for the next set of targets through her starlight scope, now over-saturated with flickering light but still just this side of ineffective.

"Left, nine o'clock, behind the statue . . . no wait!" She dialed down the aperture, trying for less light and more detail. "They're already down on the street." She checked her other targets as the first hint of smoke wafted through the open window. "So is team three. And unless I'm wrong, that's blood pooling around at least one of them."

She brought the scope down, then swung away from the window to flatten her back solidly against the paneled wall. "We have company out there."

The roaring fire covered the noise of a door opening in the outer reception area, but not the telltale click as the latch settled back into its housing.

"Arch, keep that door shut," Francesca said in a harsh whisper. She was several seconds behind Curaitis' thought process. He had already moved to cover the inner door with his tranquilizer rifle before Mr. Archie led a second man through.

Smaller than either Archie or Curaitis, the new arrival wore a standard business suit and looked as if he could have been the building owner arrived for some midnight bookkeeping. Except for the stun grenade in his hand. "The pin's been pulled," he said easily, "and I have people in the outer hall. You don't want to tranq me."

Francesca speared Mr. Archie with a hard look. "You sold us?"

He shrugged. "They came around not long after you left New Exford, trying to find out if Reg Starling was truly alive or not."

"Without us," said the man in the suit, "I doubt you could have pulled off Starling's resurrection as long as you have. We kept Loki out of the picture."

That name Francesca easily recognized. Loki was the Lyran Intelligence Corps' special-operations branch for state-sponsored terrorism, though never on the level of the Capellan Death Commandos or House Kurita's ISF. Loki had a reputation for independent operations, which had led to the formation of—

"Heimdall," Curaitis said, somehow blending certainty and suspicion in the same breath. The man in the suit nodded.

Francesca relaxed, marginally. From what little she knew of Heimdall, they weren't fanatical assassins. They worked behind the scenes, especially to keep a check on Loki's involvement in domestic affairs. But they were also the loyal opposition, known to support the Archon.

She ventured a guess. "If Heimdall has been helping us cover Starling's death, should we assume that you approve?"

"It's not as easy as that, and I think you know it. Heimdall was never quite the homogenous organization people thought it was. Even less so now, with loyalties splitting between Victor and Katrina, or falling somewhere in the middle."

Francesca thought it was a bad sign that the Heimdall agent referred to Victor's sister as Katrina. "Since we're still alive, I'm assuming your people fall into that middle ground," she said. If not, she would have to be violent and fast in her response. Her muscles tensed.

But he nodded. "That would be correct. And with the more immediate problems of the Jade Falcon attacks, we're inclined to leave it that way. So I'm here to find out exactly what you hope to accomplish with this farce."

"We intend to discover the truth," Francesca said.

"Force it into the open, where everyone can see it. If you've been following Starling's recent series, you know who stands the most to lose from his continued existence. Help us."

"What kind of help would you expect?"

"Nothing more than you've done already. Keep Lyran Intelligence from stepping on Mr. Archie. Protect his new gallery. If you can, assist the investigation into tonight's firebombing and then shout the news from the rooftops. Shake Katherine's nerves a little."

The Heimdall agent fixed Francesca and Curaitis with incredulous stares. "Hardly what I'd call an unbiased investigation."

"You're right," Francesca said. "It's biased. But who do you think arranged this night's little adventure?"

"It could be a rogue operation. It might be Nondi Steiner, or any number of alternate scenarios."

Curaitis shook his head. "I have a copy of the order, originating with Katherine's intelligence aide on New Avalon."

The Heimdall man frowned, for the first time showing a touch of unease as he shifted his weight from one foot to the other. Francesca knew that Curaitis had scored a telling shot. "Are you going to demand a copy of the order, signed in her own hand, before you'll believe it?" she asked.

"No," the man said slowly. "No. But I still don't like pointing a finger at the Archon."

Francesca waved a hand at the orange glow framed by the window. The sirens of emergency vehicles were faint, but growing louder as the place continued to burn. "The Lyran Intelligence Corps is pointing the finger," she said. "You're just sounding the alarm."

He deliberated that for nearly a full minute. No one moved except for Mr. Archie, who wrapped his arms around his body as if to reassure himself that this conversation was really happening. Francesca could think of nothing else to say that might persuade the man, and when she started to speak purely for the sake of argument, Curaitis' shook his head sternly to silence her.

Finally, the Heimdall man nodded and set the grenade down on the nearby desk. It made a hollow sound, telling Francesca that though the pin was missing, so was the explosive package. A dummy. A bluff.

"Tell me exactly what you would need," he said.

18

Lake Veil, Marik
Marik Commonwealth
Free Worlds League
10 November 3064

Victor found the Ozawa-Rickard corporate offices on the shore of Lake Veil to be a pleasant blend of the modern and the tranquil. The working areas were brightly lit and professionally decorated, while the employees went about their business with determined efficiency. There were also numerous areas for relaxation—perfumed gardens and galleries hung with the minimalist-expressionist paintings so popular on the world of Marik and also, apparently, with the Combine nationals.

Theodore Kurita had bestowed great honor on Iko Ozawa by accepting the use of Ozawa's corporate suites for the duration of his stay on Marik. Occupying the entire third floor of the building, the spacious living quarters were so simple and elegant that they might have been transplanted directly from Luthien. The wood floors were polished until they gave back a ghostly reflection, and *shoji* screens painted with scenes of samurai on horseback, rowing galleys patrolling rocky coastlines, and beautiful women in kimonos separated the rooms.

Victor and Theodore sat on traditional *tatami* mats

woven from rice straw, their knees resting on thin futons that offered some relief from the higher gravity on Marik. Facing them was a transparent wall that let them gaze out over Lake Veil. Victor could not see the other shore, but it seemed as if Theodore could, staring out into infinity as he sipped his *cha*. They had so little time before the meeting, yet the silence hung heavily over them. Victor waited until Theodore broke the silence by placing his small ceramic cup on the serving tray.

"*Sumimasen,* Theodore-*sama,*" Victor said, excusing himself for the interruption. "I am sorry to intrude on your contemplation. But may I express to you how sorry I am for your loss."

Theodore stiffened ever so slightly. Although it was nearly a year since Tomoe Sakade had committed *seppuku,* the loss still weighed heavily on Theodore's shoulders. And Hohiro's as well, apparently. Neither father nor son had been accessible thus far. At the Council's first-night reception, they'd been brusque to the point of rudeness, and they had avoided the company of others outside the conference. Victor missed their old camaraderie, the talk and martial training, but did not wish to intrude on their grief. He would share it with them, in fact, if they would allow it.

"Your wife was a very special woman."

Theodore's eyes clouded, and he glanced away. It was a furtive gesture, perhaps meant to hide his pain or perhaps his shame that it was so easily read. Hiding . . . something.

Victor took his cup in both hands. "I mean no offense."

Theodore nodded deeply, once, sketching the beginnings of a bow. "*Hai,* Victor-*san.* And I mean you no insult." He looked away, again seeking the infinite over the lake. "Your condolences are appreciated. I will pass them on to the rest of my family."

Victor seized the words as an opening. "How are they?" he asked. "Minoru? Omi?"

A longer pause this time. "Minoru works with the

Nova Cats. They are well-suited to each other. I think that he has truly surprised them with his ability to . . . understand."

Victor smiled at the euphemism. "Nothing gets by Minoru," he said. Then he waited as long as he could bear before asking, "And Omi?"

"Victor . . ." Theodore tugged at the wide sleeves of his robes as he broke off, then with obvious effort steeled himself against any further outward display. "Omi is resting in her palace," he said finally. "I'm sorry that I have no personal message from her. But I think she would want to see you focused on the greater tasks that now confront you. Now is not the time for distraction."

Which shut the door on any further discussion, and the two men sat silently with their own thoughts while awaiting Thomas Marik's arrival. Victor passed several minutes studying a tea ceremony as it was painted on a nearby *shoji*. He mentally softened the features of the lady samurai, added a touch of mischief to her eyes and the bloom of color high on her cheeks. Through half-closed eyelids, he imagined it was Omi, as he remembered her from one of a hundred evenings before the assassin's attempt on her life, before the death of his brother and the chaos that followed. It had been nearly two years since he'd last seen her—one year, eleven months, two days, and this morning.

Thomas Marik's arrival saved him from sinking into gloomy thoughts. As he had been taught by both Omi and Minoru, he set aside his personal concerns in a mental compartment, and concentrated on the present moment. The Captain-General was obviously surprised to find Victor present.

"You're here against your word, Victor Davion. No interference." The Captain-General actually sounded a touch wounded.

"Unless requested," Victor reminded him. He took a last sip of his slightly bitter *cha,* which was now only lukewarm. He set his cup on the tray, then shifted around so that his back was to the lake and he could look directly at the Captain-General. "First Lord Kurita asked for me as a witness today."

Theodore had also shifted on his mat, and bowed as an equal to the man who was simultaneously his host and guest. "That is true," he said. "I value Victor's knowledge and experience from his time as ComStar's Precentor Martial. Or would *you* prefer Gavin Dow?"

Thomas grimaced and shook his head. "So, this has to do with the Word of Blake petition to become a member of the Star League?"

"Yes, there is a problem with the petition."

"And that is?" The Captain-General had removed his shoes outside in accord with Combine tradition, but he was obviously unused to sitting in a kneeling position. Propped up on his knees and toes, he attempted to maintain a stiff bearing rather than settling back to sit on the tops of his feet.

"Candidly?" Theodore asked. "The problem is you, Captain-General. For the same reason that Katherine Steiner-Davion may not cast two votes as the head of two supposedly separate nations, I must assure the Council that you would not be allowed to do so either."

Thomas Marik looked neither surprised nor insulted. "I assume this has to do with the Word of Blake acknowledging me as their Primus-in-exile." He rubbed one hand along the left, unruined side of his face. "I allowed them to bestow that honor on me as a show of support for them, to buoy them in their time of crisis. It kept their internal factions from falling on one another. Now you would use this against them?"

Victor glanced between the two men. "It is simply a *concern*, Captain-General," he said. "That, and one other thing."

Marik nodded for him to continue.

"During my *active* time with ComStar, we followed the Word of Blake with a careful eye. They have expanded at an incredible rate, building new facilities, developing a decent army that includes hiring mercenary forces, giving aid to worlds of the Chaos March and Periphery.

Yet, even with the stockpiled resources we know were left on Terra, their organization should be bankrupt."

"Unless my Free Worlds League is supporting them," Thomas said, addressing himself to Theodore. "Which would fall under the 'undue or unfair influence' bylaws that Katrina quoted to Sun-Tzu. Yes, I see your point, but I do not foresee a problem. Word of Blake is its own entity, with a Ruling Conclave on which I have no position. I will even publicly renounce any claim to be their Primus-in-exile."

"As to the financial considerations," he went on with a shrug, "Word of Blake has a lucrative contract with the Free Worlds League, similar to the contracts ComStar has with most of the other Great Houses. They handle the shipment and sales of Free Worlds League military surplus to other nations, as arranged from the first meeting of the Star League. That gives them a source of income you may not truly appreciate."

"Can their charges and commission on those shipments make up the difference in the ledgers?" Victor asked, then immediately held up a hand in apology. "I'm sorry, Thomas. I am here to give evidence, not investigate."

Thomas' smile was thin, but it was there. "A fair question, and one I'm certain the First Lord would also have asked. However, you may have not reviewed the figures lately. Remember, the Free Worlds League has contracts with *every* Successor State of the Inner Sphere. There is more than enough profit involved in those sales. Or perhaps I should say, there *was*. With the cessation of hostilities with the Clans, that trade is finally beginning to fall off. And except to honor any final contracts, I have no intention of supporting the ongoing civil war."

"Admirable," Theodore said. "I am still going to require proof, however. Not that I doubt your word, Thomas, but as a precaution against future challenges. You will have to allow ComStar access for a full audit on your arrangements with the Word of Blake."

Thomas nodded. "If it will clear the way for the Blake petition, I see no difficulty with allowing that."

Marik spoke without hesitation, which Victor took as

either extreme confidence or a complete lack of concern. Would the ComStar audit find anything? They would have three years to look, which was the length of Word of Blake's probationary period. Thomas certainly didn't look worried, which argued well for him.

For the time being, Victor decided that he would give the ruler of the Free Worlds League the benefit of the doubt.

Dormuth, Marik
Marik Commonwealth
Free Worlds League

"An audit? You agreed to that?" Precentor William Blane demanded.

Thomas Marik looked across the small table at his friend, detecting the flush of anger crawling toward his receding hairline. As leader of the True Believers faction within Word of Blake, Blane was the man who might have become Primus if early political infighting had not made it impossible to elect any one person to the position. Naming Thomas Marik as Primus-in-exile had been his compromise, as it established Blane as mediator and therefore *de facto* ruler of Word of Blake.

"I had a choice?" Thomas asked quietly, calming his friend. Blane was a consummate politician, which was one basis for their long-time friendship. The other was that they both believed in Jerome Blake's prophetic wisdom. " 'Let he who has transgressed step into the light. If the cause is just, vindication will shine on him.' " The quote was from early, unadulterated teachings of Blake, from before the revisionists began to twist the great man's words to suit their own purposes.

Blane leaned back in his chair. "I suppose there was no way to avoid it." He laced his fingers over a slight paunch. "All right. I'll set my people to work on it right away. Top priority. With recognition from the Star League, Word of Blake will have official validation among the Inner Sphere nations. Finally." He nodded decisively, as if the matter was already settled. "ComStar won't find anything worth complaining about."

"Are you that certain, William, that there *is* nothing for them to find, or that you can hide it deep enough?" Thomas caught his friend's guilty start. "I'm not blind," he continued. "I knew what it was you needed, and was happy to give it to you when it became clear that ComStar had fallen into the hands of outsiders."

"Heretics and harlots, you mean."

Perhaps there was a *bit* more of the fanatic to Blane than to the Captain-General. "Outsiders," he said. "Focht and Mori. Jerome Blake himself promised a return of the light, no matter what treachery or dark ages might consume us, so I knew that if Word of Blake were the true path, you would win through. I looked the other way, William, no matter how hard it was at times. We both know you have your work cut out for you."

Blane nodded. "All right, Thomas. All right. We were forced to take drastic steps, but look what we have gained. We control Terra again, which was worth any risk." He brushed aside the Captain-General's concerns with a wave of his hand. "I'll put our people up against ComStar's audit team any day. They *believe*. They will prevail."

"You have more faith in them than I then. My own auditors brought the numbers to me last year. Our private arrangement was that you could siphon off an additional three percent over and above your commissions. I expected some additional skimming here and there—but William—fifteen percent?"

"Fifteen!" Blane stammered, then lapsed into silence, his mouth working but no sound coming out for a handful of long seconds. From his reaction, Thomas might just have announced that he was returning to ComStar to support Sharilar Mori.

"No, Thomas," he said, finally getting his voice back. "Five! I swear we've authorized no more than five." He sat bolt upright. "My personal files will confirm it. We siphoned away no more than five in materiel *or* monetary gains."

The Captain-General frowned. Blane's face was filled with more honest fervor than Thomas had ever seen, even at the height of debates over Jerome Blake's words. There could be no chance his friend was lying to him.

"Then . . ." he said, pausing to think for a moment, "then the Word of Blake numbers are faulty at the point of entry. If mine were incorrect, they would err in the other direction."

Blane's hazel eyes clouded with doubt, but he shook his head. "That's impossible. Who could possibly—" He broke off, the look of fear on his face promising that he knew who could have possibly perpetrated such an operation. "Damn. No . . ."

Dreading what he had come to realize not three breaths ahead of William Blane, the Captain-General bit into the idea with the reluctant strength of a man faced with only a single, terrible option. "It can only be," he said. "We've made a mistake, William."

Blane paled, his face now an ashen gray, and the leader of the Free Worlds League nodded. "It has to be Thomas Marik," he said.

$$=== 19 ===$$

Andrew Springs, Marik
Marik Commonwealth
Free Worlds League
11 November 3064

The resort at Andrew Springs had, at first, seemed an insult to Katrina Steiner-Davion. A cluster of small, fortress-grade buildings—most of them closed by her people as a security precaution—sitting on a hard, desert plain, it lacked *presence*. But that was before her full tour of the royal palace in Dormuth, which she found just as lacking.

Then Dehaver explained it to her. With its higher gravity and the terrible tornadoes and dust storms that plagued Marik during high summer, most buildings were built lower to the ground and with an eye toward strength rather than inspiration.

Her initial reaction also came before she'd tried the mud baths and the steaming hot, salty pools of the mineral springs. They were miraculous at drawing out the stress of a tired mind or the ache from her tired muscles. The world of Marik was beginning to weigh heavily on Katrina. It wasn't the physical sensation of its extra gravity, but the concessions she was forced to make on a daily basis in order to maintain the good will of the other leaders. She forced herself to do it, knowing she had to prove that her commitment to the Star League was as strong as ever and that her leadership skills were unquestioned—the civil war be damned!

And then there were days like today when the various Inner Sphere and Periphery leaders were given time to attend to the business of their own realms, to work on any private arrangements, or to spend some time in relaxation. Katrina, of course, would not be relaxing—not with her meeting with Sun-Tzu Liao hanging over her head like a headsman's axe. But she could look forward to floating in the springs later, after the meeting.

"Let's take our drinks outside on the patio," she said to Sun-Tzu, sweeping into the room where he had been waiting briefly.

Katrina was dressed for the heat of the day in a white cotton pantsuit that reflected the sun's rays and allowed her skin to breathe, while her hair was pulled off her shoulders in a severe, high ponytail that would help keep her cool. She also had an ice-cold damp cloth that she occasionally patted at the back of her neck. Sun-Tzu, however, was dressed in full Capellan fashion. His heavy brocade jacket, embroidered with gold tigers across the back and down both sleeves, had a tight Mandarin collar that must surely suffocate him in the desert heat.

At least, she could hope.

"A pleasant view," he remarked as they took seats on the flagstone terrace, she totally in the shade of an umbrella and he half in, half out.

Except for the doors back into Katrina's temporary office and a few security agents posted nearby, the only other distraction was the open desert—a blasted wasteland, in her opinion.

"It has its charms," she said, though not about to share them with the spawn of Maximilian Liao. Her arrangements so far with Sun-Tzu were purely political, giving him enough room to satisfy his nation's expansionist fervor while never letting him forget how much he needed her nation's sufferance. The Federated Suns had rolled into the Confederation once before, nearly devouring it. They could do so again.

"I appreciate your taking the time to meet with me here, Sun-Tzu. I realize that your apartments in Dormuth would have been more convenient, as they are so much nearer the Marik Palace."

"Yes. The offices over a museum devoted to Capellan culture. Endowed by Isis, and in the shadow of her vacant estate." He waved aside Katrina's concern with a lie of nonchalance. Only the hard set of his jaw gave away his irritation. "Thomas will have his petty revenge."

She nodded, already aware of the situation but wanting to hear him admit it. She personally thought Thomas' subtle display of disapproval for the way Sun-Tzu had broken off the engagement with Isis Marik well deserved. Richard Dehaver brought them each a drink, and she sipped the virgin margarita he had mixed for her from a large, bowl-shaped glass. The crushed, lime-flavored ice melted wonderfully on her tongue.

"An irritation," she finally said. "Rather like your appointing the Taurian Concordat to be a member of the Star League." She smiled at Sun-Tzu's uncertain glance. "You didn't think I would forget that, did you?"

"No. Though it does sound a bit self-serving coming from the same Archon Katrina who flatly told the First Lord that she would not condemn her Duke Robinson for acting on behalf of the security of the Federated Suns. James Sandoval still holds—what?—five Combine worlds?"

"Three. Remnants from the Seventeenth Avalon Hussars limped back from An Ting last week." And Katrina had no doubt Sun-Tzu already knew it. She mentally awarded the Capellan a point in their little game. "I have to admit that I expected more resistance from Theodore in that argument. He could have placed me in a difficult position."

The Chancellor sipped at his plum wine, the glass already sweating in the oppressive heat. He set it down on the table, having drunk barely enough to wet his lips. Katrina noticed that, like his father before him, Sun-Tzu affected long fingernails on the outer three fingers of each hand. Now, he tapped the black-painted nails against the tiled tabletop as he considered her words.

"Why should he press the issue?" he finally asked. "Theodore has taken eight of your worlds in occupying the Lyons Thumb. By all indications, you can't stop his military from eventually throwing back Sandoval's forces, and if he presses for early withdrawal, you could pressure him concerning the Thumb."

Of course! Katrina thought, annoyed that he'd out-thought her. "I missed that," she admitted. "Theodore is playing a longer game than I am at the moment."

"Theodore is the outgoing First Lord. His time in the spotlight is at an end, so of course he is looking forward. I've already held the mantle, which is why, quite honestly, I don't need to play the appeasement scenarios."

"But I do," Katrina said. "That's what you are trying to say, isn't it, Sun-Tzu?"

"I think you have greater concerns at the moment than worrying over what I am up to with my Periphery allies. Yes." He tugged at his collar, though Katrina could see it was because of the heat rather than nervousness. "We have an arrangement that suits me well enough, Katrina. I see no reason to step outside of its boundaries, and neither should you."

Rat-faced bastard of a Capellan whore! Katrina cursed silently, wanting to reach across the table to yank the forked tongue from his mouth and feed it back to him. But violence was her brother's way, she reminded herself. She could accomplish the same thing, usually, with arguments, or threats.

"That arrangement can be forgotten as easily as your engagement to Isis Marik," Katrina said, biting off the words. "If you vote against me for Thomas Marik or for that upstart Månsdotter, I promise you, Sun-Tzu, that your Periphery shield-nations will not stop the full force of the Federated Suns and Lyran Alliance from returning to finish what the Fourth Succession War began." There. About as black-and-white as she could make it.

"I would not think to vote against you," he said carefully, his face masked in a hard-set expression of neutrality.

"Then I will be First Lord. And with the weight of the Star League behind me, I can finally put to rest my brother's annoyances." Here she would have a strong ally, knowing Sun-Tzu's hatred for Victor.

"You may have trouble with that," he said. "Involving the Star League Defense Force in your civil war, that is."

Katrina looked down her nose at that idea. "As I recall, *Chancellor,* you managed quite a bit more. Your questionable use of the Star League helped you launch a war to reclaim the St. Ives Compact."

"True. But then, I had justification when the Blackwind Lancers jumped the border to try and kill me on Hustaing. What do you have?"

"It isn't what I have. It's what Victor does *not* have. Or, at least, what he has lost. Momentum."

Katrina relaxed with her drink, crunching a few ice chips and rolling the lime taste against the roof of her mouth. "Victor missed his chance by bogging down in the space around Clinton. Once, he might have struck at Tharkad or Hesperus. Now it's too late. Before a new First Lord is elected, I will officially invite the Star League in to settle the dispute. Theodore will put it to a vote, and the groundwork will be laid *before* I take office."

Sun-Tzu watched her closely, his jade green eyes showing interest and amusement. "Again, you may find that harder than you believe."

"You wouldn't be thinking to stand against me." It was hardly a question. Katrina wanted no ambiguity concerning her plans for dealing with Victor. She would have Sun-Tzu's vote, or she would have his head.

He shook his head. "I am not the person you have to worry about. After all, I could hardly stand against you, considering the latest victim of Victor's aggression."

A chill that had nothing to do with her drink ran through Katrina's body. Sun-Tzu knew something. Something she would not like. She stared at him for a moment, livid that he would dare toy with her. "What are you talking about?"

"Simply that while everyone was wondering what target Victor might hit in the Lyran Alliance, his forces have apparently used it as a diversion to bypass Skye Province and the entire Terran Corridor. Yesterday, they resurfaced. His escort force has hit *Tikonov*. My agents on-planet sent word the instant fighting began. I imagine the news will officially catch up with you by tomorrow's start of business. When Victor leaves this planet, Archon, he will be rejoining his spearhead force inside the Federated Suns."

Sun-Tzu just barely stifled a smile. "I believe, my dear Katrina, that he's on his way to New Avalon."

20

Kolcha, Tikonov
Capellan March
Federated Suns
11 November 3064

Missiles streamed in on gray contrails, blasting the ground and showering Rudolf Shakov's *Exterminator* with scorched earth. The azure stream of PPC fire slammed into the BattleMech's left hip, shoving it around. Twisting to the right, Shakov dropped his cross hairs over an on-rushing *Watchman* belonging to the Third Republican Guard. He hammered it with a flight from his LRM launcher, creating a wide band of fire and destruction down the left flank. The lightly armored machine thought better of its rash tactic and pulled back toward its own lines.

Not so a Guard *Caesar,* which had continued to move up after flaying away at Shakov's armor with its PPC. The seventy-ton design was a hunter, able to absorb damage and return solid firepower. With a gauss rifle and particle cannon at range, and pulse lasers up close, it was the most dangerous machine stalking Shakov's position.

The *Caesar* fired its gauss rifle into the *Exterminator*'s knee, crushing armor and snapping the right leg out straight, pulverizing the lower leg actuator. Not realizing that his knee was ruined, Shakov put too much weight on it as he fought against the kinetic delivery of the impact. The *Exterminator*'s leg twisted, buckled. He gave up the fight, surrendering to the fall and working his controls to make the landing as easy as possible. Rolling off his 'Mech's left shoulder, he lost more armor to the unforgiving ground, but was able to get his arms under him to push his 'Mech back upright.

The battle for Tikonov was in its fourth day, and despite Precentor Irelon's predictions, Shakov wasn't certain how it would turn out. Victor and the other regimental commanders had made a few assumptions in deciding to strike early into the Federated Suns, one being that they could expect local support in establishing a secure beachhead. That support was still long on promise and short on materializing. Their assault had turned quickly into a relief effort, with Irelon and General Killson working hard to salvage what they could from the supporters Prince Victor had remaining on Tikonov.

But no matter where they pushed through, somewhere else on planet the forces loyal to Katherine pushed back. Roughly half of the First NAIS Academy Cadre remained, and even less of the Valexa militia, which had tried to augment the First Cadre earlier in the war. Tikonov was an important planet with good resources and heavy production facilities. Katherine gave up the world of Algol in order to move the Fifteenth Deneb Light Cavalry over, and now the Third Republican was on-planet as well.

"Demi Shakov," he heard a heavily accented voice say in his earpiece before he could regain his feet. "You require assistance? *Hai?*"

"No," he said. *"Arigato."* His *Exterminator* anchored the right flank of the Prince's Men, which was joined to a battalion of the Outland Legion. The battalion commander was from the Draconis Combine, and the word for "thank you" was one of the few words Shakov knew. Of all the foreign Legion, the Combine contingent was the one he most preferred on his flank.

Careful of his ruined actuator, he levered the *Extermi-*

nator back to its feet. A silvery blur from another gauss slug streaked past, missing wide to the right. Shakov flinched away from it regardless. "Continue to encircle," he ordered, checking his HUD for rough positions on allies and enemies.

The mistakes of the First Cadre on Tikonov were plain enough that they would probably end up in an NAIS academy text some day. The Deneb aerospace caught half of the Cadre wing on the ground, and after establishing air superiority, kept the full cadre from reassembling. General Jonathan Sanchez and his entire command company had been driven into the mountains, and without him, any coordinated command fell apart.

Where the NAIS cadets had a battalion of armor, they met two battalions with 'Mech support. When they tried to rendezvous with a full company of BattleMechs with mobile infantry, it was only to discover that the Deneb Light Cavalry had already been there and mined the area. Sweeping back through, the Cavalry left nothing behind but broken machines and wounded warriors. The First Cadre and the Valexa CMM were forced to hold whatever city or strong point they were closest to, and even that tenuous grip had been slipping in the weeks before the arrival of Victor's task force.

Breaking the siege around Kolcha, one of few cities still holding out in Victor's name, had required a brute-force approach. In keeping with their earlier planned strategy, the Com Guard pilots cleared the air. A mixed battalion of armor and 'Mechs from the Prince's Men then pushed forward while the Outland Legion on the right flank bent around to entrap the Republican Guard. With General Killson's Arcturans striking at their base camp, the Guard battalion could expect no relief, and so were caught between the advancing force and the cadre-defended city.

Except that Republicans had discovered the weak link in an otherwise strong chain, sending a lance to probe the joint where the Outland Legion bent around to form a hammer against the anvil of the Prince's Men. With a pair of medium-weight BattleMechs joining the *Caesar*, all that stood between the Guard and a breech was Shakov's lamed *Exterminator* and *Chu-sa* Barnett's *Daikyu.*

"The *Caesar* is a problem, Demi Shakov," Barnett said, the end of his transmission breaking up as a PPC grazed his *Daikyu's* side. Armor sloughed to the ground under the argent fire.

"It would be less of a problem if the First Cadre would come out of Kolcha and help us," Shakov said, limping his 'Mech forward a few paces. "If they'd hit the Guard from behind right now, we'd have the Republicans on three sides and they'd shatter."

A new voice filled the speakers built into Shakov's neurohelmet. "Well, they won't do it." Precentor Irelon had apparently been listening in on the conversation. Back on active duty, Irelon in his *Crockett* held the center of the Prince's Men as they advanced into the teeth of the Republican Guard. "Without Prince Victor here, they'll stay buttoned up until rescued or routed. Whatever your problems over there, Shakov, take care of it."

"Copy that," Shakov answered. His missiles pockmarked more armor on the *Caesar's* left leg, but it just wasn't enough. Even with *Chu-sa* Barnett's PPC and autocannon added in, sooner or later the *Caesar's* gauss rifle would claim its victim.

Sooner, it seemed, as another metallic blur all but tore the *Daikyu's* right arm off. The crimson lance of the *Watchman's* laser carved in after it, severing the limb just off the shoulder. The stump pivoted around wildly, the heavy-capacity upper actuator unable to cope with the lightened load. A few ropy myomer muscles still attached to the shoulder whipped about like writhing, silver eels.

"*Chu-sa,* fall back, and I mean now!" Shakov said. "Don't argue. Give me two hundred meters." Looking into the upper-left limit of his vision, Shakov quickly blinked through preset channels, selecting his command override to the entire Outland Legion. The Optical Stimulation Technology built into his neurohelmet was activated by direct sight and simply counted the blinks. Recently developed by ComStar, OST now allowed for totally hands-free communications. And it wasn't the only new technology recently installed in the *Exterminator*.

"Outland Legion," he called out, "this is a Delta-seven order. Disengage. All units disengage and fall back." They were already moving as Shakov tracked the icons crawling over his HUD. "Swing out a half klick nor'northeast, and then hit the Guard with everything you can. Champion One," he added, knowing that Irelon would be listening in, "we are moving the hammer closer to Kolcha."

By throwing the encircling Legion out on a wider arc and ordering Barnett back, Shakov placed himself at the joint between the two units. Throttling into a backward limp, unable to keep up with the short retreat, he invited the *Caesar* forward.

Looking for the kill, unafraid of the *Exterminator*'s missile rack, the Guard 'Mechs followed. The *Caesar* and the *Watchman* moved as a team. The *Caesar*'s other playmate, a VL-5S *Vulcan*, broke cover from a thin stand of dogwood and pursued as well. Laserfire and autocannon fire from the smaller Guard BattleMechs probed for the *Exterminator*, flashing deadly light at the wounded machine. The *Caesar* whipped manmade lightning across Shakov's chest, cutting through the last of his armor, obviously saving his gauss rifle for the *coup de grace*.

Shakov tried giving himself to the count of thirty, wanting the Guard fully committed. The *Vulcan*'s autocannon chewed into his shoulder with eighty-millimeter slugs. The *Watchman* bit in with a crimson lance, drawing an angry red weal across his right side. Twenty . . . twenty-one . . . twenty-two . . . A gauss slug glanced off his left side, destroying armor in a sickening crunch that echoed up through the *Exterminator*'s torso and rattled the cockpit.

Twenty-five. Close enough. "Outland Legion, hammer them!"

Reversing his throttle, Shakov rocked the *Exterminator* back on its heels as he powered from a backward walk into a forward, hobbling sprint. He reached past the *Vulcan* with his missiles, peppering the *Caesar* across the head and shoulders. At least one warhead impacted near the wedge-shaped cockpit, cracking its ferroglass shield and hopefully rattling the other MechWarrior. Then, tying in his lasers, he unleashed a new surprise, having upgraded his medium-grade lasers for extended-range versions. With a reach almost as good as the *Watchman*'s large laser, he fired ruby daggers into the *Caesar*'s chest and arms. Armor melted and ran in orange streams.

Chu-sa Barnett's *Daikyu* was moving back up fast, chipping away at the *Vulcan* with his remaining Imperator Ultra eighty-millimeter autocannon and flaying armor with his PPC. Leaving him the two medium-class Battle-Mechs, Shakov cut in his jump jets, channeling plasma from his engine to the thrusters' reaction chambers. The *Exterminator* leapt into the air on fiery jets, arcing up and over the *Watchman*. Feathering his right-side thruster, Shakov drifted his 'Mech to the *Caesar*'s left, bringing the *Exterminator* down close by its side and just far enough that a cross-body shot with the *Caesar*'s PPC would not be possible.

The gauss rifle did damage enough, smashing square into the *Exterminator*'s chest. With little armor left, the nickel-ferrous slug spent most of its impressive kinetic force against the foamed-titanium skeleton and the physical shielding that surrounded the *Exterminator*'s fusion reactor. Support struts bent and shattered. Waste heat from the engine bled into the main body, leeching upward through the cockpit decking. Almost immediately, a heavy sweat drenched Shakov's exposed skin.

Knowing the abuse he was about to take from heat build-up, he pulled into his full salvo of four lasers. Ruby scalpels sliced deep into the *Caesar*'s left side, exploiting earlier damage and pumping megajoules of energy into the torso cavity. Half-melted gauss slugs tumbled from the wound, bouncing off the *Caesar*'s left foot with dull-sounding echoes, littering the ground as if the bird-legged 'Mech had decided to lay a nest of malformed eggs.

Wrenching his control stick and working the throttle pedals with practiced efficiency, Shakov limped the *Exterminator* around in a tight arc toward the backside of the *Caesar*. The other machine turned with him, but not quite fast enough to bring its PPC to bear, which left only the single pulse laser mounted on its left arm. Emerald light flared and stabbed into the *Exterminator*'s ruined chest, carving away more shielding and bursting a pair of internalized heat sinks.

His heat jumped directly into the red. Alarms wailing for attention, Shakov slapped at the shutdown override, gasping for breath as the scorched air drove spikes into his lungs. The battle had come down to this—his *Exterminator* wrestling with a Guard *Caesar*, holding closed a gap through which the Republicans might divide the allied forces and hold onto their siege at Kolcha. His targeting cross hairs blinked intermittently and jumped around, affected by heat-addled circuitry. He worked them to his left, approximating a mean center that bracketed the *Caesar*. Worried about cooking off his missile-rack ammunition, Shakov toggled out one of his four lasers, hitting back with the best he had available.

It was enough. One laser probed through the ruins of the *Caesar*'s left side, spilling destructive energy into the cavity. Skeleton struts softened, warped, and bent, and the leg telescoped up into the torso to crush the bulky reactor shielding. Golden fire flared deep within the wound, but then extinguished almost as quickly as the Guard MechWarrior dropped dampening fields and smothered the fusion chamber reaction. The *Caesar* toppled over, seventy tons of dead weight sprawling over the ground.

His cooling vest cold and clammy against his hot skin, Shakov gasped for breath and surveyed the immediate area through his ferroglass shield. Barnett stood over two downed BattleMechs, his *Daikyu* now missing both arms and in no condition to mount a defense against the Guard. Fortunately, it wouldn't be necessary. The Third Republican had begun a move toward them, only to find themselves smashed between the advancing Prince's Men and the Outland Legion, which had swung back in with a vengeance and crushed the Guard's left flank.

And, according to new icons painted over his heads up

display, it seemed that at least one mixed company of the First Cadre elements that had been hiding in Kolcha had speared outward from the city, harvesting a few Republicans of their own from the Third Guard's rearward line.

Two lances of VTOLs rose from between the city buildings, winging out for strafing runs and convincing the Guard that they wanted no further part of this battle. In singles and pairs, then by lances, the Third Republican turned and fled northwest, escaping the killing zone and leaving Kolcha to the victors.

"What do you think, Rudolf?" Irelon didn't sound altogether pleased with the victory.

As the *Exterminator*'s heat dropped back into the safer bands, the sweat cooled on Shakov's flesh and left his skin puckered in goose bumps. He couldn't help but feel elated to still be on his feet. He swallowed hard, bringing some moisture back to his parched throat, and blinked over to an open channel. "I think we should talk the rest of the cadre out of Kolcha and set off for the Herosoma District. Maybe we can rescue the First's command company out of the mountains there."

There were more than a few cheers and calls of support for that idea.

Irelon's voice took on the narrowed, tinny echo that meant he had selected his private circuit to Shakov. "That small company *is* the rest of the First Cadre. All the mechanized elements that survived the siege, anyway. *Now* what do you think?"

Shakov's elation died as he counted seven 'Mechs and a half-dozen armored vehicles, plus the eight VTOLs. All that was left from a reported four companies.

"I think," he began, then stopped to switch over to his private frequency with Irelon. "I think we better hope that the Sixth Lancers get here from Thorin a bit faster, and that Victor also gets here soon.

"Because if Katherine throws anything more at us right now, what we have *left* on Tikonov will never be enough."

21

Nodding for Dehaver to wait outside, Katrina preceded Gavin Dow into one of many small conference rooms located throughout the Marik palace. A ferroglass wall opened onto the corridor, and the space felt cool and sterile, as though the room had not seen much use. Dow took a seat in a low-backed chair at one end of a redwood table.

Katrina remained standing.

"If you're here to block Word of Blake's admission into the Star League, Precentor Dow, this is a waste of our time. Theodore and Thomas have both indicated their intention to allow it, and I have no good-faith reason to oppose them. Even if I did, I don't want trouble with Thomas Marik so close to the election of a new First Lord."

Dow nodded slowly, his yellow-green eyes sharp and unblinking, like a cat's. "I appreciate your candor, Archon, but I know the vote is unbreakable. Actually, I am here to help you."

Katrina was silent for a moment, guessing what he had in mind. "That rests on a very large presumption,

Precentor. That I *need* your help." She glanced back toward Dehaver, who was watching through the window. The two of them had worked out the election strategy very carefully.

"With five voting members, I need only three to become First Lord. I have assurances of support from one member and strong ties to a second, which would make opposing me difficult. What could you possibly offer me?"

Dow smiled. "Rasalhague," he said.

Katrina was stunned. "You're saying that you can—"

"Deliver the vote of Christian Månsdotter," Dow finished for her. "Last year's aggression by Clan Ghost Bear has him rightfully concerned for the independence of his Republic. He is most interested in keeping the good will of the Com Guard."

Katrina looked again toward Dehaver, suddenly wishing she'd invited him into the room. Watching her intently, he gave an almost imperceptible nod accompanied by a humorless smile. It took her a second to realize that he knew what she and Dow were saying. She couldn't figure out how, unless he knew how to read lips. She covered her surprise by walking over to take a seat at the end of the table nearest Dow.

"With Månsdotter backing you," Dow continued, "you could lose either of your other supporters and still be elected First Lord. And if you manage to keep all three, there is a very real chance that Theodore Kurita would also give you his vote to save face. That would elect you by unanimous decision."

Which would sit well three years from now when Katrina made her move to secure the First Lordship in perpetuity. Gavin Dow *did* have something that interested her after all.

"What do you want for this, Gavin?" she asked.

"I would like you to propose a resolution to make ComStar a voting member of the Council." He glanced over at Dehaver. "Would you like to consult with your intelligence aide again?"

Giving Dow her own unblinking version of a cat's

stare, she didn't take her eyes off him. "What do you suggest, Gavin?"

"You do this after Word of Blake's admission into the Star League, but before the final election of a new First Lord. Your concern is with the balance of power and fairness among the Council members. I will stand and accept the nomination, but ask that we be placed on a full term's probation, to match Word of Blake's status."

She nodded. "Which plays to Thomas Marik, who can voice no objection to such a fair-minded plan. Theodore will vote for you, hoping to offset Word of Blake joining Marik in a voting bloc. You already have Månsdotter."

Dow nodded slowly. "And we could care less what Sun-Tzu has to say. He's unpredictable, and so I try to always discount his support for my plans."

Was that a subtle warning concerning her own reliance on the Capellan Chancellor? As a high-ranking member of ComStar, Dow might know something she did not. Or he might simply be trying to sow doubt to further his own cause. "You came very well-prepared."

"I told you once, Archon, that there would come a time when you might welcome my support. From the way that conversation went, I knew I would have to do a better job of getting your attention this time."

Katrina remembered it well. The conversation had taken place via real-time HPG, though she had disconnected before it was finished. She had known that Dow's eagerness for an alliance could be made to work against him, so long as she kept him off balance. She smoothed one sleeve of her gown, then folded her hands confidently before her on the table's cold, smooth surface. "Well, you have adequately drawn my attention, Precentor. And your offer for *insurance* is . . . intriguing."

Gavin Dow flushed all the way to his silver-haired widow's peak. His appearance was truly striking, though Katrina could usually look past such superficial attributes for the more important, and dangerous, qualities. "I'm not here to play games this time, *Katrina*." He kept his tone conversational, but there was no mistaking his predatory glare. "I'm offering you everything you need, and more. Take the deal."

"And if I do not?" she asked.

He drew a small noteputer from his pocket, slid it onto the table between them. "Then you lose," he said. "I'll take my business elsewhere, and you can worry about who among your peers *will* listen to me. And I'll simply clear the report that came in this morning, which I had planned to present to you as gift."

If Dow was putting it on the table now, literally and figuratively, then it was his last—very last—offer. And he truly believed this report held value for her. Katrina tried not to look too interested as she nodded at the noteputer. "What is it?"

"Something you will find most interesting. It comes from the Draconis Combine. I believe your agents have been trying to discover the reason behind the Combine's recent communications blackout?"

"Perhaps they have," Katrina said. Her hands itched to seize the message device and read its contents, but she kept them folded tightly before her. What kind of leverage would the news give her over Theodore Kurita? "Are you saying that you know the answer?"

"That and more, Archon. That and more. If we have a deal."

Gavin Dow watched her closely, his eyes flicking away only once to check Dehaver's face through the ferroglass wall. Katrina watched him calmly, making sure that Dow knew that any decision came from her alone. Her choice. She nodded slowly, and reached out to take the missive.

"Let's see what you have," she said. "Then we had better prepare for the vote."

"And it is passed," Theodore Kurita said, casting the final vote. "Let the record show that ComStar is reaffirmed as a full member of the Star League by unanimous decision. Pending a one-term probationary period, they will be granted full voting privileges."

Applause for ComStar's new status rang louder and

longer over the Council than had Word of Blake's similar rise. A few people in the gallery stood in support of the decision, cheering. Though it was her victory as much as Dow's, Katrina met the applause with cool indifference. She watched Theodore retake his seat, damning him for the Combine's ruthless efficiency in keeping such news a secret. If she'd had possession of this information a month, a week—a day!—before, what it might have brought her besides intense personal satisfaction.

Even that had to wait. Caught up in interrogating Gavin Dow for the most minute details, followed by a hurried discussion with Richard Dehaver, Katrina had barely enough time to hurry back to the palace ballroom for the final Council session. Seeing Victor already seated in the gallery, she paused to nod in his direction and was pleased at his frown of confusion. Nondi Steiner looked equally displeased that she had bothered to recognize Victor, but Katrina ignored her questioning looks.

Gavin Dow stood, waved down the applause. "On behalf of Primus Sharilar Mori, the First Circuit, and all of ComStar, we do accept this gracious gesture. Our thanks to Archon-Princess Katrina Steiner-Davion for addressing the Council on our behalf."

"Yes, yes," Sun-Tzu said from his seat without being recognized. Today he shared the table only with Naomi Centrella, and it seemed as if his aunt's absence had removed any constraints of formality. *Or* politeness. "I'm certain we would all enjoy hearing of your *debt* to the Archon-Princess. Perhaps you could forward a report on the matter to us all."

Caught between his duty as chair and as representative of ComStar, Dow waited uncertainly, at a temporary loss for words. Thomas Marik actually rose to his defense, standing at Theodore's nod. "Chancellor Liao, your remarks are out of order *and* uncalled for. If you have a grievance, it should have been aired before the vote."

Katrina stood as Thomas sat back down, mentally chiding herself for allowing the older statesman to answer Sun-Tzu's improper challenge. She should have been on that first, but now it was better to move things along.

"As to voting, First Lord Kurita, I would like to be heard on our final matter of the day."

Sun-Tzu also stood. He wore a red robe of heavy brocade with gold dragons chasing each other over the front and the Chinese zodiac wheel emblazoned across the back. With his green eyes and cruel mouth, he looked most Capellan. "You have *another* proposal?" he scoffed. "Perhaps we should extend the Council another day."

"I was speaking of our final business to elect a new First Lord," Katrina said icily, caught halfway to the speaking podium. "If you could contain your impatience, Sun-Tzu, we won't delay you any longer than we must."

"Except that we have already been delayed overlong, and no further matters being handled here today affect me or mine. So, if you will excuse me, Katrina, I would like to be about the business of returning to my own realm." Sun-Tzu pushed his chair away with the backs of his legs, then stepped to one side and offered his arm to Naomi Centrella.

"Chancellor Liao, our official business has not been concluded," Theodore Kurita broke in, invoking his privilege as First Lord. "You are required to sit in on every public vote."

Naomi Centrella rested one hand on Sun-Tzu's arm. Whether she was attempting to pull him back to his seat or was waiting to stand with him, Katrina wasn't certain.

"I am required only to vote in a timely manner," Sun-Tzu said. "So, I shall make this simple for you all. In the matter of election of the First Lord, regardless of nominations or pleas"—he let his inscrutable gaze travel slowly around the other eight tables—"the Capellan Confederation wholly and without reservation . . . abstains."

In the silence that followed, he half-bowed, short and mockingly to Theodore Kurita. "I believe this concludes Capellan interest in this year's Council."

Treacherous, back-stabbing pit viper! Katrina wanted to scream, but she merely kept walking, past the Confederation's table and ComStar's, imagining the many things she would do to Sun-Tzu once her forces dragged him off Sian. Then, taking the speaker's table, she realized that he had lived up to the exact letter of his promise to her. He had not opposed her in any way, and in abstaining, he reclaimed his independence.

She gripped the podium with trembling hands, watching as Naomi Centrella accepted Sun-Tzu's arm, and the two pranced out of the ballroom. The small delegation from the Taurian Concordat remained at their table, though Grover Shraplen kept glancing furtively between the retreating pair and Theodore, obviously trying to decide whether or not to follow his allies out. He chose to remain, waiting to see who would respond to Sun-Tzu's withdrawal.

It had to be her. And in the same moment Katrina also realized that Sun-Tzu's action meant nothing in the grand scheme. In fact, he had all but secured the First Lordship for her. By abstaining, he left the Council divided into four voting members. It still required three votes to be elected, but now the worst-case situation would be a tie of two for and two against. In that case, Gavin Dow still held the tie-breaking vote.

And Dow owed it to *her*.

"First Lord Kurita," she said, and he acknowledged her request to speak with a curt nod. "If the Chancellor sees no benefit to his people in participating in our greatest duty and privilege of voting for your successor, we certainly cannot compel him. We can only move ahead in this matter, and it is with forward-thinking motives in mind that I would address this Council."

It wasn't *quite* the lead-in she'd wanted for her election, but in the end it would serve just as well. Always the conciliator, Katrina would now rise above Sun-Tzu's pettiness and bring to a close the Star League conference in the best interests of herself and her two realms.

"I had hoped that this year our Council would not be plagued with such petty difficulties, just as I have long hoped to come here with my thoughts directed solely toward the benefit of the Inner Sphere as a whole. Due to the arms my brother has raised against me, that hope has gone unrealized.

"Still, it is one you can help me to address. Peace benefits everyone, as we all remember so well from those few golden years after the end of the Clan invasion. A peace that came to such a sudden and shocking end when my brother, Arthur, was killed. Victor has accused me of many things since then, but truly those false charges have been nothing more than an attempt to keep me from moving toward peace." She swallowed hard, as if the memory of Arthur still pained her.

"My brother is a warrior, which is not a terrible thing. We need warriors when an enemy threatens. However, to create an enemy where one does not exist is not only folly, it is dangerous to us all. This we have also seen with the Combine annexation of the Lyons Thumb region, and in Duke Robinson's ill-fated expedition against House Kurita." She nodded respectfully to Theodore Kurita, acknowledging the wrong and making it more difficult for him to use the incident against her later.

Which he might not even try, given the distribution of the remaining votes and the futility of opposing her now. "So I am asking you for help," she said, "though not in soldiers or materiel. I would rather that no more lives were endangered. I am asking you to think about the way we want the Inner Sphere, the Periphery, and, yes, even the Clans, to view our new Star League. I am asking you to endorse me as First Lord. Not for the military strength my brother once gave up—for *that* I believe he was admirable, if ultimately misguided. I *am* asking for the political mandate, which I would hope to use to bring Victor to the peace table, to settle his grievances in a fair manner and return peace and prosperity to us all."

She drew a steadying breath and spread her hands against the podium as she looked down in a show of modesty. "I am asking you all to remember that what I have always sought is what is best for us all. Peace."

Silence followed her address, and she waited almost

too long for the Prince-regent of the Free Rasalhague Republic to stand. Christian Månsdotter saluted her with a clenched fist held to his breast. "I would second Katrina Steiner-Davion, and ask that we put her nomination to a formal vote," he said.

Victory. Katrina glanced at Theodore, saw the look of defeat flicker across his face. She also heard the rumble of voices in the gallery, and wondered how her brother would take the turn of public opinion against him. The one thing she did not consider was that the gallery was not for her, but for him.

"Point of order," Victor called out.

Katrina's self-satisfied glow faded as she looked past the tables and toward the gallery. She watched her brother stalk forward with short, determined strides. It's too late, she reassured herself. The vote had been called. There would be nothing Victor could do.

Not this time.

22

Royal Palace
Dormuth, Marik
Marik Commonwealth, Free Worlds League
14 November 3064

Victor stopped a respectful distance from the octagon of tables, staring defiantly at Katherine, who was obviously not about to give up the podium without a fight. Her confidence had waned for only an instant, a flash of doubt that vanished almost as soon as it came. Her glacial blue eyes stared through him now, a basilisk stare. Then his sister actually smiled. Secure. Supreme. Katherine truly thought she had a winning hand this time. Victor knew she just might.

Except that he planned to deal her next card from the bottom of the deck.

"I would like to address the Council," he said, turning to Theodore Kurita. The First Lord frowned, torn between protocol and reaching for the possible lifeline Victor offered.

"*First Lord*, we have before us a vote that in no way involves this person," Katherine cut in before Theodore could speak. "His presence in the gallery has been tolerated in the interest of building relations for future talks, but his interruption here, now, mocks our proceedings."

"A point of order may be called at any time to refute inaccurate facts," Victor said.

"Not by an outside party," Katherine rebutted. "The vote for First Lord is an internal matter to the Council. You have no standing here, Victor."

"I have a sponsor."

"Who?" Katherine shot an icy glance at Kurita. "Theodore? Hardly impartial, given your past history and, shall we say, personal ties?" She smiled with false kindness at the veiled reference to Omi. "If we allow you to ambush us now, what's to keep any one of us from parading in our own witnesses and turning this Council into a court room?"

Victor smiled and gave her a pitying look. "We'll have our time in a court room soon enough, Katherine. I promise you that. But in this case, you cannot argue any conflict of interest. First Lord Kurita is not my sponsor."

That stopped her cold. She had obviously not even considered the possibility that Victor had come to the conference on anyone but Theodore's coat tails. "Then who is?" she asked.

Thomas Marik stood. "I am, Katrina. I promised Victor my support if the need arose to defend his actions." He looked over at Theodore. "That promise is still good," he said.

Theodore nodded from his seat. "The Council will hear Victor Steiner-Davion."

Katherine held onto the podium as Victor made his way around the tables, as if physical possession of the platform would be enough to keep him from speaking. He ignored Gavin Dow's curious stare, and couldn't help wishing Anastasius Focht were here.

His sister finally surrendered the podium when he was only three paces away, but she placed herself directly in his path first, blocking him momentarily. "What do you think you can accomplish here, Victor?" she demanded in a harsh whisper. "What do you hope to prove?"

"I don't need to *prove* anything," he said evenly. "Accusations are damaging enough. A painful lesson I learned from you, as I recall."

"You don't know what pain is." From her greater height, Katherine looked down at him, not hiding her contempt. "But I think you will." She stepped aside, ceding the podium and returning to her own seat.

Victor's gaze followed her dignified retreat. Let her threaten him, he thought. Whatever she was planning, he would prepare for it later. Now was the time to put an end, once and for all, to Katherine's further ambitions.

"Katherine has tried to explain my mind and my actions to you," he began. "Since she has opened that door, I believe it is my duty to this Council to correct her misconceptions.

"For the record, let me remind the Council that I did not seek a civil war after my sister usurped the throne of the Lyran Alliance. I did not oppose her when she stole the Federated Suns from my regent, Yvonne Davion. I built a new life, away from the power my sister claims I crave, where I managed to live in peace. For twelve very short months."

Victor drew a steadying breath. "To my knowledge, I have never falsely accused Katherine of anything. That she has abused her position to manipulate worlds and events is self-evident. As to my references to violence against her own family, if she or anyone took that to refer to the tragic death of our brother, Arthur Steiner-Davion, that is a mistake. I freely admit that I do not know who killed Arthur."

He saw surprise ripple through the gallery, and even Thomas Marik could not totally conceal his astonishment at Victor's words. Katherine, though, tensed for the blow she knew was coming. "But I do know," Victor said, "who was behind the assassination of our mother. And I cannot stand by while this Council elects to its highest, most respected position a woman with her own mother's blood on her hands."

Katherine shot to her feet. "This is outrageous!" she cried, but her protest was all but drowned by the shouts of outrage that burst from the gallery and Theodore Kurita calling for order.

Thomas Marik was the one who finally got control of

the room, waving the gallery to silence as he rose to his feet. "Please, please." He face was as indignant as Katherine's. "Victor Davion, you cannot bring such accusations to this Council without evidence. What proof do you offer for these charges?"

Victor shook his head. "No more than Katherine offers in her baseless accusations against me. But I am not bringing formal charges against her, Thomas. Not yet. I am simply refusing to submit to the picture Katherine would like to paint of me." He held up one hand. "Do not mistake me, Lords of the Inner Sphere. I am gathering evidence. I have enough to convince but not convict."

Theodore rose slowly to his feet, bringing the number of people standing at the various tables to four. "If you are not asking for a forum to make charges, Victor, what are you asking of us?"

"Just that you consider carefully the possible bias on either side of this civil war, and take great care how you act. I ask that you take into account what you know of both my sister and me. Remember the political deals she has struck behind closed doors, the manipulations you have personally witnessed, and think of the cost you personally will have to pay in supporting her and anyone who allies with her.

"Ask yourself if this is the person you truly want for your First Lord."

Theodore Kurita glanced from one Steiner-Davion to the other. "Given the volatile nature of these conflicting accusations, I will give our current nominee for the position of First Lord the floor, if she desires. You have every right to refute your brother's unofficial charges, Katherine."

Before she could respond, Christian Månsdotter, Prince-regent of the Free Rasalhague Republic, also stood up. The final voting member of the Council, he rubbed at his chin and stared with concern toward the ComStar table. Gavin Dow and his companion, Gardner Riis, returned his look with unreadable expressions. Finally, Månsdotter seemed to come to a decision.

"First Lord," he said gravely, the dignity of his manner

and his voice winning him the floor. "The Free Rasalhague Republic withdraws its endorsement of Katherine Steiner-Davion."

With the Council ended, Victor, Theodore, Thomas Marik, and Hohiro Kurita gathered around the Rasalhague delegation. Jerrard Cranston and Morgan Kell joined them from the gallery, helping to block the table from the rest of the ballroom. Handshakes were solemnly offered, one at a time, to the new First Lord.

"Congratulations," Victor said, clasping Månsdotter's hand firmly. "What you did took courage." He followed Månsdotter's troubled gaze to the ComStar table, where Martial Gavin Dow glared back at them. "Probably more than I even know."

Christian Månsdotter nodded. The weight of his new office had already begun to weigh down his shoulders and deepen the lines around his eyes. Yet, his smile was genuine. The prestige and honor of claiming the First Lordship would be a boon to both his nation and his political future.

"Thank you, Victor," he said, then turned to Thomas Marik and offered his hand. "And I didn't thank you for the nomination, Thomas. It caught me quite by surprise. I have to admit that I figured Theodore to nominate you."

Marik shrugged and traded a meaningful look with the elder Kurita. "I expected as much also. But my history with Kath—Katrina—and with Victor, for that matter, would have made it difficult for me to be wholly impartial. Your nation has no direct ties with either the Alliance or the Federated Suns, and today you showed your willingness to act in the best interests of us all. That may be exactly what we need."

"It is still a daunting task," Månsdotter said, then traded deep bows with Theodore and Hohiro. "For now," he said to Hohiro, "I would appreciate your continuing to act as commanding general of the Star League Defense Force."

Bowing again, Hohiro said, "*Arigato*. It would be my pleasure to do so."

"Now, if you will excuse me." Månsdotter nodded toward the growing crowd also waiting to congratulate him. "I will do what I can to calm things down."

Victor watched a hint of the old Hohiro peek through the solemn mask his friend wore. "Call on me, Christian Månsdotter, if you require 'Mech support."

Thomas Marik also turned to leave, going to join his wife and Precentor Blane, who were involved in earnest conversation with Grover Shraplen of the Taurian Concordat. Victor watched, still trying to puzzle out who this man was, and again deciding that it really didn't matter. Thomas's actions had been above reproach, as usual.

Though the same could hardly be said of *him*.

"I really did not want to make this stand," he said to the tight group of friends remaining. "Not today. It's only going to buy us trouble."

Theodore Kurita shook his head. "Katherine cannot be allowed to become First Lord, Victor. Ever." He traded sharp glances with his son. "And you must not allow yourself to become distracted."

Morgan Kell reached out with his good arm to take Victor's shoulder in a solid grip. "I think it was best that you were the one who stopped her. Sun-Tzu ordered Candace offworld this morning. Now we know why." He paused, turning toward the empty Capellan table. "Candace told me she wasn't worried. That she knew you would see what was needed to win."

"Right," Victor said, with a touch of sadness. "I always win. In the end, I get what I'm after—what is needed—but others pay a high price."

"You're too hard on yourself, Victor," Jerry Cranston said.

"True," a new voice chimed in as Katherine joined the group. Trailing along was Richard Dehaver, sticking to her like some kind of living shadow. "But then, that was the way we were brought up. To make the hard decisions. Never to shirk what needed doing, no matter the personal cost." Her tone was only a few cool degrees from cordial. "Haven't you learned that after so many years at my brother's side . . . Galen?"

Victor froze, and a preternatural chill ran through his body. His sister seemed far too at ease, bringing up Jerry's past life. She was confident as ever, even in the face of her defeat. He remembered what she had said about him coming to know pain, and wondered what price she would demand of him now.

"Galen?" Hohiro Kurita asked, peering at Cranston as if meeting him for the first time. He searched the other man's face, past the blond beard and surgical alterations. "Galen Cox. You died."

"Everyone dies," Katherine said. "Some of them come back." She smiled almost shyly at Cranston, the man she had once asked to marry her and then had abandoned to an assassin's bomb. When she turned back to Hohiro, her eyes were laser-bright. "Some of them don't."

Hohiro rocked back as if slapped. He paled, then glared at Katherine as if about to eviscerate her with a draw cut.

Victor knew something important had just passed between his sister and his friend. He watched as Hohiro flexed his fingers, as though searching for the grip of his katana. "You're taking this far better than I would have thought, Katherine," he said.

"Did you think I would fly into a rage, Victor? Embarrass myself and *my* nations in front of the Star League?" Except for the slight emphasis on the possessive, Katherine's tone was almost conciliatory. "I am disappointed, yes. With you especially. You just can't admit when you're wrong, or when you've lost. But I can't be angry with you now, not after you showed such strength in front of the Council. In the face of your own tragic loss, that is."

Victor's eyes shot straight at Jerry Cranston. They had leaked the news about Galen Cox to her years before, hoping to put her on the defensive, never thinking that she might throw it back at them. Jerry gave Victor an almost imperceptible shake of his head as if to say he had no news of a military defeat on Tikonov, the only tragic loss that could set back their plans.

Or so they thought.

"Loss?" Victor asked, ready for some bluff or other manipulative ploy. His sister was like a colorful but poisonous spider spinning her web.

Watching her so closely, he almost missed the reaction of two other friends. The stiffness of their military postures and the trapped looks on their faces before they managed to reassume the impassive mask so typical of every Combine warrior gave them away. Theodore and Hohiro *knew*. Whatever Katherine was referring to, they knew.

"Yes . . ." Katherine sounded suddenly unsure, as if blundering into some social gaffe. "When I received the report from out of the Combine, I naturally assumed—"

"Victor," Theodore said urgently. "Victor you *must* come with me at once. This is not the time."

Hohiro actually laid a hand on Victor's arm, as if to compel him. Victor shook it off.

"Not the time for what?" he demanded, but icy fingers had already taken hold of his heart.

"You mean they haven't told you?" Katherine blanched, her face in shock. "Your friends . . . ? Oh, Victor, how *terrible* for you." She glanced around at the assembled men, playing the sorrowful relation to the hilt. Her poisoned gaze held Victor trapped, her ice-blue eyes seizing his, drawing him down.

"I would never have dreamed I would be the one who had to tell you," Katherine said in a rush, as though so very, very sorry for him. "Of course, it's the reason I cannot be cross with you just now. What I felt the day our mother was killed, I feel for you now, dear brother.

"Now that you have lost your dear and precious Omi."

Driven Before
the Winds

23

Rockland, Tikonov
Capellan March
Federated Suns
8 January 3065

Rudolf Shakov did not like hospitals. He'd spent far too much time in them, either in their care while recovering from battlefield injuries or, worse, visiting men and women who'd been wounded under his command.

It was always the same. You were greeted at the door by an antiseptic smell and the impersonal attitude of a reception staff who knew you were now in their domain and under their power. Both the atmosphere and the attitude usually went downhill from there. Hostile rooms of bright chrome beds and cold, bleached walls. Harried nurses with little time for questions. Novice doctors only too eager to dispense their dearly purchased knowledge, usually in long, technical terms. For the simple, factual questions most people usually wanted to ask, they referred you back to the nurses.

Shakov doubted that the Sisters of Mercy on Tikonov would be an exception.

But it was, at least in one regard. A yellow-robed ComStar adept waited to greet him near the reception desk. He was an elderly man, which was odd for an adept, with eyes of washed-out green and thin to the point of emaciation. Those eyes had obviously seen much in their time.

The man's hood was thrown back over his shoulders, his lack of vanity revealed by his long, tangled red hair. The clasp at his throat displayed the Greek *kappa* of ComStar's medical services, and his rate level of XXI years made up slightly for his advanced age. Enough that Shakov took him at face value as the adept trailed after him toward the elevators.

"The Peace of Blake be with you," the man said as the doors closed.

A Blakist! Shakov flattened his back against the elevator wall, expecting violence and feeling the lack of a weapon on his uniform belt. But the adept made no threatening moves. He simply stared back at Shakov with serene patience.

"I did not mean to alarm you. I come with a simple message, Demi-Precentor Shakov."

"Anything wrong with Word of Blake's HPG stations?" Shakov retorted, sizing the man up as a potential enemy. He relaxed slightly as he realized that the elderly adept was not just thin, but frail.

"If you would rather risk your superiors finding out we had contacted you or that the Eleventh Arcturan Guards might learn that you had been warned of their arrival on Tikonov, then we could leave this to an impersonal transmission."

The Eleventh Arcturan? On Tikonov? "You have my attention, Adept . . . ?"

The man smiled slightly. "Precentor. And my name is unimportant next to Blake's prophecy and our Master's grand design. Your attention, though, is appreciated."

The elevator slowed to a halt, and the doors opened onto the floor Shakov had selected. The Blakist nodded him forward, but did not leave the elevator. Shakov glanced down the corridor in both directions, and it was empty. "You have something you want to tell me?" he asked, confused.

"I already have. When you seek further guidance, Demi Shakov, we will be here."

The doors rolled to a close, leaving Shakov alone and bewildered. The brief encounter had left him with a great deal to think about on his short walk down the beige-tiled hall. Word of Blake had made contact, delivering important military intelligence but asking for nothing in return.

Truly, the Blakists worked in mysterious ways.

Finding the room he'd been looking for, Rudolf Shakov walked in on an argument. A man in hospital gown, his arm stuck with an IV, was banging shut an empty closet door. "Clothes!" he shouted at the doctor. His dark brown eyes flicked briefly toward Shakov, then away.

The doctor had sought refuge behind one of the nurses, a large woman with a no-nonsense air who looked as if she might have made a good field sergeant. From his position of safety, he wielded his clipboard like an armored shield. "As I told you, General, your uniform was collected by a corporal from your regiment. He will have it ready in time for your release later this afternoon."

"I'm releasing myself now, Doctor." Shakov took the patient to be Leftenant General Jonathan Sanchez, the person he'd come looking for.

"Sir, I can't authorize that just yet. You came in delirious from fluid loss and malnutrition. Twelve hours' observation is warranted."

In truth, thought Shakov, the patient did not look altogether well. His face was flushed in exasperation, but underneath the false color, the dark eyes were weary and a light sweat had already broken out on his forehead from the simple exertion. His bare arms and neck had a gray pallor to them, as if reflecting the drab gown.

"Eleven hours too long," Sanchez snapped. Though he was about the same size as the physician, his hard-bitten personality filled the room like a much larger man's. "I won't stay tied to a bottle while I have soldiers out there expecting relief." He grabbed at the IV tube that dangled from his wrist, no doubt intending to yank it out.

The nurse stopped him with an iron grip on his wrist. Shakov expected her voice to grate on the ears, stern and commanding. Instead, it was soft and filled with a kind of warm comfort that must have taken years to perfect. "General Sanchez, that's *my* work you're about to ruin. We respect your work, sir. Please respect ours."

Shakov took the opportunity afforded by Sanchez' hesitation to step forward. "General Sanchez, it's good to see you up and around. When we heard you'd been brought in on a stretcher, we feared the worst."

Shakov's white fatigues gave him away as Com Guard, but the general quickly read more from his branch and rank insignia. "Seventh Army, Epsilon. Demi-Precentor. You're a warrior with the 244th Division." A pause of respect. "You broke the siege at Kolcha."

"Precentor Irelon commanded that operation, General, but I was there. Demi-Precentor Rudolf Shakov." He bowed slightly. "We tried to pull you out of the Herosoma Mountains, but the Deneb Light Cavalry had chased you in too deep."

Sanchez frowned at the memory. "We had to sabotage our own armor units and leave them for the Cavalry. Spread my infantry to hell and gone over those mountains. You ever try to take a company of 'Mechs over knife-backed mountains in the dead of winter, Demi-Precentor? I don't recommend it." Then, almost as if in an afterthought, "Who pulled my bacon out of the fire, anyway?"

"Sixth Crucis Lancers. Their XO, Albert Jehlik, led a combined forces team that broke the Cavalry cordon."

"I'll be owing him a drink after this is all over. You too, if you can help me find some clothes."

"Nurse Anson," Shakov said, reading the name off her badge while the doctor tried edging his way out from her protection, "the general needs that IV removed and something—anything—to wear. By the time you return, I promise the doctor will have seen it our way." She hesitated. "The sooner we get him to our command center, the fewer men you'll see come in on stretchers and the fewer I'll zip into a nylon bag. Please."

Giving him a businesslike nod, she turned and left the

room with a determined stride, abandoning her superior to his fate. Shakov backed away, giving Sanchez clear access to the physician. "You going to give us an argument?" he asked the man.

"I still recommend against it," the doctor said. "But if you want to sign yourself out AMA—er, against medical advice—I can't stop you." He scribbled something on his board as Nurse Anson returned with some clothing. "Try to keep him well-hydrated for the next twenty-four hours."

Sanchez waited pointedly for the doctor and Anson to leave. "All right. What's the problem?" he asked Shakov.

"Problem?"

"You don't send a precentor, even a *demi*-precentor, down to worry the local medics without cause. Unless you have a love for hospitals."

Shakov wrestled with the problem of how much to tell him for all of two seconds. "Between our forces and what we've recovered from your cadre regiment and the Valexa CMM, we have the equivalent of four regiments on planet. Even so, we're losing Tikonov.

"The Free Tikonov Movement has resurfaced and is apparently working with the Third Republican Guard, which means we've begun fighting old Capellan loyalties as well as Katherine's loyalists. And now I have a report that the Eleventh Arcturan Guard has joined the battle. If they followed us through the Terran Corridor, they might have brought elements of other units with them from Lyran space."

With only one leg halfway through his pants, Jonathan Sanchez stopped at mention of the Eleventh Arcturan. "How reliable is that intelligence?"

"Better than I'd like to believe," Shakov said, not wanting to mention that the news came from Word of Blake. He would discuss that with Precentor Irelon only. "Most of us have been here a couple of months, at best. Morgan Kell arrived only two weeks ago. You've had almost a year to get to know Tikonov and the core of Katherine's loyalists. You held out against impressive odds."

"I was fighting for my life." The general grabbed for his shirt. "Staying on the run as much as possible, turning back to snap at the Republicans and the Cavalry whenever they thought to write us off as broken. It was all I could do to tie them down."

"It was enough. Morgan Kell wants you sitting in on our planning sessions as soon as possible."

Sanchez held up one hand. "Wait a second, Shakov. You're talking as if Prince Victor didn't make planetfall. Even in the Herosoma Mountains, we heard about *that*. For awhile it was all over the radio intercepts we picked up." Outside the room, nurses ran past in response to a muted alarm somewhere down the corridor. Sanchez stepped forward abruptly. "Has something happened to the Prince?"

"Yes, but it's not what you're thinking," Shakov said. "Prince Victor ran into some . . . trouble . . . on Marik." He didn't add that Victor was like a man whose heart had been ripped from his chest. "Let's just say that in the last two weeks, we have not seen what we need from the Prince."

The general finished dressing quickly and in silence. Shakov waited, feeling every second stretch by in miserable length as he thought again about Word of Blake and the news that the Eleventh Arcturan had arrived. The allied forces needed Sanchez, and needed him now.

"Take me to him," Sanchez finally said, managing to look impressive even in the wrinkled hospital scrubs. "Take me to Victor. You can continue filling me in on the way."

"Actually, we should stop by the command center. If the Eleventh Arcturan *have* made planetfall—"

"Victor is not at the center?" Sanchez didn't wait for an answer. "I think it's more important now than ever that I see him. And perhaps you should begin your full brief with what happened on Marik." The general gestured for the door, then followed Shakov into the hall and toward the elevators. "We'll worry about the Eleventh Arcturan and how to secure Tikonov, after."

"General," Shakov said, staring at their reflections in

the bright, polished elevator doors, "we're not exactly looking to secure Tikonov."

Sanchez frowned. "Well, what then?"

Shakov held the other man's cutting gaze steadily. There was no easy way to say it, except straight out. "We think we need to start planning our eventual retreat," he said simply, softly, as the elevator doors slid open.

He stepped forward into the small car, finding room beside an orderly pushing a young woman and her new baby in a wheelchair. Sanchez remained outside a moment longer, staring. Then he stepped into the elevator and joined the heaviest silence Rudolf Shakov had ever known.

24

The Fox's Den felt smaller than Katrina remembered from the days when it had been her father's war room. At first, she thought it was the extra terminals that had been added over the years, or that the display screens had been enlarged until they covered three walls. But none of that was enough. It felt as if the walls were physically closer, as if the entire room had shrunk in disuse.

Or maybe it was simply that the presence of Hanse Davion was missing.

Her father had had a way of filling up a room. Not stifling or overbearing—though he could be both when it suited him—but more as a catalyst. She recalled it as a warm, excited feeling. He made a place come alive. People felt more important under his gaze, and there was always that sense that great things were afoot.

Katrina began to regret her decision to hold this briefing here, though her entrance into the Fox's Den created a stir. In no small measure, she suspected, because she had her Marshal of the Armies and the Prince's Champion in tow.

A pair of lieutenants talking over coffee suddenly discovered that they had a great deal of work to do. They leaned quickly over the shoulders of the intelligence analysts, interfering with the efforts being made at the various data terminals. The workload seemed to double before her eyes, though the frantic pace lessened as Dehaver arrived and dismissed one officer and a handful of analysts.

"You have something you wished to show me?" Katrina asked Jackson Davion after the group had left.

Davion dismissed the holographic tank, and had an analyst shunt data from a terminal to be projected on the largest wall screen. The stretch of space that the Federated Suns shared with the Draconis Combine flared to life, with force-maneuver lines showing paths of attack and retreat. Katrina did not require any detailed explanation to see that forces belonging to her Draconis March lord had been forced off another Kurita world, and that the Combine had again attacked across the border into *her* realm.

"Cassias," she said in a low voice filled with irritation at the world's planetary garrison.

Jackson nodded. "It was left to the Third Crucis Lancers after the Seventeenth Hussars abandoned it. The Lancers have since moved to support Tancred Sandoval, so what's left are some under-trained militia and a regiment of armor left behind by the Seventeenth."

Simon Gallagher adjusted his square-lensed glasses. "So, we're fighting the Combine on four of our own worlds now." Never a strategic genius, the man's greatest value was being loyal to a fault. He was also underinformed.

"Three," Jackson corrected. "The Combine smashed the Eighth Urukhai on Addicks, and now they're sitting there uncontested."

"Theodore can't be thinking about keeping that world," Katrina said, fighting back the anger that was always so close to the surface these last few months. Her defeat on Marik stared back from the mirror every morning. Even without Victor's recent failures, she couldn't help thinking how much stronger would be her position with the Star League banner flying behind her.

"No," Jackson said. "The Twenty-fourth Dieron Regulars pursued the Fighting Urukhai there purely out of spite after they took back Al Na'ir. It's too far from the Combine border to properly defend, and the Davion Assault Guards have pulled half their force from the fighting on Tigress to deal with them." He paused. "But Cassias or Breed or Kesai IV—those the Coordinator might keep."

"When and if he takes them," Simon Gallagher said. "And we still have Proserpina. Or at least Duke Sandoval does, and he claims he can hold on to it indefinitely."

"If he had the full strength of his March behind him," Jackson countered, "but he doesn't. His son has drawn off most of the Woodbine Operations Area *and* the LeBlanc PDZ. Also, I remind you that the Tenth Lyran Guard has finally decided to leave Robinson, answering Morgan Kell's summons. As of this morning, they have commandeered enough transport. While it removes the threat of Victor forcibly replacing James Sandoval with Tancred, our March capital is now extremely vulnerable. If Theodore Kurita notices—"

"Theodore Kurita would not dare touch Robinson," Richard Dehaver broke in. "It would reunite Tancred with his father, and they would roll across the border with everything Tancred has built up in Victor's support."

Katrina was not a military mind, but she knew an opportunity when she heard one. "Can we arrange that?" she asked bluntly.

"I would never gamble so lightly with the security of the Draconis March," Jackson said, trying not to look appalled as he came as close as he dared to reprimanding Katrina.

Of course, he wouldn't. But Katrina could always make it happen through Simon, her "champion," if it became necessary. "What are you suggesting then, Jackson?"

He bent over one terminal and rapidly entered some input. On the large wallscreen, the Combine world of

Proserpina flared doubly bright. "Perhaps it is time to take this to the Star League. We could trade Proserpina for a complete Combine withdrawal. If we had Månsdotter's backing, Theodore would have to comply."

Being reminded of Christian Månsdotter's election was not a way to win points in this debate, but neither did Katrina intend to stick her head in the sand by denying the bitter reality of the situation. "Are we truly at the point of no other options?" she asked.

Her Marshal hesitated, which was all she needed. "Then we wait. Theodore and I have worked carefully to keep this out of the Star League's hands. If it must go there eventually, it would be better, I think, to force Theodore to sue for peace first." Also, it left open the Robinson Gambit, should she eventually need it.

"Do you have anything more for me?" she asked.

Jackson traded looks with Simon Gallagher, then shrugged. "The battles on Kathil and Wernke have swung heavily in our favor. Tikonov, in my opinion, is just a matter of time. Victor has a slightly larger force on the planet, but we currently hold all the manufacturing sites but one—Harcourt Industries—and we've shut down the Terran Corridor for now. Without solid logistic support, he can't hold."

"There is still the Tenth Lyran Guard," Katrina reminded her two officers. "The Revenants are my brother's personal unit, and we've been fortunate that Duke Sandoval had them distracted on Robinson this long. If they make it to Tikonov . . ."

"They won't," Dehaver put in.

His words caught them all off guard, though Katrina thought she was growing used to Dehaver's little surprises. "If you have information for us, Richard, let's have it now."

"The JumpShip transporting the Tenth Lyran Guard was rendered inoperable when it arrived in the Kentares system. The integrity of one of its helium tank seals was compromised." He spoke without emotion, as if reciting an intelligence briefing. "Repairs are expected to take several weeks at the local recharge station. No other nearby transport is available, due to the severe shipping shortages that have so recently plagued the Draconis March."

Simon Gallagher smiled. "When did this happen?"

"Tomorrow." Dehaver checked the chronometer, which flashed military time from one corner of the room. "In about eleven hours, to be precise."

Jackson Davion also couldn't help but smile. "Then we're even better established than I thought. So, the question is actually mine, Highness. What further do you need from me?"

She paused, considered the timing. "We must begin preparations for an assault on New Syrtis," she said. "To commence within six months."

"Six months?" Jackson didn't hide his surprise. "Highness, no matter what Duke Hasek told you on Marik, he has made no direct move to support your brother."

"I'll tell you what George Hasek told me on Marik, Jackson. He said he would never stand for my ruling the Federated Suns. He threw it in my face in public. Obviously, he meant it as a challenge."

"Why would he warn you like that?" Gallagher asked. "If he was going to throw in with Victor, you'd think he'd do it when we weren't looking." He shook his head and ran his fingers through what was left of his graying hair. "Doesn't make sense."

"It makes sense if you understand George Hasek," Katrina said. "Like my brother, he has this underlying belief that personal honor still plays some part in warfare. Giving me fair warning is his misguided attempt at chivalry." Seeing Jackson's frown, she immediately regretted speaking quite so freely in front of her Marshal of the Armies.

Jackson Davion also believed in chivalrous warfare, while Katrina considered warcraft a tool of the state, to be employed with ruthless efficiency, but only as a final option. "I've waited to see what Victor would do, but he's sitting tight on Tikonov. It's time to begin looking to the future, and that future does not hold George Hasek."

"So you want a contingency plan, in case Hasek strikes

at you," Jackson said, though he didn't sound convinced. "I can supply that."

Katrina nodded. She could pass the plans off to Simon Gallagher, when she saw the need to launch preemptively. "From what I've seen from all your reports, it comes down to this. Only Tancred Sandoval stands ready to support Victor, should he make it off Tikonov ready to drive forward." She was answered by three nods. "Excellent. Then we truly are at the beginning of the end."

"Except that if he does?" Simon asked. "What if Victor's people do secure Tikonov?"

"In that unlikely event, we deal with Sandoval first and Victor second. Remember, all we have to do is stalemate my brother until the Lyran Alliance is secured behind him. We are almost there, I think. Victor seems to have lost the big picture since the Star League Conference. As a means to fight his grief, he is obsessing about Tikonov, and in doing so, his plans are beginning to unravel in both nations. Now, work on finding all the loose threads so we can pull them a bit harder."

Katrina didn't need any further discussion, confident that at last she had the upper hand over Victor. Fate had finally intervened. Fate, and an assassin. Even if Victor escaped her forces now, she doubted he had the personal will to see the war through to the end. Nodding farewells to her officers, she left the Fox's Den to them. Victor has lost, she told herself again. He just didn't know it yet.

Looking back from the door, the war room did seem a little bit bigger.

25

Francesca Jenkins knew within two minutes of setting foot on Tikonov that something had gone wrong, just as she had feared when she and Curaitis first heard the news about Omi Kurita. It wasn't just the harassment by loyalist aerospace fighters during her DropShip's inbound run from the jump point. That was all part of the job, and those heart-in-throat minutes were all but forgotten as she saw Jerrard Cranston pull up in a ground car at the foot of the ship's exit ramp. She descended the ramp and got in, glad to trade the day's early humidity for air conditioning.

Francesca had been trained by two intelligence agencies to be a keen observer, and she read a lot into Cranston's behavior. He made no request for a preliminary brief, no attempt even at idle conversation as they drove to the city of Rockland's small military post. She couldn't help thinking that men were all alike. When times got hard, the social graces were the first thing to fall by the wayside. Instead, "the silence" would set in, its weight oppressive and stifling.

She waited, judging the severity of the situation by

how long it took Cranston to speak. It wasn't until they were actually walking into the command center that he finally broke the uncomfortable silence and gave her a thumbnail brief of how Victor had learned of the assassination and that he "wasn't taking it well."

When she finally saw the Prince, she realized that that was an understatement. Surrounding him were officers and busy aides, reminding her of a hive-mind colony swarming protectively around their leader. The walls of the command center were covered with maps displaying maneuver lines, unit names, and force strengths pinned into place with colored tacks or, when possible, magnets. Victor seemed to be directing three battles at once, or at least monitoring them, always in motion around the large planning room.

But despite this appearance of energy and control, she saw the signs of extreme exhaustion in his slow pace and the way he held himself up with arms braced on any available surface, be it table, desktop, wall, or computer terminal. He rarely stood erect except to actually move from one location to another, and even then he trailed a hand against any nearby support. When someone asked him a question, it took an obvious moment for Victor to organize his thoughts. An aide followed him around with a steaming mug—broth, it looked like—and took any chance to press it into his hands. More often than not, Victor handed it back without drinking.

Francesca was so intent on observing him that it took her a moment to spot the room's secondary focus, which branched off from Victor's personal chain of command. She read it by the occasional aide who was called over to report to the man drifting along in Victor's wake, and in the officers who nodded with respect as he passed by. Though she had never met him, Francesca easily recognized Duke Morgan Kell from her time spent in the Arc Royal Defense Cordon.

It took only a second for the lull in the room's constant buzz to draw Francesca's attention back to Victor, who had paused between maps and was now watching her watching Morgan Kell. He didn't know her at first, but seemed to recognize that she didn't fit into the room's organization. Then his memory kicked in.

"Agent Jenkins," he said, then nodded to Cranston. "Jerry told me you would arrive today." He pulled away from what he was doing. As far as she could see, the activity in the room proceeded just as smoothly without him.

"You chose a busy day for a visit," he said. "Katherine's forces are pushing hard. I don't have a lot of time . . ."

This close, Francesca saw the dark circles around his eyes and the bloodshot whites that looked almost pink. She also noticed that he held an oblong brass disk in one hand, which he rubbed and rotated in an almost obsessive manner.

"This could wait till tomorrow, Highness."

Curaitis had warned her that it might be like this, that Victor had slept rarely after his mother's death, living in a round of constant activity, most of which centered around an obsession with finding the assassin. They'd eventually caught the killer and even managed to use him against one of his employers before he escaped custody. The same assassin had carried out Omi Kurita's death, no doubt hired by a vengeful Katherine, and Curaitis had predicted the result. On top of his grief, Victor would have to deal with the fact that he had once held the assassin in his grasp—might have stopped him from ever killing again—and then lost him.

"I doubt tomorrow will be any better," he said. "We've received word that the Tenth Lyran Guard has been delayed, again, and Harcourt Industries is shaping up into a disaster." His voice cracked a bit from overuse. He took the mug from his aide, sipping just enough to soothe his throat.

"Highness, when did you last sleep?" Francesca couldn't help asking

He took a second sip of what smelled like beef broth. "No time," he said vaguely, setting the mug aside on a table. "We have to be ready for the Revenants. And at least one WarShip we can't account for is still prowling about the system somewhere. I don't suppose your in-bound run detected it?" He waited for Francesca to shake her head. "I didn't think so, but you never know. So, what can you tell me?"

"We've been working Katherine's nerves for more than a year now, Highness. Curaitis checked with his contacts on New Avalon, and it seems that she's been more angry than threatened by Reg Starling's resurrection. Except that she authorized a large covert op against Starling's art dealer a few months back, which we're taking as a sign of her increased agitation. So we're upgrading to Phase Three."

Francesca paused when Victor shook his head once, violently, obviously trying to ward off the creeping stupor of sleep-deprivation. She checked to see that he was still following her words. "Curaitis has gone ahead to New Avalon. I'll join him there for our final play."

The Prince seemed to perk up. "So you have the evidence?"

"We can prove that she has tried to suppress Starling's works, with lethal intent in at least one case. Now we need to establish her more personal ties to his old identity as Sven Newmark. Once we have that, we can prove obstruction of justice. We need to validate Newmark's original files that implicate her in the plot . . ." She trailed off, cursing herself for skating so close to the subject of Melissa Davion's assassination ". . . in Ryan Steiner's plot. The chain is almost complete, Highness."

Victor's energy level had risen, and he shifted uncomfortably in his obvious desire to return to his interrupted activities. Or perhaps mention of his mother's death had him on edge. "Very good, Francesca. And please pass on my appreciation to Agent Curaitis as well."

He stopped fumbling with the object in his hands long enough for Francesca to see that it was a *tsuba*, a sword-guard, meant to slide over the blade of a katana. The brass circle was fashioned in the shape of a dragon, coiled around to bite its own tail. Victor glanced over his shoulder, as if missing someone, then said, "I will leave it to Jerry to get the full details of your plans."

She waited for him to move from earshot, then turned to Morgan Kell, who'd stepped over to join her and Cranston. "What is he running on?" she asked quietly.

"Vapors," Kell said. "Vitamin supplements and four hours of exhausted sleep, if he's lucky. Victor is holding himself together right now by staying busy, Ms. Jenkins. It's enough to provide some direction, keep the troops occupied, but he keeps bogging down in the nuts and bolts of the daily routine." He glanced at Jerrard Cranston, who had also come over. "And you can tell Agent Curaitis that it's going to get worse before it gets better—*if* it gets better."

Cranston shook his head. "We saw Victor through this once before. He can pull out of it. He will."

"It's different this time, Jerry," said Kell. Francesca found him difficult to read, with a natural poker face earned in a lifetime of secrets and hard decisions.

"What makes you so certain?" she asked.

"I've been there," he said. "Victor's strong. One of the strongest men I've ever known. But there are some truths even he can't fight." He looked from Francesca to Cranston. "No matter what, he can't *win* this one."

"And Tikonov?" she asked. She and Curaitis would need some idea of when Victor might move forward toward New Avalon. "What about Tikonov?"

"It depends on whether the Tenth Lyran Guard can find their way here in time, on whether we can keep Harcourt Industries or maybe free up some other production facilities to establish a new logistics center here. And it depends on whether we can convince the Eleventh Arcturan Guard to pack up and head back to the Alliance." He shook his head. "Too many things can still go wrong, and I have to admit that inspiration has been lacking from everyone of late."

Morgan took a step closer and lowered his voice. "What it comes to, Agent Jenkins, is that you need to get to New Avalon as soon as you've briefed us thoroughly. We're going to need any evidence against Katherine you can eventually hand over.

"If things don't improve soon, it may be all we have to stop her."

Gray smoke from the woods burning to the east drifted in piles and thinning streams across the Tukwila Valley, barely overriding the acrid, burnt-cordite smell of ordnance that hovered over the battlefield. Enemy artillery fire continued to pummel the no-man's land separating Brevet-General Linda McDonald's loyalists from the allied forces, forcing her to stay her hand while the Crucis Lancers and the Com Guards desperately tried to buy time for a counterattack.

The enemy had not given up the city of Tukwila easily—and with it, control of the Harcourt production facilities—and they wanted it back. Both sides knew its value to the battle for Tikonov. McDonald's infantry forces controlled it now, and at the moment there was nothing to which she was more dedicated than continuing to deny Victor the armor-producing factories.

And that shift in her priorities was only one of an entire host of new difficulties.

As it turned out, she cared much less about her field promotion to brevet-general than she would ever have imagined. It was everything Leutnant-General Maria Esteban had groomed her for, but it also took her beyond the more hands-on role of a MechWarrior. Strapped into the secondary seat of her *King Crab,* at the mercy of Colonel Vance Evans, who was still getting used to the controls of her hundred-ton machine, McDonald's primary concern had to be for the greater strategy. When missiles rained down hard on the *King's* broad back, when Evans failed to turn inside to bring the 'Mech's twelve-centimeter autocannon into play against a flanking Goblin support vehicle, all she could do was clench her teeth and grip her armrests as if she could pilot the 'Mech with them herself.

Some officers, she knew, could hold an entire battle in their heads while also fighting their 'Mech in combat. Victor Davion was one of those, by all reports. As was the commander of the Com Guard 244th Division, who had stalked opposite her position most of the day in his *Crockett.* Precentor Irelon and Rudolf Shakov, his surviving command-level officer in an *Exterminator,* had already cost her twice the 'Mech's tonnage in casualties.

The problem wasn't just that she couldn't participate as fully in a combat role, but that the Eleventh Arcturan Guards had never functioned well in large-scale engagements. Regimental maneuvers had atrophied their abilities rather than improved them, forcing them to rely heavily on strength of numbers and a brute-force battle of attrition. Not the ideal situation, and one she hoped to quickly improve.

Maria Esteban was counting on her, having left McDonald in command on Tikonov while she returned to Lyran space with one of their two WarShips to marshal further resistance against Victor Davion. The plan was for Esteban to slam shut the back door, while McDonald burned the house down around Victor's head.

"The Lancers are bending around again," Leutnant Friedrickson, one of her new lance commanders, warned. His voice broke up every few words in a crackle of static as PPC discharges interfered with communications. "Falling back for reinforcement."

The man was far too cautious. Reading her tactical screen, McDonald knew that her left flank was in no real danger from the Crucis Lancers. It was a probe attempt, no real offensive.

"Disregard that, Leutnant," she snapped. "Push forward and concentrate fire." She read the code designations attached to the Lancer icons. "Bring down that *Penetrator* or don't bother reporting back to base."

On her screen, she watched as the Lancers played out further west, shifting from a straight echelon-right formation to a right-flank advance. The Lancers' main force could hurt her if she let them get around her flankers. Friedrickson was in the wrong place, her weakest officer in a critical position, but there was no moving him now and she could compensate.

"Hauptmann Sergei," she ordered, "take command of the left flank and move forward to support the push."

Watching a battle play out at the strategic level was no substitute for the lethal reality of fighting in it, but it had its advantages. The Lancer probe turned out to be a diversion that allowed the 244th to reorganize into an arrowhead formation, moving armor to the front and backing it up with their short column of BattleMechs and armored infantry. They would be coming soon, slamming into her line, attempting to cut her forces apart so that the Lancers could roll up one entire flank.

McDonald sent two squadrons of VTOLs stinging in against the Prince's Men, harassing their point and blunting it when a pair of Yellow Jacket gunships gutted a Demolisher. Fire belched out of the hole where the tank's turret had been, roiling greasy smoke into an already-hazy sky. She ordered her right flank to curl forward, but they had trouble holding a solid line and clumped into company-sized units, her MechWarriors habitually outpacing the slower armor support. Still, they were learning. And so was she. Maybe she *should* try taking the cockpit controls next time.

The thought kept her company right up until the entire world shook apart and her carefully laid plans spilled out in a jumble of panicked thoughts.

Whatever had happened, it happened fast. One moment her line was holding, even pressing forward to push the allied forces further away from Tukwila. The next, her headset was flooded with overlapping communications and the *King Crab* was knocked to the ground. Colonel Evans was trying to get the 'Mech back on its feet by rocking onto its front. Vertigo gripped McDonald for a moment as her equilibrium trailed behind Evans' attempts to right the armored behemoth.

"Evans, what the hell was that?" She shook her head clear, wincing as a spasm pained her neck. She remembered a violent shove into the left side of her command chair, and the spinning sensation of the fall. She put together what had happened even before Evans replied.

"Took a glancing blow from an Arrow IV missile. Ah, it's a nightmare out here, General."

That she could see for herself. The chaos visible through her ferroglass shield left little doubt that the 244th had slammed ahead as she'd suspected, though not directly for her center. She checked tactical, saw that the Com Guard armor battalion had cut through her right flank and opened a hole into her rearward lines. McDonald chewed her lower lip as she worked to mentally untangle the communications mess while her officers tried to pull together as a regiment.

To blazes with that, she decided. If the Prince's Men wanted to break her regiment up, she'd oblige.

"Reserves, seal that breech," she ordered, calling up elements from the two militia units still appended to her Arcturan Guard. "Pull out in a secondary line and back both flanks. Hauptmann Sergei, you will lead the left flank forward. Now, by companies, charge the Lancers and keep them back. Two-minute press, then fall back for Tukwila." It would cost her a few machines, breaking down her command into its component parts, but she knew the kind of damage and chaos her team could inflict if released from artificial restraints.

"Striker Battalion," she continued, "break up and hunt armor. Ignore the 244th 'Mechs as much as you are able. If they're going to throw armor around like it can solve their problems, I want them to know the cost."

Evans had the *King Crab* on its feet again, lumbering forward at the head of another company to meet the oncoming BattleMechs of the Prince's Men. "And us, General?" he asked.

She didn't bother with the comm, selecting to mute her mic and simply shouting between the *King Crab*'s two cockpits. "If I have to change whatever you're doing, Vance, you'll be first to know."

In the meantime, she ordered her armor support to push forward, outpacing the slower *King Crab* and worrying the Com Guard line before the *King*'s assault-class autocannon could acquire range. It pinned the 244th in place, though at a cost as an Elemental leapt from concealment to ride the back of an Arcturan Pegasus hovertank.

McDonald had mistaken the armored infantryman's smoky, gray-blue color for a mere boulder a moment ago. Now it reminded her of a tick, crawling over the armored hide of her hovertank, looking for blood. And finding it, as the Elemental tore a hatch cover away with its claw and pumped laserfire into the tank crew's cockpit. Then the Elemental jumped away, disappearing behind the legs of a Com Guard *Excalibur* as the Pegasus veered to one side. The hovertank flipped end-over to roll through the Com Guard line in a fury of shedding armor and spraying dirt.

Inspired by that action, a lance from the Sixth Crucis Lancers thought they'd be smart, nipping in behind the armor in an attempt to relieve the harried Com Guard. They'd waited too long. From the edge of the *King Crab*'s range, Evans belched out a furious firestorm of depleted-uranium slugs that chewed into the left flank of what looked like a fresh-from-the-factory Federated Suns *Templar*. The OmniMech shed armor in a rain of splinters and shards, littering the ground with razor-thin steel and leaving its side bare of protection. McDonald clenched her hand with her thumb, as though that would let her fire the *King Crab*'s laser. Evans was on top of it, though, skewering the ruby lance into the *Templar*'s side, probing for the engine shielding.

The laser missed the engine, and gray-green coolant erupted from ruptured heat sinks in a sickly spray. Meanwhile, the *Templar* not only kept to its feet but claimed a Fulcrum heavy hovertank. Its rotary autocannons chewed into the hovertank skirting, spilling its cushion of air and grounding the blades into the earth. The Fulcrum lifted one more time as its high-velocity blades spent their kinetic energy in a single, violent instant. Then the tank dropped on its side before rolling over on itself.

Wounded and desperate, the *Templar* tried to escape on its plasma jets, taking to the air and leaving its comrades behind. With her detached perspective on the battle, McDonald might have let it go, the better to concentrate on closer threats. Evans had no such thought. Running into the thick of battle, he reached out again with his pair of assault autocannon. This time, one of them blew all the way through the *Templar*'s flank, completely eviscerating the left-side chest cavity while the machine was still in the air. There was nothing left for it but a graceless tumble back to the ground, crushing one arm beneath it and piling up in a heap of metal, myomer, and MechWarrior.

The battle had turned into a brawl. Linda McDonald watched it play out on her tactical screen, counting up destroyed machines and lost lives. She traded two crippled or destroyed BattleMechs for every one claimed from the enemy, making up for it slightly in Com Guard armor. As with most brawls, though, the bigger opponent had the advantage and that meant her Arcturan Guards. Plus the fact that her people would fight with greater efficiency the more they were whittled down. It was a bloodless way of looking at it, but it helped her to realize that even if the enemy commanders were willing to pay the butcher's price, they couldn't win.

A fact they realized in the next second as the Com Guard armor force finally broke. The vehicles streamed away on random paths, hovercraft bolting first and fastest while the tracked vehicles followed in a more cautious retreat. A few companies made a dash for Tukwila, thinking to end-run Linda McDonald's fractured command. They were beaten back and sent into a rout by the militia reserve she'd left in place.

"The Crucis Lancers are falling back, General!" Leutnant Friedrickson shouted, his cry giving way to pure elation. "We took down the *Penetrator* and a *Jager-Mech*."

Other calls echoed the leutnant's report as the allied forces fell back in haphazard fashion from Tukwila. Added to the list of kills was Precentor Irelon's *Crockett*, though he had apparently ejected clean and was picked up by a fast-moving *Exterminator* that leapt in the air and caught the slowly descending warrior by the parafoil.

"We pursue?" Colonel Evans asked, anticipating her by throttling the *King* forward.

McDonald might have agreed under ordinary circumstances, but her mission objectives overrode her warrior instincts. "No," she said, the hardest order she'd had to give since landing on Tikonov, and it seemed to cheapen their victory. For the moment.

"We don't pursue. Our job here was to deny the allied forces any resources from Harcourt Industries. If we chase them, that objective is endangered." It was the kind of call she'd seen Maria Esteban make so many times. Hearing similar words come from her own mouth gave McDonald a mixed rush of pride and frustration. She weathered some grumbling, but cut it off after only a few seconds.

"Fall back to Tukwila," she ordered, "and call out the salvage teams. Let's see what we can put back together." Then, they'd see just how far Victor was willing to go to keep Tikonov.

McDonald's only real concern was the WarShip *Melissa Davion,* which Victor could still call in from the nadir jump point. Maybe it was time to call in the *Fox*-class corvette she had hidden in-system. General Esteban had doubted that Victor would use his cruiser for orbital support. It was his one secure way off-planet, if he ever chose to run. Perhaps he wouldn't, though. The renegade Prince could have decided to make his last stand on Tikonov.

And if that were the case, Linda McDonald was here to oblige him.

26

Rockland, Tikonov
Capellan March
Federated Suns
16 February 3065

Sitting cramped on one side of the long conference table, Rudolf Shakov rocked his chair onto its back legs, trying to escape the claustrophobic feel of sixteen men and women packed into a room meant for half their number. At the back wall of Outpost 23, a small air conditioning unit hummed and wheezed, laboring against so much body heat. It managed to keep the room temperature bearable, but that didn't help the odor of so many bodies packed in tight, especially with some people still in sweaty MechWarrior garb.

"You've all read the same reports I have," Morgan Kell said as he brought the strategy meeting to order. Conversation dropped off to a few last whispers barely audible over the struggling AC unit. "You all know what we're up against. Now I want to hear from you."

He swept his iron gaze down one side of the table and back up the other. "Can we hold Tikonov?"

Shakov did a quick head count in the silence that followed. To the usual cabal of regular-army commanders and their regimental aides, Morgan Kell and Jerrard Cranston had added Captain Harsch, the ranking officer left to the Valexa CMM. Also present were two commanders from the Outland Legion, which he had formed up into a pair of rump battalions with combined-arms support.

Notably missing was Prince Victor, a loss everyone seemed to feel as they glanced now and then at the closed doors at the end of the narrow room. Tiaret stood an impassive guard before the doors, which *seemed* normal. But the fact that she wasn't personally watching over Victor, and hadn't been for several weeks, only underscored the sense of emptiness eating at the task force from within.

Captain Harsch cleared his throat, waited to see if any senior officer would jump in ahead of him, then began to speak when no one else pulled rank. "We've been waiting for reinforcements," he said. "Any chance we'll see them soon? It might help to know how long we've got to hold."

As the senior Com Guard officer overseeing all communications, Precentor Irelon took the question. "There is no easy answer, Captain. The civil war has a score of worlds up in arms and fighting their own battles over whom they support. The units we've been depending on are the ones we knew would come to Victor's side, eventually. The Tenth Lyran and any of the Davion Guard regiments. But the Revenants are still isolated at Kentares, and the Third Guard are caught up trying to push the Combine forces off Cassias."

He paused. "This report is new," he said by way of apology to Morgan Kell, "but the Fifth is dead."

That silenced the room for a number of painful heartbeats. Morgan waved down the excited outbursts that followed, waiting for an explanation. Irelon looked the question to Shakov, who called up the more detailed reports from memory. They had hoped to give Morgan the news in private, after the meeting. There had been no time before, and also no impetus to hold up the others as this assembly was supposed to be discussing Tikonov.

"The Fifth Guards broke yesterday on Kathil," he said, "after Katherine's Eight Donegal Guards and the

First Chisholm Raiders combined to push them back against the Olympic Ocean. Loyalists are hunting down stragglers now."

This made the regiment the second of the stalwart Davion Guards to fall in the civil war. The assembled officers gave the Fifth a moment of silence.

Shakov waited them out, continuing only when most eyes had turned back to Morgan or himself. "The Davion Heavy Guards are still stranded on Galax, though Tancred Sandoval promises to bring them transport. Eventually. Our best hope right now are the Assault Guards. They were willing to let the Combine unit retreat from Addicks in order to make it to us, but then Katherine hit them in place with the Achernar Militia *and* the Fifth Lyran Guard. It may be enough to tie them up indefinitely."

"Which demonstrates our ultimate problem," Morgan said, picking up the thread. "No matter what we *might* bring to Tikonov just now, Katherine—currently—has access to more free regiments. If we can't do it with what we have, we can't count on a victory here at all."

Shakov watched Morgan carefully, studied him, seeing the gifts that had made him an accomplished mercenary commander in his time. No matter the differences in rank, position, or nationality, Morgan made everyone feel like they were a part of the grand strategy and that they might hold a special role in what was to come. And all the while, Shakov suddenly felt certain, Morgan Kell had already decided. Already knew.

"Tikonov is the most strategically placed world for Victor's stab toward New Avalon." Shakov stroked his goatee, knowing it needed a trim. "We knew that coming in, and it's twice as true now."

Across the open stretch of table, Jonathan Sanchez nodded agreement. "We can't leave Katherine basing from Tikonov behind us. We're going to have to win this fight now or later, Morgan."

Jerrard Cranston leaned forward. "And if we win it now, General, what then? I know you've fought hard for this planet, but do we just sit here, exposed, while the prince recovers?"

"Victor is in no shape to lead us forward," Morgan said, his tone brooking no debate, not even from Nadine Killson, who had looked ready to argue.

Shakov maintained a solid mask for form's sake, but if Victor's state hurt *his* confidence, he could only imagine what it was doing to the rank and file. "Where else could you take him, Morgan?"

"Back into the Alliance. Into the Arc Royal Defense Cordon if necessary. Now that the Jade Falcons have been contained again, it's the most secure location we have." Morgan met the gaze of every officer in the room, one by one. "Victor needs time. We can wait that out here, but the longer we do so, the more important this world becomes and the greater the chance that this entire civil war will ultimately be decided by Tikonov, not on New Avalon."

Jonathan Sanchez nodded. "Then Victor should leave. But the First NAIS Cadre stays on Tikonov. We'll make certain Katherine's forces don't get too comfortable." He looked around the table, accepted Captain Harsch's nod as a pledge for continued support by the Valexa CMM, then came back to Morgan Kell. "My cadets and Harsch's militia are seasoned veterans by now. We can hold. Give me a second regiment, Morgan, and we can keep a secure beachhead open until you return."

The plan, though desperate, could work. Shakov considered the loyalist forces on Tikonov, counted half of them who would no doubt chase Victor back into the Alliance and so leave Sanchez the chance to make good on his promise. "It's worth it," he said, then gave his reasoning, with the probable reactions by General Esteban and Linda McDonald.

Morgan nodded. "I won't order anyone to stay, but if there is a volunteer . . ."

Patricia Vineman stood up immediately, just edging out General Killson. "The Sixth Crucis will stay," she said. "My Tsamma Lancers will wait for Victor here. They wouldn't dare fail the prince."

"I can try to find you more support," Morgan promised. "With the Free Tikonov Movement springing up again, perhaps I can get Treyhang Liao to back us with Free Capella. I don't know."

He combed through his gray beard with his fingers, then seemed to make up his mind. "Here's how we'll do it. We pull out in one week. Before that time, I want the forces remaining behind brought up to the best level of materiel readiness we can offer. Also, we need to prepare against Linda McDonald's WarShip, which is moving in from the zenith, and maybe bloody the general's nose a bit to make certain she follows us. General Sanchez"—he looked to the First NAIS commanding officer—"is there anything else you need from us?"

"Yes, there is, Morgan." Sanchez sounded a touch disappointed, but had his answer already prepared. "Give me Tukwila and Harcourt Industries." He smiled grimly. "Then keep Victor safe, and make it back to relieve us."

Shakov watched Morgan's slow nod, and knew it was more than a simple acknowledgment. It was a private promise as well. The word of Morgan Kell.

"With pleasure, General," he said. "To all of the above."

27

Outpost Twenty-Three
Rockland, Tikonov
Capellan March, Federated Suns
21 February 3065

Rockland's small military outpost could never hope to house a tenth of the machines and supplies belonging to the allied forces, and the local spaceport had been commandeered by General Killson's Twenty-third Arcturan Guards. Rudolf Shakov jumped onto the running board of a slow-moving fuel truck and hitched a ride the final hundred meters to where the Prince's Men had secured a few thousand square meters of cleared earth. He held onto his narrow perch with one hand on the truck's grimy door handle, while the other clasped his foul-weather jacket tight at the throat to fend off a chill morning mist. The dampness clung to his hair and condensed to the occasional droplet that trickled down his neck with a cold, lazy finger.

The gray sky stretched from horizon to horizon, and by reports would not improve between Rockland and Tukwila. Not that it really mattered. Ahead, MechWarriors sealed themselves into cockpits while tank crews buttoned up against the declining weather. Infantry loaded onto warmed transport carriers. They were in hovercraft, mostly, but a few VTOL craft as well.

The first 'Mechs made their way clear of the open-air staging area, forming up for the quick-march south. A scout lance walked cautiously between two armor squads, wary of any straggling ground crew, then picked up the pace and ran for a forward position on the assembling column.

Shakov counted fifteen BattleMechs as he jumped free of the truck, and not much more in armor. Two battlesuit squads headed up a rump battalion of infantry. That was all that remained of the Com Guard 244th Division—something like forty percent operational. Not counting aerospace fighters, of course, which were already heading up to intercept the WarShip *Katrina Davion*. Air support today would fall to the Sixth Crucis Lancers and some Com Guard VTOLs. It would be enough. It had to be.

Walking past Victor's *Daishi*, Shakov swiped his right hand against the sleeve of his other arm, trying unsuccessfully to wipe off the oily residue he'd picked up from the fuel truck. The 'Mech was an impressive design, even among the other avatars of war that surrounded it. Lethal and majestic, and remaining behind, he reminded himself. After the field emptied, some technician would use the BattleMech's maintenance mode to walk it over to the spaceport and load it aboard a DropShip, ready for the exodus.

Then he saw Victor, and for a moment, he had cause to hope.

The prince stood near the foot of his 'Mech, talking with the division's senior weapons technician. Heavy mist beaded his green trench coat, and his sandy-blond hair was starting to darken and flatten out with moisture. A pair of security agents stood off to one side, exchanging uncertain glances. Two nearby MechWarriors and a trio of technicians were more discreet. They stood grouped together as if discussing some last-minute problems with their machines, but were just as obviously waiting to see why the prince had come out to the field. Shakov walked over quickly to join the conversation between Victor and the master tech.

"It doesn't matter what you were told concerning my

'Mech," Victor said, his patience obviously wearing thin. "I'm taking him out."

Shakov's hope died in the second it took to size up Victor's physical condition. The prince shifted slightly from one foot to the other, a constant motion no doubt meant to fight off his exhaustion. His eyes sunken in a drawn face said more than any medical review could. There was still strength behind them—that Victor was still on his feet after the abuses he'd put his body through in the last few months was testament enough to his drive—but no hunger. No sharp-edged steel, or burning, that promised that Victor was ready for combat. He was not even in combat togs, but still dressed for the command center. If he wanted to take to the field, however, who would tell him no?

Besides the division's senior tech, that is.

"Yes, Highness." The man nodded in agreement, even as he framed an argument to Victor's order. "And it would do a lot for the men for you to lead them. But your *Daishi* isn't ready."

"Looks ready to me," Victor said. He acknowledged Shakov's presence with a curt nod, not yet ready to give up his argument. "Armored and armed."

"Not *fully* armed, Highness. When we were told that your 'Mech would not be needed, we stripped it of all ammunition as well as the focusing lenses on two pulse lasers in order to bring other machines up to full military readiness." He looked over at Shakov and then at the nearby MechWarriors. "We thought you would want the men as prepared for combat as possible."

"I do," Victor said, doubt beginning to creep into his voice. In his right hand he still gripped the swordguard Omi Kurita had given him, rubbing it as if it might bring him luck or courage. "Of course I do. But ammunition can be loaded quickly—"

"Begging your pardon, Highness," the tech broke in, "but it can't. Not today. Duke Kell ordered that all excess munitions be transferred to the First NAIS and to the Sixth Lancers. We've cleaned out our stores. Completely."

Victor looked ready to argue further, and everyone

around seemed to hold their breath while they waited for the explosion. They expected him to order that munitions and parts be stripped from other 'Mechs or that supplies be retrieved from the Sixth Lancers. Then he suddenly rocked back on his heels and nodded perfunctorily. "I see. No arguing with efficiency, is there?"

He looked again toward the *Daishi*, wistful and yet without his usual force. "I should get to control, then, to help Morgan coordinate."

The prince traded nods and salutes all around, then clasped hands with Shakov and wished him luck. The security agents trailed after him as he finally retired from the staging grounds.

"I want those forms on file by the end of the day," Shakov said at once to the tech, startling him. He pulled the man along as he began walking to his *Exterminator*. "All the transfers and the authorizations to strip the *Daishi* of essential parts."

The senior technician looked confused. "Sir?"

"I don't want this incident to become a problem." They came under the physical protection of Shakov's BattleMech, and the mist lightened somewhat. "Let's keep it as aboveboard as possible."

"Demi Shakov, I don't know what you mean," the tech said, but Shakov knew from his eyes that he was lying. "There was no incident. Nothing happened." He glanced over Shakov's shoulder, following Victor's retreat, then looked down and away. "Prince Victor was never here," he said in a much quieter voice.

Shakov considered that, recognized the truth in it, and then nodded the other man on his way. Climbing up on the foot of his 'Mech, he reached for the chain-link ladder that would take him up the side of his 'Mech. His hand slipped off the first rung, and he grabbed at it again. Scaling the ladder from rung to rung, he climbed toward the *Exterminator*'s cockpit, thinking darkly that the senior tech was right.

Prince Victor wasn't here.

General Linda McDonald paced her command operations room, striding from the data terminals to the display tables to the wallscreen monitors and then back to the data terminals. Already this morning she was overseeing four separate battles as Victor Davion's Outland Legion and battalion-strength elements from the Twenty-third Arcturan Guards staged hard-hitting strikes against the loyalist forces on Tikonov. Already she had spoken with Captain Siddig on the *Katrina Steiner*, who updated her on the harassment attacks plaguing the WarShip.

Already she *knew* that these were diversions for a much bigger operation.

Large-scale ops, she was quickly discovering, did not differ so much from tactical-level combat. You put out pickets and flankers. You engaged at a distance, trying to pull the enemy off balance. Though the product of a grander vision, these were strategies with which she was familiar. And when you didn't know the design of an attacking force, you waited them out.

The waiting was the hard part.

"On the field," she muttered aloud, "I'd be waiting in a 'Mech with targets painted and my thumb on the firing stud."

A tech looked up from his screen. "What was that, General?"

General. She was the one in command here, not just of a single battle or a single regiment, but over an entire world. The old lady. McDonald winced, thinking how often she referred to Maria Esteban in those terms, just as her officers and support staff no doubt were thinking of her. The used-to-be-MechWarrior who had traded her cockpit for a swivel chair and guaranteed retirement. Well, *that* was a notion of which she would disabuse them very quickly.

"I said I want to be out in the battle." She made her voice loud enough to carry across her COR. "Can someone find it for me? Because I guarantee you we haven't seen their main thrust yet."

A fighting general. That was what she would be. Esteban had always said that once you had the floor, you discovered your own command style. It had taken her mentor's absence for McDonald to find out what hers was. She wanted to wed the responsibilities of command to the satisfaction of personal victory. Not to be a hero, because heroes most often died brutally and fast, and at lower ranks. But she didn't just want to command respect. She wanted to plunge in and get her hands dirty, and *win* respect.

She wanted, she realized suddenly, what Victor Davion already had. The same strength that had allowed him to foment this rebellion. That bothered her. It wasn't wrong to respect—even admire—an enemy, but it was unsettling nonetheless. Mostly because it meant that somewhere in the past Victor had been worthy of devotion, and it reminded her that she herself had given it to him right up until he crossed the line from ruler to would-be conqueror.

"Our reconnaissance flights still show a great deal of activity around Rockland," Lieutenant Franklin told her. An intelligence analyst, he was often quicker with the reporting than the analyzing. "DropShip activity as well as infantry maneuvers."

McDonald shook her head. " 'All warfare is based on deception,' " she said, quoting one of her favorite military texts. "I won't make it *quite* so easy on them as to believe everything they show us."

Where would Victor attack? Here at Tukwila or at Hang-Than or Volobus? He or one of his command staff had something tricky in mind. "Vance," she said, motioning to her newly appointed exec. "Where would you attack? What can hurt us right now?"

Brevet-Colonel Vance Evans reflected on the question as diligently as he pursued everything else. It wasn't his flash and daring that recommended him, but his steadfastness. Another reason McDonald had decided to move him back to his own 'Mech, leaving her to pilot the *King Crab* alone. If she stumbled, she wanted someone there to pick up the pieces.

"The largest production site on planet is the Ceres Metals facility on Arano Bay. We've allowed Sun-Tzu's Free Tikonov Movement to hold it, as a status symbol, but that does mean the site is under-defended."

She nodded. "It's also a long-distance strike, requiring DropShips to make a ballistic hop or a three-day maneuver over one of five passes. I don't see how they could pull that off without us seeing." She ran the fingers of both hands up through her hair, tugging at it in frustration. Maybe she was asking the wrong question.

"Where *wouldn't* you attack?" she asked.

"Tukwila," he said without hesitation. "It's our strongest point nearest Rockland. We have the equivalent of two regiments here, with supporting forces." He shook his head. "You don't attack the opposition where the enemy is strongest."

"Not without superior forces," she appended, "or surprise. Damn it, Vance, that's exactly what they're planning. To kick us in the teeth." Of course, they were coming back to the Tukwila Valley. Victor's people needed a morale boost, and this was the site of their latest defeat.

McDonald turned to the nearest communications officer. "Recall any nearby patrols and pull in our overflight reconnaissance to within fifty klicks. I want adequate warning of any approach, and nothing slipping through until we're assembled."

Then she turned back to her exec. "Get our people ready and fielded." Then she grabbed a personal comm set and tugged it over her head while making for the door. She was finished in the operations room. There wasn't anything more she could accomplish here that she couldn't do by remote. And the sooner she got back onto the field, the better. She wanted that extra time—she needed that extra time—to plan a warm reception for Victor's allied forces.

"And once they're in, we slam the door," she said.

"General?" a voice said over her headset. She'd spoken loud enough to be picked up by the voice-activated mic.

"I said get me Captain Siddig on the *Katrina Steiner*," Linda McDonald said harshly, covering her slip with an order. Another sound military practice, just like the old adage about controlling the ground by controlling the skies. "Patch me through to the WarShip, and keep the line on standby once we have them."

A plan was already forming in her head. With a bit of luck, and some accurate orbital fire-support, the site of the allied forces' latest defeat would also be the site of their last.

28

Holding high station over Tikonov, Captain Handal Siddig controlled his bridge crew with an iron hand as the WarShip *Katrina Steiner* dove through a new wave of enemy aerospace fighters like a shark among barracuda. The fighters, no match for the savage strength of the corvette's naval-grade autocannon and lasers, were instantly gutted and turned into blasted or burned-out husks. Chased by loyalist fightercraft the entire way, all the enemy could hope to do was slip in, nip at the corvette's flanks, and flee.

Still, the little bites they took added up. Siddig held on tight to the arms of his bridge chair, feeling every bump and shudder that trembled up from the *Katrina Steiner*'s deck plates. The bridge was a cacophony of alarms, shouted reports, and the occasional command—his commands—on how the *Fox*-class corvette should fight the scissors-wave attack strategy employed by Prince Victor's allied aerospace. Staggered runs lanced in at the WarShip's belly, then angled aft to avoid the corvette's broadside weapons array. The next run to break through his screen of fightercraft and assault DropShips always came in from behind.

"Forty-five-degree starboard roll," Siddig ordered. "Call it by fives. At twenty, give me a lateral burn and a ninety-degree port turn."

"Roll forty-five, come around ninety," Helm repeated the order. "Aye, sir."

The aerospace fighters worked hard at penetrating the WarShip's engineering sections, at once the heart of the vessel but also protected by the thickest armor. By rolling and turning, Siddig ruined their approach vectors and gave them fresh armor whenever possible.

It also brought more weapons to bear against a new wave of fightercraft. On his starboard screens, Siddig watched as streamers of crimson energy reached out. One of them burned into the nose of an inbound *Lucifer* medium fighter, lancing all the way in to the fusion chamber. The flare of a reactor overload momentarily brightened the screen. One of the WarShip's sensor technicians focused in on higher magnification. The blackened, twisted remains that tumbled out of the wash of energies resembled less a state-of-the-art aerospace fighter and more a crumpled, half-melted can. Several sharp edges glowed orange, cooling toward a dull red as they trailed small globules of molten metal into the surrounding space, all of it streaming forward on the fighter's original path.

All heading directly into the side of the *Katrina Steiner*.

A great deal of the fighter's mass had burned away, but even a few tons could do serious damage at those speeds. Siddig tensed for the impact. The cooling mass struck a glancing blow amidships, tearing through armor and several compartments before falling back into open space. The WarShip trembled, but no calls came in reporting critical damage.

"Guns!" Siddig called out to his weapons officer. "You get that idiot relieved at once! We are *not* going to Robert this WarShip into Tikonov just because someone has an itchy finger and can't wait for the turn."

"Copy *that*," Weapons said, catching Siddig's slang. No

one wanted to be crewing the next *Robert Davion*, the WarShip that had reportedly burned into Kathil's atmosphere after being rammed by a gutted DropShip at the start of the civil war.

"Roll twenty," Helm called out. "Coming around."

Siddig leaned into the turn as the fusion drive routed power through lateral port thrusters and applied a quarter-gravity push to the WarShip's aft. The projected image of Tikonov swung from the monitor's left, drifting low but still visible as a white-blue arc at the trailing edge of the screens as the WarShip finished its roll. A distant white sphere hung above the planet, moving slowly toward the monitor's upper-right corner. It was an escaping DropShip, *Union*-class, one of several making runs for the nadir jump point and Prince Victor's WarShip-protected fleet of JumpShips in the last four hours.

"Captain-sir," Comms yelled for attention. "General McDonald calling in for you."

Siddig shook off the call. "Hold," he said. "Guns, can we reach that DropShip?" He didn't care what it was up to—resupply, administrative, communications courier—there was no good reason to let Victor Davion's forces have easy contact with other worlds. Anyway, General McDonald had ordered a quarantine and—more important—Maria Esteban had concurred.

"It's at extreme range, Captain. No promises."

"Begin bracketing it with forty-fives and fifty-fives. Donate two Barracuda missiles to it as well. Try to target engines if you can."

"Missiles away," the weapons officer reported almost at once. "I need five degrees more port turn to bring our lasers into reach."

"Helm, make it happen."

"Five degrees port, aye, sir."

The capital-class lasers stabbed out in brilliant colors, reaching out of sight to try and worry armor from the escaping DropShip. The *Katrina Steiner* shook as another fighter flight rolled beneath and scraped armor from the corvette's underside. Siddig looked to Comms, nodded, and turned aside to the small, flat-screen video he reserved for the brevet-general's calls.

Linda McDonald's face was half-masked by her neuro-helmet, and from the way the video image jumped and blurred with gray static, Siddig knew she was deep in battle herself. "Not a lot of time, Handal," she said between clenched teeth. "I need that promised fire support."

"We're working on it, General."

McDonald was not hearing excuses or empty promises. "I have two regiments pushing us slowly back toward Tukwila, Handal. I want orbital support. Now give me a time frame."

A new alarm joined the background noise. "Contact," Sensors called over most of the bridge chatter. "We have an IR signature out there."

"Barracuda missiles," Weapons said. "Twenty seconds to impact."

The captain of a WarShip had to be an expert at multitasking. A good officer crew could only shield him from so much. Handal Siddig seized on the more important thread first, turning from the screen to find his main sensors station. "Distance and strength on that IR signature?" he asked, hands twitching with nervous energy.

Infrared pulses were the only indicator of an arriving jump-capable vessel. If Victor's allies were bringing in a ship now, it was either to meet the escaping DropShip—which meant it was far more important than he'd thought—or to support the fighter assault against his corvette.

"Six thousand klicks. Right on top of us." As interplanetary distances went, the sensors officer was not far wrong. "It's big—it's here! Intrasystem jump! One hundred-five degrees, mark eighty."

No need to order the sensor shift. An auxiliary screen painted the target, read its IFF codes, and attached appropriate tags. Siddig had known what it would be, though. The FCS Cruiser *Melissa Davion*.

"Report, Captain Siddig." Linda McDonald's voice was compelling enough to drag him back around to the comms screen. A frown creased her brow. She had obviously heard enough to worry.

So had he, but his duty lay somewhere between the immediate threat to his vessel and his obligation to the troops on the ground.

"Helm, turn us away from that cruiser," Siddig ordered. "Give me a hard approach to Tikonov." He didn't wait for the repeat-back before returning to McDonald. "General, you'll get your fire support, and you'll have it within fifteen. But I won't guarantee much more than ten minutes on station. After that," he said, "you're on your own, and I have a cruiser to kill.

"Before," he said under his breath, making sure no one heard him, "it kills us."

Tikonov's drizzle had never turned into a full rain, and the tiny drops that beaded and ran down Rudolf Shakov's ferroglass shield were like a pale reflection of the sweat that drenched him. Perspiration rolled off his brow, streaming down his face to pool in the small cavity formed between his skin and the collar of his cooling vest. The salty taste burned on his lips. A few small rivulets filtered through his goatee, leaving behind an itching deposit of flash-dried salt. A similar white scale showed on the back of his wrists where sweat did not wash it away often enough.

That was the drawback to upgrading his *Exterminator*'s medium lasers to an extended-range class. The 'Mechs double-strength heat sinks could handle the increased heat generation, but only barely. Combined with his missile rack and the occasional use of jump jets, heat build-up was inevitable. But the upgrade also gave his sixty-five-ton machine sharper teeth. Already he had claimed a Carlisle Militia *Starslayer* and a Fulcrum hovertank, neither of which were prepared for his longer reach. Word was spreading, however, and the awkward-looking *Night Hawk* he was fighting at the moment spent more time falling back to long range than it did returning fire with its own farther-reaching weapons.

Shakov smiled grimly as he checked his heads up. His

battle computer painted the holographic display in a wide band across the *Exterminator*'s overhead ferroglass shield, giving him more detail than the usual HUD, which was confined to an auxiliary monitor or, worse, a narrow ribbon painted on the inside of a neurohelmet face shield. As good as his sensor-fed display was, it was still cluttered with icons and threat markers. At a glance, though, it seemed that the plans drafted by Morgan Kell and Colonel Vineman were working.

The Com Guard forces had again vaulted ahead of the main allied lines, and Shakov rode the very edge of that push. Linda McDonald's loyalist forces were falling steadily back toward Tukwila. The small city that existed to service Harcourt Industries was now only two kilometers distant, down a shallow slope, and just beyond some low foothills. Every time one of the loyalist MechWarriors retreated, it placed Victor's allies that much closer to their goal. A steady push into and through Tukwila was all part of their plans.

Unfortunately, up to this point, it was part of the enemy plans as well.

A lance of ruby energy fell down from the skies like the glare of some angry god, scorching the earth and leaving a scar along the ground and across a Com Guard jump-capable Kanga hovercraft. It split open under the naval-class laserfire, engine erupting in a brilliant fireball that quickly burned off into a dark, oily cloud. Its heavy ammunition stores detonated in sympathetic explosions, shredding armor and hurling large chunks of the vehicle up to a quarter-kilometer distant. One of its jump thrusters smashed into the side of a Lyran *Barghest*, destroying armor and claiming some retribution, but hardly enough.

"That was Adept Dawson!" someone called over the general Com Guard frequency, riding the forward edge of a wave of confused chatter.

". . . came from above . . ." another warrior verified.

". . . we lose our screen?"

"I didn't see . . ."

". . . no aerospace fighter . . ."

Shakov seized on this last transmission, able to agree

with at least *that* much. Whatever that had been, it was no aerospace fighter. He twisted his controls hard against their physical stop, turning his *Exterminator* away from the wrecked Kanga and whatever had killed it.

Additional lances of crimson terror carved into the allied lines and the surrounding battlefield. Trees exploded as moisture at their cores flashed to steam faster than the wood could burn away. Rocks split, melted. A forty-ton *Sentry* belonging to the First NAIS cadre simply disappeared under one orbital strike, its fusion reactor mushrooming up in a display of fire and ground-shaking thunder. The Sixth Crucis Lancers lost two BattleMechs in quick succession as well as a squad of Infiltrator battle armor, who were burned down to a tortured composite of half-melted armor, crisped flesh, and ash.

Realization dawned on Shakov at about the same time the retreating Lyrans firmed up their lines and set themselves for a solid defense of Tukwila. He felt like firing blindly up into the gray skies. The slow retreat of Katherine's loyalists had kept the allied forces grouped together in tight units, and Linda McDonald had called in the *Katrina Steiner* to provide fire support. A dangerous tactic, but not impossible. Victor had proven during the Clan homeworlds campaign that accurate support fire could be called down from orbit if you had a clear fire zone and a captain you trusted. McDonald obviously had both.

But for how long? Morgan Kell was on top of things, his voice calm and reassuring. "The *Melissa* is moving in to engage their WarShip, force it off. Can you hold firm for fifteen minutes?"

Well, maybe not *that* reassuring, Shakov thought. The allied line wavered as warriors milled about, unsure. Already the probing lasers searched for their next victim, found it in another NAIS cadet. The laserfire took an arm from his *Watchman*. It might have cut the 'Mech down its entire length but for the *Watchman*'s speed and the lightning reactions of the cadet, who jerked his machine mostly out of the beam's path.

"A quarter-hour?" Precentor Irelon broke in. "We won't make five minutes."

Jonathan Sanchez was only slightly more sanguine. "We don't get a second chance at this, people." His voice was strong, coming over the frequency reserved for command officers and senior staff. "Can we absorb the losses?"

The question hung unanswered as McDonald's forces made several small, discouraging pushes. A gray blur blasted into the ground near the feet of Shakov's *Exterminator*, striking up a shower of earth and spattering clods of dirt against his ferroglass shield. Across the no-man's zone being held by the Lyrans, a loyalist *Barghest* had leapt forward to support a *Night Hawk*'s advance. The *Barghest* bounded forward again, then hunched back on its four legs to set itself for firing its heavy gauss. This time, the nickel-ferrous slug took Shakov's 'Mech in the left arm, all but tearing it out of the shoulder socket.

He turned into the *Barghest*'s line of attack, ignoring the *Night Hawk*'s probing lasers as he concentrated on the greater threat. His missiles fell in a wide spread over the other 'Mech's broad back. Two lasers managed to scar a forward leg, hardly enough to send it fleeing for Tukwila.

Tukwila! Shakov toggled for the Com Guard's tactical channel. "Prince's Men, form up and hold your ground. 'Mechs on the right, armor wide left flank." He switched back over to the command level. "General, we have to move forward against Tukwila. Now!" He dodged his 'Mech back to the left, vying for the head of a hastily assembled arrowhead formation. Ahead of him, a squad of Com Guard's battlesuit infantry raced forward to harass the loyalist forward lines.

"Our infantry hasn't penetrated the city yet," Colonel Vineman said. The full infantry assets of her Lancers were set to flank the loyalist line, but it was too soon. According to the original plan, at least. "McDonald still controls Tukwila. What do you expect us to do against a well-defended city?"

"A lot better than against an unreachable WarShip," Irelon cut in again as he moved his commandeered *Excalibur* up from the backfield. "And they won't dare use orbital support in the midst of a populated city. General Sanchez, pull your lines west and be ready to follow us through."

"There's no open corridor to the west," Sanchez said.

Which was true. Shakov had an up-close-and-personal view of the western flank as he began pacing his people forward. The loyalist forces defending Tukwila at this point were roughly fifty percent stronger than the advancing Prince's Men.

"There will be," he promised, kicking the *Exterminator* into a forward run.

Consisting of a company each of armor and 'Mechs, a few VTOLs, and a double-handful of battlesuit infantry, the Prince's Men threw themselves straight into the path of the Lyran western flank. Grinding his teeth in defiance, Rudolf Shakov divided his fire between the *Night Hawk* and, whenever he could get a targeting lock, the *Barghest*. A laser brightened the armor over his left leg, carving off a half-ton of his protective shell. The *Barghest* missed again with its heavy gauss, the recoil throwing the seventy-ton 'Mech back on its armored haunches and nearly knocking it to the ground.

Around Shakov, the Com Guard MechWarriors had all chosen targets of their own. Armor tended to match against opposing vehicles, but when possible concentrated fire on enemy 'Mechs. The battle raged at close, violent quarters. An Arcturan *Cestus* fell back under the combined assault of two Burke assault vehicles. A *Talon* joined the *Cestus* a moment later when a Com Guard *Raijin* took its head off with a carefully aimed PPC. Then the Prince's Men suffered another casualty when a *Wyvern*'s fusion reactor lost containment and exploded itself across the battlefield.

Locked into the narrow focus of his own private battle, Shakov scarred twin cuts across the *Barghest*'s chest. It leapt aside and hunkered down within some trees to break sensor contact. Shakov pulled his targeting cross hairs over the *Night Hawk* again, waiting for the reticle to burn deep and gold and then spread missiles out to pummel the top-heavy design. He was about to follow up with lasers when the *Night Hawk* slowed, began firing at its own feet, and then shuddered as four Infiltrators and one Elemental swarmed over it.

How would Tiaret explain her butting in this time? That the Lyrans had never bid a WarShip? Not that he was about to bring it up now, too grateful for the help. Cutting in his jump jets, Shakov left the *Night Hawk* to her attention and leapt forward for the *Barghest*, hoping to crowd the other BattleMech and slip in beneath the heavy gauss's optimum targeting ability.

Rearing into a guarded crouch, the *Barghest* smashed a new slug into the *Exterminator*'s right leg, knocking the limb out from under Shakov. The *Exterminator* spun a lazy pirouette, coming down hard on its left side and throwing him against the seat harness. His breath rushed out between clenched teeth as the harness buckle dug into his abdomen.

Fighting for breath as well as for his life, he rolled onto his chest and pushed himself upright, drawing molten scars over the *Barghest*'s chest and legs as he worked the sixty-five-ton *Exterminator* back to its feet. Seeing the electrical discharge of the heavy gauss coils pointed directly at him, he set one giant 'Mech leg behind him to brace for the impact. The slug caught him in the chest this time, crushing armor with a metallic crunch and impacting several support struts in his engine shielding. Waste heat bled free into his machine, raising the temperature in the cockpit by another degree.

His eyes felt dry and scratchy, and what little breath he pulled into his lungs burned as if were eating fire. Shakov squinted at his forward shield, saw the flashing cross hairs settle over the *Barghest*, and decided it was close enough. Despite his heat curve and the close range, he cut loose with missiles and lasers both. Half of the warheads actually struck, chipping away that much more armor while one of his lasers was finally able to probe into the interior of the *Barghest*'s chest. It found nothing there that it liked.

But his next brace of lasers did. Pressing forward so close that he rendered the *Barghest*'s heavy gauss all but useless, he made that a permanent condition as two ruby lances speared into the ruined flank of the quadruped 'Mech. They bored through the hole smashed in earlier by the exploding Kanga's jump thruster and directly into the exposed guts of the heavy gauss rifle. The lasers flooded the gauss capacitors' bank, rupturing it, freeing the stored energy, which dumped into the *Barghest*'s chest. The combined discharge carved away at the fusion reactor's physical shielding and finally ate into the very core of the 'Mech.

The only way to salvage such a disaster was to drop the emergency dampening fields in place and hope for the best, which was what the *Barghest*'s MechWarrior did. Then he punched out, just for good measure. The skull of the forward-thrust head exploded outward, and the command couch ejected on a tongue of orange flame that carried it up and away from a potential disaster. But the fields did drop in time, and the *Barghest* simply fell over, lying still, dying not with a banshee scream but silently. It was the last loyalist 'Mech that stood in their way.

Shakov stood at the eastern edge of the gap the Prince's Men had forced through the enemy lines, shaken and battered but still on his feet and with a battle to fight. The narrow corridor still had to be held.

"Prop it open," he called out to the rest of the Prince's Men. Rounding on the eastern edge of the loyalist lines, he led the shrinking battalion forward, again on the attack.

Behind him, the allied forces poured in toward Tukwila.

29

Tikonov System
Capellan March
Federated Suns
21 February 3065

"She's coming around," Sensors yelled, "full brakes!"

Handal Siddig saw that for himself on the *Katrina Steiner's* primary viewscreen, which showed a computer-generated model of the FCS *Melissa Davion* swinging around on her attitude thrusters, swapping end for end, with the main drive glowing brilliant white. She would hit his ship with a full broadside and then power into another forward run. His fingers gripped the armrests of his chair with knuckle-whitening strength. The *Katrina Steiner* might be able to stand up to one more pass, but it was a risk and he knew it.

Then again, in space battles, every maneuver was a risk.

"Give her our nose," he ordered the helmsman. "Forward guns ignore everything but a continuous fire pattern on the *Melissa's* beam. Helm, full thrust and ready our own turn." His orders given, Captain Siddig braced for impact.

His enemy did not disappoint. From long range, the *Avalon*-class cruiser hit him with naval-grade lasers and gauss rifles, slamming the nose of his *Fox*-class corvette with stunning destructive power. Then the full force of its capital-class autocannon powered in behind, chewing through armor and support structure, ripping open spaces and spilling the ship's hoarded atmosphere into cold, unforgiving space. Lights flickered and alarms screamed for attention. The corvette bucked as if it had slammed into a solid wall, spilling several of Siddig's bridge crew to the floor. His own safety harness held, digging painfully into his abdomen and no doubt making a nice bruise across his thighs. His teeth slammed together, and he felt the grinding of chips between his back molars.

A fire sparked to life in the back of his auxiliary communications station. Two petty officers had it under control with short bursts of frosted powder expelled from an extinguisher. The bridge smelled of overheated electronics, scorched plastic, and the acrid bite of the smothering agent.

The main screens were dark. Siddig saw his bridge damage-control people hard at work under the eye of his executive officer, Commander Jeremy Franklin, and knew there was no way to hurry them. "Sensors, tell me you still have feed."

"Aye, Captain. We're holding a direct path at the cruiser. Shallowing a bit on our approach."

"Forward guns still firing," Weapons reported. "We lost one of our naval cannon."

Siddig nodded as the tactical screen winked back to life, then felt his heart leap up into his throat as a new barrage worried his vessel like a furious mastiff with a rag doll in its teeth. Separated by a mere half-dozen kilometers, the two ships continued to spar with their capital-class weapons while fightercraft and assault-design DropShips darted in and around them both.

The *Katrina Steiner* had less reason than the cruiser to worry about smaller craft, as its point-defense weaponry was enough to deter most fighter jocks. Siddig's entire strategy, in fact, had relied on overpowering attacks by the aerospace fighters under his command, but he wasn't getting that. The Eleventh Arcturan Aerospace Brigade—what little Maria Esteban had not taken with her—had no experience fighting a capital ship. The cruiser constantly intimidated them into aborted runs, despite all the recommendations of battle theory. As for his large contingent of militia aerospace, the less said about them the better. Several militia officers flat-out refused to engage the *Melissa*, turning instead for the assault-class DropShips she had ferried in with her. They were smaller than the cruiser, certainly, but their full array of point-defense weaponry made them ultimately more dangerous to fightercraft.

Despite this lack of support, Captain Siddig was left with no choice but to engage the enemy. He couldn't avoid the fact that, WarShip to WarShip, the *Katrina Steiner* was outgunned better than three to one. All he could do was try to fight his vessel three times better than the opposing captain, though in his heart he knew he had only managed a two-to-one gain. That was not enough.

But it didn't stop him from trying.

The *Melissa*'s maneuver had hurt the smaller corvette, but it had also robbed the cruiser of its momentum, hanging the vessel dead in space for several long, critical seconds. Siddig slashed the *Katrina Steiner* across her bow at close range, angling for the enemy ship's underside.

"Cut the main engines," he shouted at his helmsman. "Pitch up ten and roll over ninety."

"Main engines are dark," Helm answered. "Angling for broadside, aye!" The officer relayed orders to thruster stations at the fore and aft of the vessel, turning the corvette until it was coasting past and beneath the *Melissa Davion* at a range of only two kilometers, presenting a full broadside at the other WarShip's underbelly.

"Fire!" Siddig ordered. Though his weapons officer had certainly relayed the command before he ever gave it, his bridge crew had to be reminded occasionally of who held full authority on the corvette.

"Firing broadside," Weapons answered.

Main screens cut out intermittently as a new salvo

struck from the cruiser, shaking the corvette. Damning his own lack of caution, Siddig released himself from his seat restraints and half-stumbled, half-swam over to the weapons station. With the corvette no longer under thrust, gravity had fled the ship. Anchoring himself in the null gravity, he grabbed the edge of the console and hung on for dear life, watching the countdowns as his capital-class autocannon sent several tons of munitions into the cruiser's underside. Lasers probed the ruined cavities for critical systems. Fires glowed briefly in a few scars, but died almost instantly as the vacuum of space robbed them of air.

"Again," Siddig barked into the ear of his weapons officer. "Hit them again! Helm, ten degrees starboard, hold our angle!"

But the ships were quickly drifting apart as the *Melissa* refused to turn after the agile corvette. Momentum pushed the *Katrina Steiner* into the cruiser's wake and beyond reach of Siddig's main guns. Not out of reach of the cruiser's teleoperated missiles, though. A trio of short, sharp jounces shook the vessel and nearly dislodged Siddig's grip on the weapons station.

"We lost aft maneuvering thrusters," Helm shouted.

"Two more missiles inbound, fifteen seconds to impact," Sensors called. "Cruiser is not—*not*—turning yet."

Siddig shoved himself off from the weapons station, then went flying with practiced ease back to his chair. Twisting around mid-flight, he landed almost perfectly in the seat. "Light up the engines. Maneuver with forward thrusters."

"Bridge, Damage Control." The voice that crackled over the closed-circuit comm was not that of Lieutenant Charles, Siddig's Damage Control Officer. "Main engines are down."

Two more violent tremors shook the ship as the *Melissa Davion*'s parting shot of missiles struck them amidships. Siddig stabbed at a button mounted to his personal comm station. "Who is this? And you better know *exactly* what is wrong with my engines."

"Sir, this is Chief Sorence," said the senior enlisted

man. "The DCO is working on the problem. It looks like the last barrage we took might have damaged containment systems and the safeties kicked in."

A fairly calm way of saying that the *Katrina Steiner* was dead in space and might not recover engines for some time. Although the chief phrased it as a possibility, his tone sounded completely certain.

Siddig slammed one open hand down on his armrest in frustration. With his ship crippled, his carefully crafted strategy was in a shambles, and he easily imagined the *Melissa Davion* coming around at a leisurely pace to destroy the *Katrina Steiner* and crew. Siddig grabbed up his handheld, cutting off the over-speaker conversation.

"Can you start them without safeties?" he asked sotto voce. Two nearby officers swapped anxious glances. Siddig glared them back to their duties and waited for the chief's reply.

"It's possible," the man said after a long pause, "yes sir. But any severe damage to the reactor *or* any of its support systems will cut all of our careers short." As if to underscore the warning, the *Katrina Steiner* trembled again from a close-in fighter attack. "I wouldn't recommend anything more than two gees of thrust."

"Do it," Siddig ordered. "Give me what you can." He rammed the handset back into its secure cradle, not caring that he gouged skin from his knuckle.

"Captain," Sensors called out, "new signals coming through. Multiple contacts rising from the planet surface. Five, maybe six DropShips flying in a tight formation. Heavy fighter cover."

"Recovery mission?" Franklin asked, gliding over to anchor himself with one hand on the back of the captain's chair.

"Could be anything from resupply to reinforcements to help polish us off." Siddig shook his head, silently calling curses down on Prince Victor. With or without those DropShips, though, his course of action was clear.

"Helm, plot a course to the zenith jump point. Stand ready to make an intra-system jump if that cruiser comes around on our tail. Comms! Recall all fightercraft and

DropShips!" His decision made, Siddig's voice took on new strength. "I want a screen between us and the *Melissa* so tight it would make a *Sparrowhawk* nervous. Make it happen, people."

"We're retreating?" Franklin asked.

"Falling back to the jump point," Siddig corrected his exec. "We're dead in space, Jerry. Even if we had full engines, we couldn't stand up to that damned cruiser without veteran aerospace support. And that's nothing we're going to get anytime soon." He watched the flickering main screens as his auxiliary forces regrouped to form a protective blockade.

"It's time to extend and escape, and fight another day," he said softly. "Whatever's happening down there on Tikonov, it's in General McDonald's hands now."

═══ 30 ═══

Tukwila, Tikonov
Capellan March
Federated Suns
21 February 3065

Riding the plasma streams from his jump jets, Rudolf Shakov drew up the legs of his *Exterminator*, preparing to cushion his landing with a crouch. Two ruby lances speared after him, but the *Gallowglas* firing from the ground missed high.

Landing safely, the *Exterminator*'s diamond-tread feet bit into the slab roof of Tukwila's tallest building. At six stories high, Courtyard Towers was twice as tall as any other structure and was so near the center of town that it made for the perfect spotting platform. In one direction, Shakov caught sight of a Valexan *Enforcer* harassing the retreat of two Arcturan *Falconers*. Along another side street, he saw an enemy *Talon* and a newer *Stiletto* racing for the city's edge. Then, the icon of a *King Crab* flashed briefly over his heads up display, standing out from the rest. As it patrolled up the street from the east, it flashed an intermittent signal as his sensors found it in between buildings.

Another of the *Gallowglas*'s lasers scored a blackened wound down the side of the building. Then the electrical wash of a particle projection cannon cut at Shakov's right arm, fusing his hand actuator into a cast of half-melted armor and ruined myomer. He thumbed his firing stud and threw a double-handful of long-range missiles back at the *Gallowglas*. The warheads rained down onto the other 'Mech's head and shoulders, buying Shakov time as it was forced back around the corner of a nearby department store.

Tukwila belonged to the allied forces by sheer weight of numbers. The Sixth Crucis Lancers had poured into the city through the gap Shakov's warriors had forced in the enemy lines, followed by Irelon's Com Guard and General Sanchez's hybrid of the First NAIS and Valexa militia. The desperate maneuver caught a majority of the Lyran loyalists out of position and unable to regain the city in time. Several companies fought their way back in via the industrial sector and an abandoned warehouse district, but more still remained outside. The battle had since degenerated into a waiting game for the allied forces—waiting for Prince Victor to make his escape and for Linda McDonald to give up Tukwila as a lost cause. Shakov only had to last a handful of minutes, a quarter of an hour at most, and the city, at least, would be won.

Not that Linda McDonald would allow such an easy conclusion to the battle. Though lacking 'Mechs, she did have a well-placed and highly motivated regiment of assault infantry in Tukwila. In these narrow streets, even unaugmented soldiers were a threat to BattleMechs. Laser-rifle squads and anti-'Mech jump troops worried the allied force, running up the cost of holding the city. Two lances of armored vehicles and a *Penetrator* had already fallen victim to such tactics. Another half-dozen MechWarriors reported injuries to their machines stemming from similar traps and ambushes.

But that battle was also shifting in the favor of the Sixth Lancers as Colonel Vineman ordered her motorized infantry to make desperate runs for the protection of the city. Slowly, like peeling an onion layer by layer, the allied forces were skinning away the enemy numbers. Loyalist infantry at the edge of Tukwila were reportedly in flight, offering less resistance as they sought escape from the press of Vineman's veteran troops. Meanwhile, Com Guard battlesuit soldiers were ferreting out loyalist command posts and securing as much of the inner city and industrial sector as possible, buying some relief for the beleaguered 'Mechs.

But not for Shakov. With his HUD so cluttered with targets and threats, he missed the pair of Yellow Jacket gunboats that came beating a rapid path down the street below. The Eleventh Arcturan was big on VTOL squads, and McDonald wasn't wasting them in reserve. Twin gauss slugs slammed into the *Exterminator*, one smashing through his back and the other crushing armor just behind the left knee.

He fought for balance, keeping his 'Mech on its feet more by luck than skill. His return fire cut two scarlet beams over one VTOL, missing the rotor but nearly taking off its stabilizer. Then both machines banked away low, disappearing into the shadow of Courtyard Towers.

They would be back, of course, and Shakov knew better than to stay overlong in such an exposed position. He touched off his jump jets and rocketed back and away from the high building, then let himself fall toward the street below. This time, he noticed when his tactical sensors painted the double-icon of the Yellow Jackets on his HUD, catching them as they tried to sneak low around the close corner of the building. With a light touch to his controls, Shakov drifted his *Exterminator* to the left and then cut the plasma jets completely, dropping sixty-five tons of unsecured BattleMech straight down into the rotors of one VTOL.

It was never a contest. The fragile craft folded under so much weight, the rotor blades snapping off and the cockpit crushed inward. Shakov feathered his jets enough for a rough-but-adequate landing on the street below. The crushed gunboat looked nothing like the state-of-the-art craft it had been a moment before. Its companion was nowhere to be found.

Alarms screamed for attention, allowing no more time for looking around. The *Gallowglas* was back, having slipped around the department store and down a tight alleyway, determined to claim one more victim before leaving the city. Energy bathed the nearby facades with artificial light as the twisting arc of the 'Mech's PPC snaked down the street to crisp more armor from Shakov's chest. He braced for the certain follow-up by the *Gallowglas*'s lasers. He figured the 'Mech would remain secure at the mouth of the alley, forcing him to retreat or run a gauntlet of severe fire. The enemy 'Mech surprised him by stumbling into the street, its lasers missing wide.

Then Shakov saw that it had been shoved into the street, actually. A salvaged *Starslayer*, repainted in Com Guard colors, followed behind the *Gallowglas*, lasers stabbing into the back of the Lyran machine. Damning his heat curve, Shakov added to the enemy pilot's misery by stabbing out with his four lasers. One sliced up into the head of the *Gallowglas*, while both of the *Starslayer*'s main weapons cored through the 'Mech's back. Rattled, nearly decapitated, and caught in an untenable position, the *Gallowglas* pilot punched out of the cockpit before a second salvo from either machine deprived him of the option. The struggling *Gallowglas* crumpled onto the street, striking sparks from the ferrocrete before it lay there motionless in an untidy—but salvageable—pile.

"Maybe now we can get Adept Deluca back into a cockpit," the *Starslayer* MechWarrior offered. Shakov recognized the voice of Adept Bills, piloting a different 'Mech since losing his *Raijin* on Furillo. Few of the Prince's Men were fighting in their original machines. Too many of them were no longer fighting at all.

Shakov swallowed dryly as waste heat bled past his damaged reactor shielding and radiated up through the metal deck plates of his cockpit. His breath came fast and shallow as he blinked away sweat, trusting his cooling vest to keep his core body temperature at a safe level.

"Worry about Deluca later," he said. "Worry about the Arcturan Guard right now."

There wasn't much left to worry about, however. At the next corner, a pair of *Fenrir* battlesuit troops made the mistake of choosing fight over flight. Their spreads of short-range missiles blasted more armor from Shakov's *Exterminator*. One spanged off the 'Mech's head, shaking him and leaving behind a light ringing in his ears. Another warhead smashed into his right arm, exploiting earlier damage and destroying one of his lasers.

But three lasers were enough to cut apart one of the infantrymen, and Bills kicked the other through a nearby wall before the trooper could fire a new barrage. Shakov hated to see such a waste of fine men and material. "Give it up," he murmured, his voice low enough not to be heard.

Another block down, and through the nearby intersection, a full company of VTOLs screamed past at right angles to Shakov and Bills. Each gunboat was there and gone before either MechWarrior could target it. Likewise, none of the Lyran pilots seemed eager to turn into the teeth of the two 'Mechs. Hardly an attack run, Shakov decided. Those craft were in full flight. He remembered his intermittent contact with the *King Crab*. Had General McDonald finally recalled her forces?

Whether or not she had, the VTOL pilots seemed perfectly willing to avoid engagement. A limping *Cobra* and the pair of Hunter support tanks that followed the aircraft had less of a choice. Shakov's lasers dug into the armor guard that protected the lead tank's treads while the second Hunter turned in to launch a full spread of thirty LRMs into the face of Adept Bills' *Starslayer*. The *Cobra* tried to follow suit, bringing up its two launchers and pivoting hard on its good leg. But the tread refused to bite into the ferrocrete, and the leg slid out from under the Arcturan BattleMech. It crashed to the street, one arm wrenched so far back in its shoulder socket that it froze in place.

The lead tank abandoned its companions and poured on its best speed as it raced after the fleeing VTOLs. Shakov and Bills pressed the remaining Hunter, crowding the effective range of its targeting computer as they sliced it apart. After the tank's next missile spread flew wildly about due to a lack of solid targeting informatio the Hunter's crew called out their surrender over an open frequency and powered down.

The *Cobra* MechWarrior took more convincing. Even with the arrival of a Valexan *Hunchback*, the Arcturan Guard MechWarrior refused to admit defeat as it struggled back to its knees. He also managed to slam a double-handful of missiles into Shakov's right flank, blasting away the last of the *Exterminator*'s armor on that side. Then the *Starslayer* cut the *Cobra*'s crippled leg out from under it while Shakov's lasers sliced off its only good arm. As the valiant machine toppled backward, the *Hunchback*'s twelve-centimeter autocannon tore off its remaining leg for good measure. The allied MechWarriors left it on the street, helpless in the path of an approaching Sixth Lancer infantry platoon.

"All forces, this . . . General Sanchez." The transmission was scratchy and cut out intermittently, telling Shakov that the general had to be on the far side of Tukwila. He dialed up the gain, and worked the filters to clear up the signal. ". . . in retreat," Sanchez went on. "We've also heard . . . the *Melissa Davion*. Prince Victor is clear. Again, the prince is safely away and the Lyrans . . . abandoning Tukwila."

Shakov felt a heavy load lift from his shoulders at hearing those words. All the pressures that had built up with Victor's downward slide, all the twists and turns they'd been handed on Tikonov, faded back until he saw with utter clarity what he had to do now. All that mattered from here on was staying alive and getting off Tikonov to rendezvous with the Prince's escort.

Bills apparently shared his thoughts. "And we're out of here as well," he said, slowing the *Starslayer* to an easy walk. "Salvage, load, and burn for the nadir jump point. Thorin, here we come."

Bills was right. This should be it for the allied forces, the word Shakov himself had been waiting for—demanding—in the last hour. But a chance comment Morgan Kell had made back in Rockland niggled at the back of his mind. It sparked something inside him, something more than simple duty. He throttled his *Exterminator* into a faster walk, rolling with the 'Mech's swaggering gait as he gained the next intersection and cut toward the eastern edge of the city.

"Not yet," he said over the allied forces' open channel, bringing the *Hunchback* pilot into the conversation. "We aren't finished here."

Both pilots fell in behind him, accepting his command without question. Three blocks further on, Shakov added a Sixth Lancer *Rakshasa* and a trio of Cavalier battlesuit troopers to his line. He spread them out in a search pattern over several blocks, avoiding the retreating loyalists at every turn as he sought his target.

"It might help if we knew what we were looking for," Adept Bills said after being called away from a *Zeus*.

"You'll know it when we find it," Shakov said, then lapsed into silence for several long strides. "We have Tukwila, which means we have Harcourt Industries. That gives General Sanchez the support base he wanted. But there's one more thing we need to do. One final gesture."

He saw a new icon flash onto his HUD, read the tagline of information attached to it, and knew he had found her.

KGC-000.

Rudolf Shakov smiled thin and hard, took a new grip on his controls, and throttled up into a run. "Per Morgan Kell's request, we still need to bloody General McDonald's nose."

Giving the order to abandon Tukwila was one of Linda McDonald's most difficult moments on Tikonov. It meant admitting that she'd been caught unprepared, that she'd been beaten by a single warrior, the one who'd spearheaded the charge that broke her line and allowed Victor's force to spread quickly into the city, behind her back. And it all happened while she was drawing the enemy forces into a position where the *Katrina Steiner* could decimate their line—her moment of greatest achievement.

She tried convincing herself that none of it mattered. If reports were to be believed, a half dozen DropShips had fled the system on the spine of the *Melissa Davion*. That could only mean that Prince Victor had decided to fall back, and so Tikonov wouldn't be the final battle of the civil war after all. If that was the case, Tukwila meant very little in the greater scheme of things. It was only one failed objective and one bruised ego. She would get another opportunity to set things right.

She pulled her *King Crab* around a new corner, within sight of the city's edge and a few trailing 'Mechs belonging to her loyalist force. She took one hand off the throttle and rubbed at the gritty residue of dried sweat that itched at her neck and along the exposed skin of her arms and legs. Another score of long, bow-legged strides and she was finally free of Tukwila. No plan survives contact with the enemy, she told herself.

The tried and true wisdom failed to comfort, however, and the siren that suddenly screamed for attention interrupted any additional pep talk she might have generated. The tactical screen flashed a handful of new threats as her proximity alarm warned of incoming missiles. She turned her 'Mech into the attack, taking the first spread of LRMs along the *King Crab*'s left side instead of its wide back. The machine bucked and trembled as half a hundred warheads enveloped it, pitting armor and tearing up the surrounding ground. Dirt pattered against her wide ferroglass shield.

Reading the information from her heads up with practiced skill, McDonald saw that her attackers consisted of four 'Mechs and a short squad of battle armor. She dropped her targeting cross hairs over the *Exterminator* in the lead, wondering if it was the same one that had broken her line earlier?

Com Guard, the IFF tag confirmed. It had to be.

Grinding her teeth, she pulled into her two long-range triggers even as she realized that her situation was hopeless, that she was caught out of position, again. If she allowed the *Hunchback* to get too close, she was outgunned by some seventy-five percent, and there was no way to prevent it. At her best speed, she could manage maybe fifty-five kilometers per hour. The hard-hitting *Hunchback* had another ten over that. The other three BattleMechs edged her out by even more.

Her torso-mounted laser stabbed a ruby lance into the *Exterminator*'s chest, splashing armor to the ground in a pattern of fiery runnels and molten drops. A flight of fifteen LRMs also arced up and over, pasting small blooms of fire over the left side of the enemy 'Mech. Its left arm fell uselessly at its side, but the 'Mech continued its advance.

"In a hurry, General?" a mocking voice asked over an open frequency.

McDonald might have expected anything from a demand for surrender to an ultimatum for her release, but not banter. Not from a member of Com Guard, whose members were often dour, even by Lyran standards.

"I've got time," she said, bringing her laser back on a short cycle. The beam of coherent light sliced across the *Exterminator*'s thigh, gimping the faster machine, which limped forward at the head of its makeshift lance.

The return fire came hot and lethal. The *Exterminator*'s missile launcher spat out a new flight of ten warheads, but was the least of McDonald's worries. The *Rakshasa*, content until now to remain in the *Exterminator*'s shadow, threw out three times the missile coverage *and* stabbed at her with a pair of cherry-red lasers. One cut into each of her legs, peeling away nearly the last of her lower armor. The *Starslayer* also wanted to have its say. It sliced across the *King Crab*'s forward cockpit with one of its two large lasers, drawing a molten line across her transparent cockpit shield. Runners of melted ferro-glass blurred her view.

McDonald recognized too late that she'd made the mistake of falling back into her old routine of warrior first, commander second. She had issued no calls to her nearby warriors, a few of whom were moving in now of their own accord, but not as many as she might have summoned. She had also scope-locked on the *Extermina-*

tor, turning it into a personal nemesis, when any of the other three 'Mechs presented a greater threat.

"Never too old to learn," she muttered, not caring that she'd broadcast over the open channel.

Heading back toward the city's edge, she left any possible reinforcements behind while attempting to bring her assault-class autocannon into range. Her own laser-and-missile pairing stung at the *Rakshasa* once . . . twice.

She stumbled under another intense barrage, one leg shaky as it nearly folded beneath her, but the hundred-ton assault 'Mech weathered the storm even while extending its claw-like hands toward the green-painted Lancer BattleMech. The pincers opened, and a stream of depleted-uranium slugs traced destructive lines from each of the *King Crab*'s autocannon to the *Rakshasa*'s main body. The hot metal ripped into already-weak armor, chewing through support structure and into the ammunition bin that fed the 'Mech's right-shoulder missile rack.

Ruptured fuel cells lit a hot-burning fire that cooked off several warheads. The *Rakshasa* staggered forward, its body jerking with spasms as more of the stored missiles exploded in a violent cascade of raw force. The BattleMech's cockpit split open under explosive charges, and the MechWarrior ejected his command couch on booster rockets. He rose above his rapidly disintegrating machine, then a parafoil extended at his apogee, letting him glide safely back toward Tukwila. The *Rakshasa* fell onto its right side, then flipped up and around as a blossom of fire from the erupting munitions tossed it in the other direction. The cartwheeling BattleMech tore itself to pieces against the ground.

Too little, too late, and Linda McDonald knew it. Bringing her autocannon around against the *Hunchback*, she managed to scour away a large swath of its armor before the other 'Mech's autocannon bit into her left leg and cut if off at the femur. The *King Crab* overbalanced and toppled right. As she came down hard on her right side, that arm and its weapon were pinned, useless, under her. The *Exterminator* brought its foot down on her other arm, crushing the autocannon barrel. Twisting under the impact, the *King Crab* lost its other leg when it was torn from the hip socket. The 'Mech's wide body slammed onto its stomach, throwing her forward in her restraint harness, then came to rest like a beached whale.

McDonald shook her head to clear it and peered through her ruined ferroglass shield. She saw the *Exterminator*'s shovel-blade feet lumbering toward her. Her gaze traveled up the legs and the ripped-open torso to the wedge-shaped head. Dark ferroglass stared back at her, though she could almost see the expression of disdain on the other MechWarrior's face. It felt as if she might have cracked a rib, and the acrid smoke of scorched wiring filled her cockpit. But her comm system was still functioning.

"With Prince Victor's compliments," the Com Guard warrior said.

Then, all three remaining BattleMechs turned their backs on her and began heading toward Tukwila. At the edge of town, they paused to look back and watch her humiliating departure.

At first she worried for the trio of Cavalier armored infantry, thinking they might have stayed behind to drag her from the cockpit as a prisoner of war. Then, she saw them holding back a respectful distance as well, making no move to interfere as two loyalist 'Mechs and a Centipede scout car pulled up alongside her. McDonald extracted herself from the *King Crab*'s cockpit and swung down to the ground.

Painfully conscious of every humiliating step, she mustered what was left of her dignity and walked calmly toward the scout vehicle. Any of the remaining allied MechWarriors could have finished her off easily, but they left her alone to live with the failure.

If it was meant to intimidate her, she didn't let it. The fates had tempted her with the possibility of a heroic victory on Tikonov, then stripped it away when just within reach. That did not detract from what she *had* accomplished in her first solo command. Her task force had blunted Victor Davion's push into the Federated Suns and all but secured Tikonov for the Archon. More important, McDonald understood now more than ever what it would take to win a final victory. Which would make her that much better at command.

Pausing with one foot on the running board of the Centipede, she spared one last glance for Tukwila. Leaving her alive to fight another day might be the worst mistake Victor's force ever made. She learned from her mistakes. She would find Victor Davion, wherever he had gone, and prove that to him personally. She would hunt him down. Bring him to justice.

One way or another, Linda McDonald would see this civil war through to the end.

Epilogue

Avalon City, New Avalon
Crucis March
Federated Suns
8 April 3065

Katrina nodded curtly at the salutes of the two uniformed and very well-armed palace sentries, passing between them and under a metal-lined arch that buzzed a slight warning. She stopped at the head of the next corridor, looking a sharp question at Richard Dehaver, who followed.

"Your jewelry," he explained. "I had the sensitivity turned up." A large window of mirrored ferroglass was set into the wall nearby, and he nodded at his reflection. A section of the window lit up green. "Highness," he said, and gestured for Katrina to move on ahead of him again.

This section of the palace was reserved for the local offices of her Ministry of Information, Intelligence, and Operations. It consisted of four short corridors arranged in a series of T-junctions that created a number of blind corners the deeper in one moved. Katrina studied the arrangement as if she'd never seen it. In fact, it had been nearly a year since her last visit to these offices. MIIO data came to her through Dehaver and a few others. There was usually no need for her to interfere with the local agents or disrupt their routines.

Today, however, there was.

"Do we know where he is yet?" she asked.

"Jackson Davion thinks your brother is on Thorin, which he used as a staging base for his drive into the Federated Suns. Thorin and Muphrid are both secure worlds for him, and with General Sanchez still making trouble on Tikonov, we think Victor will want to remain at his forward-most base. Also, the Prince's Men and the Outland Legion are there, and we've made an ID on the Clanner woman, Tiaret." Dehaver shrugged. "We still have agents working to confirm Victor's physical presence."

"Morgan Kell?"

"Dropped from sight. He may be on his way back to the Arc Royal Defense Cordon." Dehaver brushed at the front of his suit, straightened his jacket. "The ARDC is another *possible* destination for Victor. By all accounts, Highness, your brother is in need of serious rest and recuperation."

She nodded, then let the conversation wane as Dehaver paced ahead of her to reach the door and to tap in the correct code on a wall terminal. A buzzing sound indicated that the locks had disengaged, and the door opened with an easy shove.

Katrina had never visited Dehaver's office, but had always assumed it was a place befitting her chief intelligence aide. Roomy and with plenty of aides to keep him well-informed of recent happenings and reports on operations. Wood paneling and quiet carpets. Pictures on the wall of dignitaries he knew—and certainly one of her.

The truth, as it always seemed to be of late, was less impressive than her fantasies.

Dehaver entered and slipped around the side of a small, metal desk hardly wider than his chair. He had to, in order to make room for her. Closing the door behind her, Katrina found the place positively claustrophobic even with only the two of them as its occupants. Three meters to a side, with stark, plastered walls and no windows, it could just as easily have been converted closet space. Her walk-in wardrobe was larger.

Dehaver did have the pictures, though. One wall was covered with surveillance shots of Victor, Tancred Sandoval, Jerrard Cranston *and* Galen Cox, Morgan Kell, George Hasek, and Robert Kelswa-Steiner. She also found her sister Yvonne, some Com Guard officers, and a large, dark-skinned woman who had to be her brother's Clan bodyguard. Her own portrait hung next to the door, so close to the frame that it looked like she was peering into the room, spying on herself with Dehaver to make sure everything was being properly handled.

He picked up the unframed canvas that leaned against the side of his desk and dropped it onto one corner of the desktop. "Here it is," he said. "I would have brought it to you."

Of course, he would have. But Katrina did not feel like waiting when she heard that the latest Starling had been delivered to her palace. She leaned over for a look at it as one might a venomous serpent in the zoo, respectfully cautious even though the creature was behind glass. Dehaver tilted it up for her to see. The painting was more realistic than the usual Reginald Starling style.

Katrina was caricatured in Bloody Princess IX as a withered crone with bloodshot eyes and blackened stumps for teeth. Two gaudy crowns sat askew atop her head. Gem-studded clothes hung awkwardly on a skeletal frame. Her golden hair, though beautiful and lustrous, fell out in large hanks to pile over her shoulders or drift in tangled wisps around her feet. The entire scene spoke of vanity and inner rot, and would have been enough to order Starling's death, again, even without all the rest.

In one of her claw-like hands, the Bloody Princess held a world, her fingers digging into the crust to slowly crumble the planet. Drops of blood rained down from the dying orb. Her other hand was stretched out before her, working puppeteer rods from which dangled a marionette. The marionette could only be Reg Starling himself, wielding a painter's knife globbed with red paint and using a second blade to saw at the strings that bound him to his evil mistress. Looking closer, Katrina saw that her distorted doppelganger was actually hauling the marionette not from a box, but from a coffin at graveside. The tombstone in the background was the most perfect item in the entire piece, inked onto a blank bit of canvas.

The name on the stone read, "Sven Newmark."

"This is not the original?" she asked, her voice tight.

"No, Highness. We have already found the artist employed in making the copy, and have detained him accordingly. His comment was that the original is even more disturbing."

"Found him where?"

"Here in Avalon City," he said. "He said he'd been hired by phone and dealt only through intermediaries. Starling, or whoever this really is, has apparently taken up residence on New Avalon."

Katrina glared at her intelligence aide. "And how much is this person asking for?"

He spun the painting around. The blackmail note was painted on the backside of the canvas, signed with an artistic flourish. "Ten million kroner. According to the note, that is half what you and Ryan Steiner paid for the assassination of your mother. Ten million, and he disappears into the Periphery with the original, safe and secure unless we 'disturb' him again."

Katrina crossed her arms and frowned. "Ever since Victor's *performance* at the Star League conference, these accusations are getting out of hand . . ."

Dehaver showed no sign that he cared or even heard. "What are your orders, Highness?"

"Find the man, Richard. Do whatever you must to lure him into the open. Then take him." Her hard gaze caught his, held it until he nodded.

Dehaver knew what she wanted. He would see to it. In a few short months, Katrina hoped to be free of the storms that had lately piled up on the horizon, darkening the skies. Victor had apparently folded, and the civil war seemed to be dying out like a guttering candle. There might be a few rogue knights to deal with, people like George Hasek and Tancred Sandoval, but they could hardly stand alone.

Pausing for only one last look at the disgusting canvas, she turned toward the door. So much for Sven Newmark . . .

Now it was time to sweep the board clear of the remaining pawns.

* * *

Hawkins Estates, Muphrid
Freedom Theater
Lyran Alliance

Staying at the Hawkins Estates on Muphrid made Jerrard Cranston nervous. The world was drastically underdefended, relying on the illusion of poor strategic value to protect itself from Katherine's loyalists. And the Hawkins estate had all the physical security of a public park. Its vineyards were spread over open countryside, currently under harvest by a flood of seasonal workers. The winery was in full operation, the current stock being laid down while selections from previous years were drawn up from the massive underground cellars and shipped away. Owners Todd and Shelley Hawkins threw lavish parties, which brought nobles, corporate executives, and holo-stars as weekend guests.

Cranston could only hope that none of them knew they were sharing the mansion with Victor Steiner-Davion.

This was the best they could come up with, wanting to keep Victor close to their forward base on Thorin without having to worry unduly about his safety. Hiding in plain sight, a scheme concocted by Tiaret, Morgan Kell, and himself. It seemed to be working, but it still made him nervous.

Cranston met Kai Allard-Liao just leaving Victor's

suite in a deserted wing of the house. "He's waiting for you," Kai said.

As if Victor, or any of them, were doing much else these days. "Any change?" Cranston asked.

Kai shrugged, a rather lop-sided effort without his right arm. "He eats when he's given food. Reads a lot—battle reports, news items from different worlds, personal messages. He's always working on plans for retaking Tikonov or for an assault on New Avalon, but there isn't a lot of heart behind it. More of a mental exercise."

"Busy work," Cranston said. "Another man might do crosswords or build a matchstick house. It's a diversion."

Morgan nodded. "Other than that, he gets up in the morning, breathes in, breathes out, and eventually sleeps again."

"He's sleeping too much," Cranston said, his words coming out with a sharpness he didn't intend. He wasn't mad at Victor, of course, who'd been made to bear more than his share in recent years. If he was angry, it was against the fates for their latest, most cruel torture.

"You prefer him the way he was when he wasn't sleeping?" Kai asked. "He hit the wall hard. It will take some time for him to put things back together. It's part of the grieving process. People tend to go along normally, coping, or so they think. After a few months, they simply stop and the entire backwash of emotion rolls over them. No one's immune. Not even Victor Davion." Morgan looked back toward the door. "His obsessive drive on Tikonov distracted him for almost six months, but the pain has finally caught up with him."

Cranston nodded absently. "I should see what he wants. You're heading out for Thorin?" Morgan nodded, and they traded left-handed grips. "Give everyone our best," Cranston said in parting, then opened the door to Victor's suite.

The place was actually designed as one large room, with sleeping quarters and a small living area spread over the carpeted side of the room and a small office sectioned off by the beige-tiled floor. The draperies were closed, shutting out the midday sun and leaving only a pair of lamps for illumination. Victor sat at his desk, leaning back in a swivel chair to stare up at the ceiling. He swiveled back and forth in a slow arc. A jade pendant hung around the collar of his white turtleneck, where he could see it, touch it if he wanted.

"I haven't seen you wear that in awhile." Cranston said. It was an old gift from Kai.

"Sun Hou-tzu. The King of the Monkeys." Victor's voice wasn't exactly lifeless, but it was definitely flat. "It's to remind me to be true to myself."

If Cranston remembered right, Sun Hou-tzu was said to hold some power over the realm of death. He also saw the oblong sword guard Omi Kurita had given Victor on Outreach. It sat on the desk in front of him, holding down a stack of papers and maps. It was to keep Victor safe, she had said. Cranston had been there, too, during those years when Victor had held life by the throat and wrung from it all he could. Not just for himself, but for his friends and those he loved.

And now here he was, sitting in a dim room, surrounded by impotent talismans.

Victor glanced over. "You lost your parents to the Combine, didn't you, Galen?"

Being called by his given name threw Cranston off for a moment. "Yes, I did. In the War of 'Thirty-nine."

"And you didn't hate my father for starting that war?"

Cranston drew a deep breath. "Oh, I did, Victor. I did. For a long time. The pain needed someone to focus on, and I fed it Hanse Davion and House Kurita. It weighed on me for years."

"But you're my friend. And Hohiro's. Our fathers cost you your family."

Cranston shrugged. "What would you like me to say, Victor? It hurt, and I was angry, but eventually I stopped blaming others. A stray artillery round destroyed my parents' home. Whether it was defective material or even carelessness, I'll never know. I wanted to prevent more needless deaths, and that's how I came to join the military. I think I've been able to do that." He shook his head, chasing away the memory. "And the pain eventually faded."

"How?" Victor sat up, his eyes suddenly charged with more energy than Cranston had seen in weeks. "How does it fade, Galen?"

Cranston took it as a good sign that Victor at least *wanted* to get better, but he knew there wasn't much he could say. "It simply does, Victor."

Victor settled back again, drained. "There is so much I have to do still. On Thorin and Tikonov. On New Avalon, if I ever get there. Katherine has to be dealt with, and the Clans can't be forgotten either. And then there is Omi . . ." Victor trailed off into thought. "I'm sending you to Luthien, Jerry."

The words caught Cranston by surprise, the second time in as many minutes. "Luthien? My place is here, Victor. Why send me?"

"Because I cannot go myself, and I need someone I can trust implicitly. I don't want Theodore deciding again what it is I need to know, and when I need to know it." He held up his hands to forestall any argument. "He meant well, Jerry, but Theodore has his own agenda and his own nation to safeguard. If he and I agree on anything right now, it's the need to seek justice for Omi. You will help him do that, on my behalf."

Cranston nodded. "If you ask me to, Victor, I'll go. I'll dig out what I can, but I won't even know where to start."

Victor rocked forward from his chair and stood up. "I do," he said.

Simply, and with such calm assurance that Cranston believed him.

"I've had time to think of nothing else." Victor stepped away from his desk. "It came to me when I thought about your plans for my safety here on Muphrid. No large guard. No armed convoy into the ARDC. It all made sense."

He walked past Cranston to the window, where he drew aside the curtain just enough to stare out onto the well-kept grounds. Light flooded into the room, back-lighting Victor. Cranston felt a spark light in him, too, stirring the embers of hope.

"This assassin is a predator most of the time," Victor went on, his voice stronger, "and that is how we have treated him. As someone dangerous and cunning. As someone stalking us in the shadows, waiting for the perfect moment to strike. But we seem to have forgotten something. That once he strikes, then he becomes the prey. The Draconis Combine is dangerous ground, and he will know the truth that the prey distinguishes itself through *movement*. Tell Theodore that, Jerry. Make him understand.

"The assassin is still on Luthien."

About the Author

Loren L. Coleman first began writing fiction in high school, but it was during his enlistment in the U.S. Navy that he began to work seriously at the craft. For eight years now, he has built up a bibliography that includes (at the time of this printing) eleven published novels, a great deal of shorter fiction, and involvement with several computer games.

Storms of Fate is his eighth BattleTech® novel, and his second since taking over the main story line of the BattleTech® universe. His previous books in the series include *Double-Blind, Binding Force, Threads of Ambition, Killing Fields, Illusions of Victory, Flashpoint,* and *Patriots and Tyrants.* He is also the author of *Into the Maelstrom,* the first novel of the Vor™ series, and *Rogue Flyer* in the fascinating universe of Crimson Skies™.

Having lived in many parts of the country, Loren currently resides in Washington State. His family includes: his wife, Heather Joy; two sons, Talon LaRon and Conner Rhys Monroe; and a young daughter, Alexia Joy. The household also includes three Siamese cats, Chaos, Rumor, and Ranger, who are beginning to demand top billing.

BATTLETECH®

Loren L. Coleman

THREADS OF AMBITION

Sun-Tzu Liao is the First Lord of the resurrected
Star League. In the last year of his reign, he
decides to milk his power for every ounce of ben-
efit to himself. His dream to rebuild his Capellan
Confederation at any cost is about to become a
reality. His first victim: his own aunt, Candace
Liao, who deserted the Confederation in the
Fourth Succession War, taking the St. Ives
Compact with her. And as Capellan fights
Capellan, the high price of glory will be paid
in full....

(0-451-45744-7)

To order call: 1-800-788-6262

Don't miss out on any of the deep-space adventure
of the Bestselling **BATTLETECH**® Series.